Number 34 Appleton Close

By

Gillian Jackson

Published in 2016 by FeedARead.com Publishing

Copyright © The author as named on the book cover.

The author or authors assert their moral right under the Copyright, Designs and Patents Act, 1988, to be identified as the author or authors of this work.

All Rights reserved. No part of this publication may be reproduced, copied, stored in a retrieval system, or transmitted, in any form or by any means, without the prior written consent of the copyright holder, nor be otherwise circulated in any form of binding or cover other than that in which it is published and without a similar condition being imposed on the subsequent purchaser.

A CIP catalogue record for this title is available from the British Library.

Acknowledgements

With grateful thanks to my family for their encouragement
and support, particularly Derek, who has to live, not only with me,
but with the characters I create.
Thanks also to those who read my books and give such valued feedback.

Chapter 1
Maggie Sayer

It was exactly as I remembered from a decade ago, uninspiring and unwelcoming. Of course the weather didn't help, with the dismal pewter sky a perfect match to the ugly concrete building, a throwback to the 1960s when anything in architecture seemed to go. The gravel drive was badly in need of maintenance, and avoiding the potholes in my little car could almost become an art form. High narrow windows along the front of the single-storey building were crying out to be replaced, but money for all public building was scarce and a young offenders' institute would almost certainly be low on the priority list. Huge drops of rain were starting to fall from the dense grey sky as I pulled my car into a visitors' spot on the car park then hurried to the main entrance, thoughts of the next hour filling my mind with the potential challenge it could hold.

I'd visited Redwood Young Offenders' Institute only a few times in the past, the last time to see a teenage mother who had been arrested on several occasions for possession and dealing in drugs. As far as I was aware the young woman had beaten her addiction and with the help and support available at Redwood moved on to a drug-free life, an outcome which certainly painted the institute in a good light. All previous visits had been as part of my counselling training, when a sulky teenager barely engaged with me at all and was obviously only attending as a condition of her sentence. I can still recall her petulant expression and dark piercing eyes; she was certainly a testing client but a challenge and therefore valuable experience in those early days of training. Today's client, however, was a seventeen-year-old girl who was incarcerated for repeated shoplifting, which was the only information I knew or wanted to know. It's always preferable to have an open mind when commencing a counselling relationship, which offers the client a chance to be heard and believed without preconceived ideas on the therapist's part. After passing through the security gate I found myself in a square, high-ceilinged lobby, the height of which gave a hollow feel to the space, and the sound of my shoes echoed as I approached the reception desk to sign in. Nothing had changed here either, not even the decor. When the appointment was verified I was led to a small room, simply furnished with two easy chairs and a coffee table, where I was to wait for my newest client to arrive.

Lindy Baker was a waif of a girl, barely over five feet tall, with a slim almost boyish figure and hair cut short which gave an overall pixie-like appearance. Her face was oval with clear skin, high cheekbones and pale blue eyes filled with an expression of resignation as the warder steered her towards the vacant chair. For a moment it seemed that the warder intended to stay, or at least say something but my surprised look had the effect of the woman leaving the room and closing the door firmly behind her. The girl's eyes scrutinized her new surroundings before meeting my own, and with arms crossed over her chest, a typical defensive pose, she waited for something to be said.

'Hello, Lindy, my name is Maggie Sayer and I'm here for about an hour today. There are one or two things to tell you before we can get started, mainly about the confidentiality of our meetings.' I began to outline the triple harm clause, the three things which would cause me to breach any confidences shared in our times together, which were if the client intended to harm herself or someone else, or in particular, if a child was at risk. Of course this seemed unnecessary as Lindy was in a secure environment and monitored twenty-four hours a day, but each session needed to set this out, and once it was out of the way I smiled at the girl and asked,

'I'm here today because you requested to see a counsellor, would you like to tell me why you wanted this?' There was a pause while Lindy considered the question, chewing on her bottom lip and drawing in a few deep breaths.

'Sally, my roommate, suggested I try it. She sees someone each week and says it really helps and looks good when they are considering release, you know, shows you're conforming or whatever.'

'So you want to conform?'

'No, not really, I don't want an early release but Sally says it's helping her get rid of stuff, baggage and whatever, you know?'

'And you have baggage you'd like to get rid of?'

'How long have you got?' Lindy's tone held only a little sarcasm and more than a little resignation but I answered anyway.

'Well, as I said, an hour today but if you want to continue our sessions I can come each week at about the same time.'

Lindy unfolded her arms and rested her hands in her lap, hopefully a sign that she was relaxing.

'So what does a counsellor do then?' This is so often one of the first questions a new client asks, as counselling is a new concept for many.

'I'm here to help, which can be done in several different ways. Generally I listen, really listen to what you have to say and reflect your words to ensure I've understood what you're saying. Hopefully together we can give you a greater understanding of your feelings and why you act in certain ways. Surprisingly, we often know very little about ourselves, and our time together may prompt you into a greater understanding of yourself.'

'What do you know about me then? What have they told you?'

'Who are 'they', Lindy?'

'The police, the warders in here, social services, don't they have a file on me or something?'

'If they do I haven't seen it and don't want to. All I know is that you're here for repeated shoplifting offences, is that right?'

'Yes, but surely they've told you more than that.'

'Is there more? If so I'd rather hear it from you than anyone else.' A silence followed and Lindy crossed her arms again, shifting in the chair and turning her body slightly away from me. I waited for a while before trying a gentle prompt.

'This is your time, Lindy, and for your benefit only. You can tell me anything you like and if I ask questions it's only to make sure I understand what you're telling me. I know nothing about your background, whether you have family, how you got on at school or even why you began to shoplift, so perhaps you'd like to tell me something about yourself?'

Lindy again shuffled in the chair but raised her head to meet my eyes.

'I don't have any family, or none that want to know me anyway, except for my brother Jack and I don't know where he is now.' Her pale blue eyes moistened and a wistful expression crossed her face. 'School was okay but I moved around a lot from one school to another, usually when my foster parents didn't want me anymore and I was sent to another place.'

'That must have been difficult for you.'

'You get used to it, I suppose.'

'Would you like to tell me about some of your foster homes?'

'Not really.' Another silence lingered for a few moments, broken by Lindy who seemed to have had a change of heart.

'Most of them were only in it for the money. When they thought I was too much trouble they had me moved on, preferring to get babies or very young children, older kids are too challenging. I could tell you some tales about foster carers that you wouldn't believe.'

'If that's what you want to talk about then please, go ahead.'

'Seriously? You'd want to listen to all that?'

'Yes, sharing it could help you to feel better. I meant it when I said that you can talk about anything.' I was already warming to Lindy. Being moved around to several different foster homes couldn't have been easy and there must be a reason why she was in foster care to begin with. After a few moments of silence she seemed to decide I could be trusted and began to talk again.

'My mother's a drug addict and even she doesn't know who my father is. Social services took us into care when I was seven and my little brother was almost two. During the past ten years I've been with five different families, the longest was with the first foster parents who kept me until I went to secondary school when they said I became disruptive. What they wouldn't admit was that she was pregnant by that time and I was no longer wanted, I think they were trying their parenting skills out on me. The second family were an older couple with grown-up children, tough on discipline which I didn't mind, at least they felt I was worth the effort... but then they got to retirement age and gave up being foster parents. I presumed they no longer needed the money when their pensions began and I'd obviously just been a 'job' to them. My next home was with a couple who couldn't have children, as was the one after that but both couples were waiting for a baby to adopt and again I wasn't welcome when that happened. The fifth foster home seemed great at first but it wasn't long before I found out why they wanted me there, particularly him... and I only stayed for a few weeks before running away. That was when the shoplifting began... but only for food. I was living on the streets by then, which isn't as bad as it sounds although I was dreading winter. The first shoplifting incident got me into trouble with the police but they decided not to prosecute and I was returned to social services. Not wanting to go through the humiliation of another foster home, I ran away again after stealing some money from a social worker's bag. I hated doing that but needed it to buy food. When the money ran out I had to steal again and that's how I ended up here.'

Listening silently to her, I could feel this girl's pain at being unwanted and passed around like a parcel, sometimes to serve other people's needs rather than her own. Lindy had only outlined her story but she'd done so coherently and without the bitterness many others would have felt justified in harbouring. She struck me as an intelligent girl, fluent in recounting her history and without feeling sorry for herself in any way, and there was obviously much more which would hopefully come out in later sessions. With a start in life like Lindy had experienced, I wondered what the future would hold for her. She was obviously resourceful, having lived on the streets for a time but that was no sort of life to go back to. I asked how much longer she would be in Redwood, and was told it was for another four months.

'How do you feel about being here?' I asked.

'I like it, it's the best place I've ever lived in and much warmer than the streets. I'm enjoying the chance to study and the library's great. I can do as many courses as I like as long as I go to the offender behaviour sessions.'

I knew that Redwood offered a wide choice of courses both academic and vocational which were organised through The Manchester College and tailored to suit all abilities. I'd sat in on a couple of the offender behaviour courses during my own training, and remembered being impressed by the way they aimed to give these young people an understanding of why they offended and in doing so they would hopefully be enabled to change their behaviour.

'Do you have any plans for the future, Lindy, any ambitions for when you are released?'

'That's easy, I'll do my best to get sent back here which will probably mean I'll start shoplifting again. It beats the alternatives of either going back into care or living on the streets. The magistrate thought he was locking me away from the world but actually he was locking the world away from me.'

Chapter 2
Maggie

Approaching Fenbridge, my thoughts remained with Lindy Baker. It was incredible and rather sad that so many people had failed this girl who was still only a child. Inconceivably, Redwood seemed to be the best place she'd ever lived and her only ambition in life was to be returned there again after her release. The concept that she would actually reoffend to go back to an institution spoke more about this client's former life than her words had done. Lindy missed out on much of the schooling she should have had in past years but was certainly not unintelligent and in fact her take on life seemed almost profound. It was as if she was battling the system after falling through the cracks of what should have been a safe upbringing. Lindy was learning about life the hard way yet was not embittered by it. She was reasonably articulate and had none of the moodiness or attitude which many teenagers display. These thoughts were interrupted by my mobile phone and as it was hands-free I answered immediately.

'Maggie, where are you?' My friend Sue sounded anxious.

'Hi, what's wrong?'

'I've gone into labour, that's what's wrong and Alan isn't answering his phone!'

'But you've another two weeks to go yet, haven't you?'

'You and I know that but apparently this little chap doesn't! Can you pick me up or shall I ring for an ambulance?'

'I can be with you in ten minutes, okay?'

'That's great, thanks, Maggie; I knew I could rely on you.'

Turning the car towards the west side of town I couldn't help but smile, all thoughts of Lindy pushed to the back of my mind for now and replaced with the excitement of this new arrival. It was Sue and Alan's third child, another boy to complete their family. Rose, their eldest child, was five and at school, then came George at nearly two, who attended nursery when Sue was working at the health centre where I was based, and now another boy who seemed to be in a hurry to arrive. Rose had longed for a sister rather than another brother, but unless the scans were wrong, a boy this would be.

Running down the path of their large rambling old family house, I found the door unlocked and Sue waiting in the hall, one hand leaning on the wall for support and the other on her back, moaning as another contraction brought the familiar stab of pain.

'Waters have broken,' she uttered between gasps, so this was not a false alarm. Propping Sue up as best as I could, I helped her to the car and when she was settled inside, attempting to breathe correctly, I ran back into the house to grab her bag and lock the door.

'Have you managed to get hold of Alan yet?' I asked.

'No, his bloody phone's switched off... I'll kill him!' Another groan interrupted her words.

'Hang on in there, Sue, we'll soon be at the hospital and then I'll try to ring him for you. And you can concentrate on having this baby.'

We parked in the only available spot near the entrance, one reserved for volunteer drivers. I would usually observe such signs but the situation was an emergency, I didn't want my friend to give birth in the car! Sue stumbled towards the entrance, leaning heavily on my arm, and I was glad to see a nurse coming towards us to help. Within ten minutes of our arrival, Sue was being examined by a midwife while I tried to reach Alan. On about the tenth time of ringing, he eventually answered.

'Alan? It's Maggie, I'm at the hospital with Sue, it looks as if your son is arriving!'

'What? But we've got another couple of weeks yet, is everything okay?'

'Yes, she's with the midwife now, he seems to be in a hurry.'

'I'll be there in half an hour. Sue's going to kill me for this, isn't she?'

'Well, she wasn't happy that your mobile was off.'

'But I was in court! Oh, never mind, I'll grovel when I get there.' The call ended and I asked the nurse if she would give my friend a message.

'You can go in if you like, she'll be glad of the company, it's a bit of a waiting game now.'

Tentatively I knocked on the door, opening it slightly to see if all was well.

'Come in, Maggie. Have you got hold of Alan yet?'

'Yes, he's on his way and should be here in half an hour or so. He's been in court, that's why his phone was switched off.'

'Don't make excuses for him! Oh no, here comes another one...'

She gripped my hand, her nails digging into the palm. Trust Sue to want to share the pain! As the contraction eased she turned over on her side, releasing the breath she was holding.

'This is the last, the very last; if Alan wants any more children he can have them himself!'

I stifled a laugh and began to rub Sue's back in an attempt to relax her. Having no children of my own I could only imagine what labour pains felt like, something I would now never experience. Staying with

Sue through the next four contractions, I began to wonder if the apparent intensity was normal, particularly as this was Sue's third baby. She herself had expected this birth would be as easy as shelling peas, but it certainly didn't look like it. Within the half hour, Alan arrived, sheepishly peering into the room just as his wife was experiencing another contraction. Looking at her husband she struggled to speak.

'Don't think you're ever going to touch me again... you're sleeping in the spare room from now on!' I smiled, remembering Sue making a similar statement when George was born. Poor Alan blushed but was allowed to kiss his wife's cheek and as the pain lessened took over the massage while I quietly left the room.

It was three-thirty and pointless going back to the surgery, so I decided to wait in the corridor, assuming it wouldn't be long if the intensity and frequency of the contractions were anything to go by. I thought of Alan rushing to the hospital and wondered if he had used the blue light to speed his journey. It wouldn't surprise me, it was an emergency and if he didn't arrive in time for the birth his wife would never let him forget such a crime. Sue and Alan were actually one of the happiest couples I knew. They had met at the police station when Sue accompanied me to report a case of harassment and Alan was the detective sergeant who took my statement. He was so unlike the kind of man she usually went for but they proved to be a perfect match and were married in a romantic surprise wedding at Gretna Green nearly seven years ago. I had been there too although unaware of Alan's scheme. My then partner, Peter, had been in on the surprise and the Boxing Day wedding had been a magical event. Peter and I were married ourselves within a few months, a second marriage for both of us. I had been widowed in my twenties, after three blissful years with Chris, whose surname, Sayer, I still use for work.

Peter Lloyd had been divorced after over twenty years of marriage and had two grown-up daughters. Having remained a widow for fourteen years and thinking I would never fall in love again, meeting Peter was a wonderful experience. My time for having children, however, had passed by but I'm fortunate enough to have a close relationship with Peter's two daughters and I'm very much a hands-on granny to my two step-grandchildren. Peter and I are also godparents to Rose and George and had been asked to fulfil this role again when the new baby arrived, a delightful responsibility which we both take seriously.

Waiting in hospitals is certainly not my favourite occupation. Chris died in this very hospital after suffering a massive brain haemorrhage but at least today's wait was for a much happier reason. I rang Peter to tell him where I was, and as Sue's mum Ruby was picking the children up from school and nursery, there was nothing more to do except wait. The midwife entered and left the delivery room several times, smiling at me on each occasion and as the door opened Sue could be heard moaning and Alan trying to placate her. Both of us knew Sue well enough to know that this was her way, she played the tough woman to the world but was actually one of the most caring, sensitive people I have ever known and it's a privilege to call her a friend. As if to endorse this, Alan appeared to tell me that it wouldn't be long now and Sue wondered if I would like to be present for the birth. It took no thinking about and after an assurance from Alan that he didn't mind, I jumped up and we both went back in to the delivery room.

The experience has to rank as one of the most amazing I have ever witnessed. In the latter stages of labour I held Sue's hand, whilst Alan was being used as a wall for his wife to push against with her right foot and a maternity nurse was posted at her left foot leaving the midwife free to deliver the baby. All four of us constantly encouraged Sue, telling her how well she was doing and that it was nearly over, which proved to be true as James Hurst suddenly entered the world. His first cry was the sweetest sound I have ever heard and there were tears all round as the new baby was weighed, (a healthy eight pounds four ounces) and had his face cleaned before being placed into his mother's arms for the first time. I tactfully took my leave, kissing both my friends and their new arrival before leaving them to enjoy the moment as I made my way home to tell Peter all about it.

Naturally there have been times when I've regretted not having children of my own, times when I indulged in dreaming of what my own offspring would have looked like but generally it was not an issue. I have so many wonderful people in my life to love and who love me, and little James was another very welcome addition to my circle of friends and family. Sue was always happy to let me share in her family's milestones and have her children on occasions. (Others call it babysitting!) And there were Peter's daughters and his grandchildren too; when I thought of all these positives there became no room in my life for regrets. Pulling into the courtyard of my home, I hurried inside to tell Peter all about the baby.

Chapter 3
Maggie

'He's gorgeous,' I babbled to my husband, 'Fair like Sue and a good weight, especially as he was a couple of weeks early. Alan had tears in his eyes and I struggled to contain mine, it was such an emotional experience!' Peter smiled; he would get to see the new addition soon enough but his thoughts quickly moved on to more practical things.

'Let's eat out tonight. I didn't start anything as I wasn't sure when you'd be home so we'll call it a celebration and go to The Duck shall we?'
I didn't need asking twice and was too excited to cook a meal anyway, so going out was perfect.

'I'll just change and be with you in a few minutes.' I kissed him on the cheek and happily went down the hall to our bedroom. We live in a bungalow, a relatively new build which his colleagues designed as a wedding present for us with Peter's needs in mind. Shortly before we were married, Peter was diagnosed with multiple sclerosis and our life together was uncertain. He, wanting to spare me the possibility of another loss, tried to end our relationship, but I refused to accept such a decision and we were married shortly after. Peter's condition has of course caused concern at times but he's responding well to a comparatively new drug, Gilenya, which has made such a difference to the symptoms he was previously experiencing. Now he can continue the work he loves as an architect, as long as he limits his hours and works from home whenever possible.

True to my word and with the thought of a good meal as an incentive, I was ready in just a few minutes and we set off to eat at one of our favourite places. The Duck is a gastro pub, recently refurbished to incorporate both a cosy traditional pub and a bright conservatory restaurant offering an excellent choice of food. We were early enough to get a table without having booked and were shown to seats at the far end of the room. The bright lighting and warmth of the restaurant belied the falling temperature outside as the grey day had turned into a dark, wet evening. The temperature was low even for late March, but my mood was buoyant as I again described the miracle of James's birth which I had been so privileged to witness. When the food arrived we ate during gaps in the conversation, both of us animated by the events of the day. As the evening wore on we were oblivious of the people arriving at regular intervals until the waiter brought us the bill, an undisguised hint that he needed the table for other diners. Hurrying to make our way out, Peter left a large tip by way of apology and the waiter's mood softened as he bade us a good evening.

'I'll give Alan a ring when we get home, see what's happening with them,' Peter said.

'It's Saturday tomorrow so if they need anyone to look after Rose and George, I'll be happy to volunteer.' I didn't know how long Sue would be in hospital; they hadn't really decided on a time line, thinking they had another couple of weeks to make plans.

Alan answered the phone almost immediately and Peter passed on his congratulations before asking how Sue was.

'She's here if you want to talk to her.'

'What, home already?'

'Yes, they get you out as soon as possible these days. I thought she would want to stay overnight, which was an option but she doesn't seem to trust me and Ruby to look after the children!' Alan laughed. Ruby, Sue's mother, possessed a similar temperament to her daughter which often led to friction between the two strong-minded women. Alan was glad to chat to Peter for a while, then Sue came on the phone and I took over to speak to her.

'Are you all right? It seems very soon, and to send you home at night too?'

'It was my decision, I could have stayed the night but then goodness only knows what I would have come back to. Mum's staying here for a few days so I'm off to bed myself now. Alan bathed the children and put them to bed so I only have James to worry about. I'll have to get up to feed him though, it's a shame that fathers aren't equipped to breastfeed then I could have a real rest.'

'Would you like me to take Rose and George out tomorrow?'

'Thanks, Maggie, but Mum's already planned the day and Alan will be around to help; he's taken a couple of weeks paternity leave but I bet he'll be glad to get back to work after it! You'd be very welcome to call and see James properly though. He looks so different now he's been cleaned up, he's a little peach.'

'I'll come after lunch then you can have a good rest in the morning, okay?'

'Great, I'll look forward to seeing you and thanks for today.'

'No need to thank me, it was wonderful, that's the first birth I've ever witnessed and it will probably be the last too.'

'It will if you're counting on me for another round of birthing entertainment, I'm finished on that front!' Sue said goodbye and rang off.

'Want to come with me tomorrow to visit?' I asked Peter.

'Try stopping me, I should think Alan could do with a bit of moral support too, having his wife and mother-in-law under the same roof.'

I sat on the sofa beside my husband, leaning my head back and closing my eyes. It had been an eventful day and I was tired. Just as I was about to suggest an early night, Tara, our cat leapt up and curled herself up on my lap, and instinctively I began to stroke her silky coat. Tara was missing Ben almost as much as we did. Ben was our dog, mine originally, a wonderfully loyal friend when I lived alone but sadly now no longer with us. He had reached the grand old age of sixteen which was a long life for a dog, but parting with him had been so hard. However, he had been in so much pain that the vet left us in no doubt that to try and keep him going much longer would be cruel. During those last few weeks we all made a fuss of him but he no longer wanted to go outside, as walking was such an effort and so painful. Tara spent hours curled up against his warm body, somehow sensing that her friend and often partner in crime was suffering. In the end the vet came to take Ben away whilst I was at work; it was a sad day and I cried bitterly when I returned home and he was gone. Peter tried to console me, reminding me of what a wonderful life I'd given him and how happy he had been. I knew this to be true, Ben had been a rescue dog and we were therefore unsure of his previous life, but from the first day I brought him home we became the best of friends and as it was only a couple of weeks since he died the pain still caught me unawares at times. For Tara it was also a loss. I know that cats are only supposed to live in the moment but Tara searched for Ben for days after he went, I knew she missed him too.

Saturday was bathed in sunshine. It began very weakly but by mid-morning was strong enough to warm the air and dry the ground from the overnight rain. I had risen early and was in the kitchen baking when Peter got up.

'Is this one of your special occasion cakes?' he asked.

'It is. I know they won't be short of anything, especially with Ruby there, but I thought perhaps a chocolate cake and a few scones would be welcome. And don't look like that, there's one in the oven for you as well and we'll keep a couple of the scones.'

Peter kissed me then poured some coffee and sat down to watch me work.

'We'll have to think of something to buy for James. I know he'll have everything he needs from George's old clothes and equipment but I'd like to look for something new.' My obvious delight at the arrival of Sue's baby made Peter smile. He knew how much I enjoyed being with the children in our lives, his own grandchildren and Sue's expanding family.

After a light lunch we set off. Sue and Alan lived on the west side of Fenbridge in a detached Victorian villa which sounds grander than it actually is. It was certainly a project when they bought it but Alan relished the challenge and slowly they have breathed new life into the place. With much still to do, it was now however comfortable enough to live in, and offered the space that their growing family needed.

Ruby answered the door, a huge smile on her face.

'Congratulations on becoming a third time granny!' I bent to kiss the slightly shorter, older version of Sue.

'Thank you, come in. Sue's upstairs feeding the baby but Alan and the children are in the lounge.' Ruby led us down the hallway where we found Alan flat on his back while George jumped up and down on his chest and

Rose laughed uncontrollably. He lifted George off and stood to greet us.

'Hi, you've just saved me from a fate worse than death!'

I went to put the cake and scones in the kitchen with Rose following behind, asking if the chocolate cake was for her.

'For you all,' I told her, 'A special treat to say welcome to baby James.'

'He doesn't eat cake, only milk.' Rose's face was serious. 'He's getting it from Mummy now but then he'll have some bottles.'

I couldn't help but smile at Rose's serious expression and I picked my little goddaughter up. She was as light as thistle down and smelled of soap and talcum powder. Planting a kiss on her cheek, I asked what she thought of her new baby brother.

'Well I really wanted a sister, but he is sweet. Mummy says I can help her to look after him, she let me hold him this morning while Daddy took some photographs.'

'He's a very lucky boy, having a big sister like you. When he's older you'll be able to teach him all sorts of things and I'm sure you'll be a big help to Mummy and Daddy.' I carried Rose through to the lounge at the same time as Sue was coming downstairs with James. I kept Rose on my knee as I sat down, not wanting to make too much fuss of the baby while his big sister wanted my attention. When Rose jumped down, I stood to hug Sue and have my first real cuddle with James. He seemed contented and rightly so, he had just been fed. A little milky bubble played on his lips, which were pursed as if ready to bestow a kiss. Gazing down at this little miracle, I silently wished him a safe and happy life. James had the best start any child could have, with doting parents and surrounded by family and friends who would always be there for him. I hoped he would always feel this and know how much he was loved.

Peter broke into my thoughts by reaching to take the baby from me; confidently holding the tiny bundle, he proclaimed that the new arrival looked just like his father.

'I should hope so, Peter, if he looked like the milkman I'd be worried!' Alan laughed but then noticed his daughter trying to figure that out and quickly changed the subject.

'I've rung in to work and fixed up to start paternity leave from Monday, two weeks, I can't wait.'

'Don't think it's going to be a picnic, Alan,' Sue chipped in. 'The decorating in the little back bedroom needs finishing and I'll probably need lots of rest so there'll be plenty to keep you occupied.' She grinned at me as Alan rolled his eyes. Sue came over as the bossy wife but we all knew she doted on Alan; it would be good for them to have some family time. For that same reason we didn't stay long. Ruby made coffee and after drinking it we left them alone. Sue did look tired and as James had settled in his Moses basket and was fast asleep, my friend would be able to rest too.

'If you need anything just ring,' I said as we left, but I could see that Sue was well supported for the time being.

Chapter 4

Carol Jacobs was seated in the practice waiting room for the second time in a week. Dr Williams, however, didn't appear to mind how many times she visited the surgery and appeared genuinely anxious for her welfare, which was exactly what Carol needed at that point in time. A few of the other patients in the waiting room glanced in her direction then turned swiftly away, embarrassed to see the cut on her forehead and the darkly swollen eye. Her turn came just a couple of minutes after the appointment time and she soon found herself sitting in a warm, comfortable room, hearing the doctor's soothing Scottish lilt and the concern in his rich voice.

'This is twice this week, Carol, don't you think it's time to sort this out permanently?' he asked with real empathy as if she was important to him. She lifted her head and shrugged dejectedly, leaving him to draw his own conclusions. Tom Williams stood up and moved beside his patient to gently lift her hair and see the open wound on her forehead.

'I'll get a nurse to clean that for you before you go and I suggest an ice pack for your eye, but it's going to be a real shiner in the morning. Would you like to tell me what happened this time?'
Carol lowered her head again and replied quietly,
'It looks worse than it is but it wasn't Bill's fault. I'd forgotten he was on early shift and didn't have breakfast ready soon enough, he got annoyed... but he didn't mean to hurt me. I fell onto the door jamb and did this.'

'We can get you help, Carol, there are so many places for vulnerable women to go these days and plenty of support. There are choices, you know, you don't have to stay with Bill.'

'No, I couldn't leave him! He loves me and it's just that sometimes I do silly things which annoy him, but he would never really hurt me.'

'From the state of you on your last few visits I would say he's already hurt you enough, and seriously too. He shouldn't be allowed to get away with this; are you sure you don't want help?'

'Really, I'm fine. We have a nice home and I don't have to go out to work, Bill's a good provider and besides there's nowhere else to go even if I wanted to.' Dr William's patient looked thoughtful and somewhat weary.

'Will you at least see a counsellor? We have two excellent ones here at the surgery, Steve Franks and Maggie Sayer. I could make an appointment if you like?'

'Oh, I couldn't talk to a man... perhaps Ms Sayer if you think it will help?'

'I'm sure it will help. Now I'll just get a nurse to clean that cut for you.'

Dr Williams picked up his phone and asked for a nurse to do a dressing before taking Carol from his room to the reception desk. The appointment with Maggie was made and then a nurse took her to a treatment room to clean and dress the wound. She left the surgery feeling so much better; the visit had gone well and seeing a counsellor was a bonus, it could only help. Carol wondered what Maggie Sayer would be like and if she was as kind and sympathetic as Dr Williams, but there were only four days to wait before she'd find out for herself.

During those four days Carol's eye turned various shades of blue, black and yellow, and the bruising was still very noticeable when she returned to the health centre again on Thursday morning. If she had expected a reaction to her bruises from Maggie, she was disappointed as the counsellor showed her into a small comfortable room and offered a chair. When they were both seated, Maggie began to outline the confidentiality of the sessions and the exceptions to it.

'So, anything I tell you will stay in this room?' Carol asked.

'Yes, but do you understand the exceptions to this?'

'Yes, thank you.' There was a brief silence then Carol opened her mouth to speak but suddenly broke down sobbing, which did take Maggie a little by surprise. The counsellor calmly nudged a box of tissues towards Carol and moved her chair slightly closer, waiting for the outburst to cease and her client to calm down. After a couple of minutes she blew her nose and lifted her head to meet Maggie's eyes.

'I'm so sorry!'

'There's no need to apologise, tears can be cathartic at times. Would you like to tell me how you are feeling today?'

'Rather silly now.' She attempted a smile and continued. 'I suppose Dr Williams told you that my husband sometimes hits me?'

'No, he hasn't told me that but if you would like to talk about it perhaps it will help.'

Carol was rather surprised that Maggie had no background information on her until she explained,

'I try to begin a relationship with my clients knowing nothing except what they want to tell me. It enables me to get to know you from what you share and not from other people's opinions, which could be biased. If I do ask any questions it will be to clarify what you're telling me so that I can understand how you are feeling, and perhaps enable you to look at things from a different perspective. This time is for you to use exactly as you wish so do you want to talk about your relationship with your husband?'

'Well you know now that Bill hits me but he's not a bad husband really.'

'You seem defensive. In what way do you mean that he's not a bad husband?'

'He provides well for me and we have a really lovely house.' She was deliberately avoiding eye contact, and tearing little pieces off the crumpled tissue in her hands.

'And is that important to you?'

'Well...yes I suppose it is. I don't need to work, in fact Bill insists that I don't as he likes me to keep the house clean and tidy and have his meals ready for him after work.' Scrunching the tissue pieces into a tight little ball she looked expectantly at Maggie, waiting for some kind of reaction, but was given only the briefest of nods, encouraging her to continue.

'Bill's sixteen years older than me and a bit old-fashioned in his views; he has high standards and certain expectations.'

'And do you share his views, Carol?'

'Mostly, yes I would say so, although sometimes it would be nice to be able to meet friends for coffee or something but Bill doesn't approve of me going out without him. He doesn't give me enough money for that sort of thing either.'

'So you don't have money of your own, only what Bill gives you?'

'Well yes, but he can be generous in most things. I can buy nice food to cook, as long as I keep the receipts to show him.'

'And are you happy with this arrangement?'

'Well, I've never really thought about it but I suppose so. We go out shopping together for things for the house and Bill likes to choose my clothes for me, he's really very generous at times.'

'Bill chooses your clothes for you?' Maggie wondered if she had misheard. Carol was a very attractive young woman and was dressed rather conservatively in muted colours which presented a rather old-fashioned appearance and did nothing to enhance her rich chestnut hair and slim figure.

'Yes and they're always good quality; he doesn't mind spending money on me.'

'But he doesn't give you money to spend for yourself?'

'Well, I don't need it, do I? I have the housekeeping money for food and he takes care of all the bills and things.'

'Apart from Bill, do you have any other family who you're close to?' Maggie wanted to build up a picture of Carol's life and find out if she had support from parents or siblings.

'My father died when I was sixteen and my mother lives with my sister, not too far away, but Bill doesn't get on with them and prefers it if I don't see them.' The answer was almost whispered.

'And is that okay with you?'

'Oh yes, it's always better to go along with what Bill wants, it makes life so much easier.'

For the rest of the hour Maggie listened carefully to what Carol shared, showing little or no reaction and only occasionally asking for clarification of particular points. By the time this new client left she had presented a detailed account of her home life, leaving Maggie in no doubt that things were not at all right within the Jacobses' marriage and wondering what Carol really wanted from counselling or even from life itse

Chapter 5
Maggie

There was something about Carol Jacobs's acceptance of her situation and willingness to talk about it yesterday which was unusual. For a first meeting she'd been very open, which generally was not the case with abused wives, who very often needed their story drawing out of them over a few sessions. But then everyone is different and no two clients are ever the same, even if they share the same problem which in this case was an abusive husband. Carol appeared to want me to know all the facts and details of her life, relating them so quickly that she almost tripped over the words. This could simply be because she had no one else to talk to and as so often happens once the floodgates are open, it all poured out. There was almost too much for me to take in, and when she left yesterday I found it necessary to make a few notes to remind myself of her circumstances and jot down anything which I felt needed exploring at a later date.

The physical abuse was plain to see and from what Carol described of her life, there was evidence of psychological abuse too. Limiting money, isolation from friends and family and making all the decisions were classic indicators of this and Carol, although very much aware of what was happening, for some reason was unable to break free from the marriage and the circle of abuse. She also seemed to have some knowledge of the psychology behind domestic abuse and a good understanding of what was happening to her yet she was unable, or didn't want, to stop it. However it was early in our relationship, too early perhaps to draw conclusions and as she was keen to come back again we'd hopefully be able to work on some of these issues to her benefit at a later date.

Joyce Patterson has proved to be a great friend to me over the years I have known her. She is my counselling supervisor and I was due to spend the morning with her. All counsellors need supervision sessions for their own mental health and often their sanity. We made contact shortly after the completion of my training when I was seeking a supervisor and hit it off from our very first meeting. She is about fifteen years older than me and has always been an energetic, cheerful person. Although I didn't know until a few months into our relationship, Joyce too had been widowed at a young age, a shared heartache that went someway to help our bonding. I have of course remarried whereas she has remained single and lived alone in the bungalow to which I was heading. We understand each other and have a similar outlook on life, in fact I could see myself becoming just like her in fifteen or twenty years' time, clinging on to the job I love and resisting retirement for as long as possible. Of course I had a husband to consider so maybe for me retirement would be more welcome. Joyce often knew my thoughts before I voiced them which could sometimes be disconcerting but her wisdom has helped me through many situations and I have the highest regard for her professionalism and value her friendship greatly.

After ringing the doorbell I tried the handle and found it open so went in. Joyce was recovering from a hip replacement operation and I followed the sound of her voice into the lounge and bent to kiss my friend's cheek.

'Could you get the coffee, Maggie? The tray's all ready in the kitchen.'

'Of course, but you didn't need to bother, I'm fine without.'

'It was me I was thinking of, I was up early with this blasted hip. Sleeping is the biggest problem!'

I smiled and went to make the coffee. Five minutes later we were both seated, catching up on news before our work began. The first topic of conversation was Sue and Alan's baby. Joyce was delighted for them and wanted all the details which I was glad to replay once again. She asked about Peter's health and also about my mother who was still coming to terms with my father's death a little over a year ago. I was able to answer positively on all fronts. Now that Mum has got that first year over without Dad she seems much improved. The first year after bereavement is generally the hardest, full of anniversaries, the first birthday, the first Christmas and so on. At least Mum is now living in Fenbridge where I can keep an eye on her. My parents had retired to Scotland, living their dream in a small market town in the border regions but when Dad became ill they moved back to Fenbridge so I could offer the help and support they needed. Their bungalow in Scotland is still in the family; Mum was reluctant to sell it so we decided to keep it as a holiday retreat and we've already had some relaxing weekends there.

Once the personal enquiries were out of the way it was time to tell her what was on my mind. I had a couple of clients who were coming to the end of their sessions with me and it was good to be able to report that they had both made progress. Then I began to tell Joyce about Lindy and Carol. Describing my hour with Lindy took me right back to that rather soulless detention centre which to me seemed stark and unfriendly. To Lindy, however, it was apparently the best place she'd ever lived in her short life, a fact which spoke volumes about the girl's childhood. Joyce found it as incredible as I did that my new client intended to re-offend when she left Redwood in order to return.

'You know your role with this girl is only temporary, Maggie?' Joyce reminded me. 'You can't take on all of your clients as friends.'

I smiled, knowing she was referring to Julie, a young mother who had been in an abusive relationship when she came to me several years ago. Both she and her son were badly beaten by her bully of a husband who ended up dying in an accident after putting them both in hospital. My relationship with this young family crossed the boundaries usually in place between client and counsellor and became a friendship. Julie is now happily remarried and we remain good friends.

I moved on to tell Joyce about Carol Jacobs, as always using only her first name to maintain confidentiality. Verbalizing my thoughts and first impressions of Carol helped me to understand my own feelings towards this new client.

'She seems to look at things objectively and talked almost as if she was telling the story of someone else's marriage. And she makes excuses for her husband, insisting that he loves her which in Carol's eyes seems to make everything right. Sadly she had some rather nasty bruises and a cut to her forehead which must have been painful. She's an intelligent girl with a good understanding of what's happening to her yet she still makes excuses for her husband and blames herself for the abuse. She appears to be unable or unwilling to make any changes.'

Joyce listened carefully and nodded.

'Perhaps she just wants to get you on her side before feeling comfortable enough to work with you? I've known clients who have a good understanding of their problems and only needed counselling to validate their feelings or simply to feel normal again. I remember one young woman, years ago now, who took regular beatings from her partner and even provoked him into doing so. She eventually admitted that to herself the beatings proved that he loved her. She worried when he didn't beat her regularly, thinking he was indifferent about their relationship. To the poor girl her partner's violence was a sign that she was worth the effort to him and that he loved her. Typically that particular girl had grown up in a home with a violent father and taken on board those destructive introjected values without knowing what they were. Many of these women need rescuing from themselves rather than from their partners. They disregard their own and often their children's safety, perpetuating the cycle when they won't break free. Sadly though that is a decision which only they can make, and offering all the help in the world still won't persuade some women to leave an abusive relationship.'

'Well it's early days with Carol and no doubt I'll get a better understanding of her as time goes by, and she did seem keen to come again which can only be a good thing.'

When it was time for me to leave Joyce insisted on getting up to see me out in spite of my protestations.

'I need to move about or I'll seize up!' she explained as we walked towards the hall.

'Well don't forget to lock the door,' I reminded her as we said our goodbyes.

Chapter 6

Lindy Baker hadn't known what to expect when she first arrived at Redwood. The custodial sentence was expected, her solicitor had prepared her for that but the reality of the impending detention was unfamiliar and therefore something she dreaded. The first one to admit that her life was a mess, Lindy, who felt so alone in the world, had no idea of how to sort it out. Living on the streets was not a long term solution or a prospect she relished and yet the thought of being sent to another foster home was even more frightening. As it turned out her pessimism was unfounded and there were aspects of life at Redwood that she actually enjoyed. A clean bed to sleep in and hot showers readily available was certainly a plus, as well as regular meals. But the best thing for Lindy was meeting Tracey, who occupied one of the two rooms at the end of the corridor with her six-month-old son Sam. It had been something of a surprise to find facilities for mothers and babies at Redwood in the form of two mini 'bedsits' each boasting en-suite toilet and shower plus a fridge for bottle preparation. Tracey had taken up residence in one of these rooms the day after Lindy arrived. Perhaps because they were the two latest inmates of the wing or maybe because Lindy was drawn to the baby, they formed a friendship of sorts and began spending time together. Over the first few weeks of Lindy's incarceration she found herself enjoying the routine of studying then spending time with Sam during her free hours. It struck her as strange that a mother could be sent to a place like Redwood with her baby but Tracey was a habitual offender who had broken licence conditions several times. She was delighted to find in Lindy someone to share responsibility for her son and even though the others teased them, calling them a 'lady' and her nanny, neither really minded and Lindy did seem to possess a soothing touch, settling a fractious Sam when his mother failed to do so. The warders were flexible in allowing her to help too; they didn't enjoy listening to a crying baby any more than the other girls did. The purpose of having facilities for babies was to allow mother and child to bond, but over the weeks it was Lindy who bonded with Sam and he became an important part of her life in Redwood. Although aware of the fact that any relationship with him could only ever be temporary, it became increasingly difficult for her to be objective in her relationship with Sam. She chided herself for this yet with every passing day she grew closer to the little boy who reminded her so much of her brother.

In the days after Lindy's first session with Maggie her thoughts were often directed back to that frightening day when she thought her little brother might die, and she wondered if that was something she could share with Maggie. Lindy had never told anyone about it and as her roommate said it might do her good to offload 'stuff'. The counsellor seemed to really listen and wanted to know about her, which was such a different experience from all the social workers and foster carers she'd had. They expected her to be the one to listen and were never interested in what she had to say. All they ever did was talk at her, issuing instructions as to what she should be doing and how she should be behaving and they were always too busy to listen and take the time to find out what she wanted or how she was feeling. Lindy expected Maggie to be surprised when she told her that Redwood was the best place she'd ever lived, but if she was it certainly didn't show.

In reality the girl knew that she wouldn't last long living on the streets. The summer weather might be okay but it would be incredibly hard in winter and the thought of the long dark nights made her shiver with fear. Lindy was unsure what would happen to her when the time came to leave Redwood. Was there another alternative now that she was seventeen? Perhaps she was too old for foster care but with not having much of an education it would be hard to find a job. There might be benefits she could apply for but finding somewhere to live was a whole new ball game and Lindy didn't know where to begin. At least Redwood was warm and although the meals were not brilliant they were better than many places she'd lived and it was safe too. Going back to shoplifting in the hope of being sent back wasn't much of an ambition but no matter how much she thought about it, she could come up with no alternative idea.

Lindy made a conscious decision to trust Maggie, which was a big step for her. Sadly, childhood years had taught her that adults were generally not to be trusted. Initially she was unsure about continuing the counselling sessions but eventually decided to attend and see how it worked out, and so a week later she found Maggie waiting for her in the same room, a continuity which brought a small degree of comfort to the teenager.

After a brief reminder of the confidentiality of their conversations, Maggie asked what she would like to talk about. Having had a week to ponder this, Lindy jumped right in and began to describe her feelings at being at Redwood. She was quite animated as she talked about Tracey and baby Sam and how much she loved helping to care for him and how much he reminded her of her own younger brother.

'Sam reminds me of Jack, who I miss so much. When Jack was a baby, even though I was only six or seven, I looked after him more than our mother did. She was very often stoned or out with her latest boyfriend so it was up to me to find something for Jack to eat and change his nappies when they were dirty. My baby brother was the most important person in my life. Even at seven years old I knew that our mother didn't care about us. Her next drink or latest boyfriend was the only thing she thought about. The flat we lived in was dirty, I did my best to keep Jack clean but he didn't have many clothes. Sometimes I had to just wrap him in a blanket to keep him warm and he always seemed to have a cold, his nose was runny and he coughed a lot. I really loved my brother and miss him so much.'

'How old will he be now, Lindy?' Maggie gently probed.

'Almost eleven and moving into secondary school in September but I have no idea where he is and probably no chance of ever seeing him again.'

Maggie had to swallow the lump rising in her throat. Lindy, head bowed now, was focussing on her hands which were clasped tightly in her lap, as she appeared to be transported back to that difficult time in her childhood.

'The day we were taken away was the worst day of my life. Jack had another cold, his breathing was raspy and I was worried about him. Mum had been out until late the night before leaving me to babysit as usual. She'd not been to bed and was still asleep on the sofa when I got up early the next morning. I remember shaking her quite hard but she wouldn't wake up even though I kept on and on shaking her. Jack was crying and struggling to breathe and I knew he needed to see a doctor even though I was only seven. Not knowing what to do I opened the front door of the flat, which was never locked, and went to knock on our neighbour's door. An elderly couple lived there and they came in to see what was happening. The lady, I can't remember her name now, took one look at Jack and rang for an ambulance. Soon our little flat was filled with people, I stood in the corner opposite the door, afraid of what was happening and wondering if I'd done the right thing or if I would be in trouble. The paramedics were first to arrive and spoke kindly as they assessed the situation, putting an oxygen mask over Jack's little face and wrapping him in silver foil to keep him warm. By the time they were ready to leave for the hospital, the police and a social worker had also arrived. I knew that things would never be the same again and cried bitterly when they took Jack away, desperately wanting to go with him. The social worker said I must go with her to somewhere where it was warm and there were other children to play with. A policeman managed to wake Mum but she was struggling to talk properly. The lady took me away and I cried for my brother, even though she said I would see him when he was better. I was scared that the paramedics wouldn't know where I was to bring him back to me, and refused to be comforted for hours. Even now, with an understanding of what happened and why, that awful feeling still returns. Jack was the only person I loved and the pain of not being with him was almost unbearable. Looking back, it wasn't surprising that we were taken into care. The flat was filthy, there was no food in the fridge except a bottle of milk which had curdled, and a seven-year-old was the main caregiver for a one-year-old baby. I know now that it was right to seek help, if I hadn't gone to our neighbours that day Jack could have died but I was to lose my brother either way. When he'd recovered we were together for only a few weeks before he was moved into foster care and later adopted. I only had myself to blame, it was me who asked for the help, which eventually led to us being separated. I still have no idea where he is and probably no chance of seeing him ever again and I've never seen our mother since that day either.

'When I asked the social workers about my mother they told me she'd moved away from the area. At seven years old I couldn't understand why she didn't come back for us but over the years it's become clear that she never had any feelings for us. But I don't care!' Lindy's tone changed and she lifted her face and spoke almost angrily.

'All I care about is Jack even though they have never told me where he is. I cried for him at night for months afterwards but I haven't cried again since then!' The sudden defiance left as swiftly as it had come, she lowered her head again and continued,

'There was nothing I could have done to keep us together at the time but it's been so hard to accept that Jack's moved on and I'll never see him again. He may not even know he has a sister; he was too young to have any memories of me. I can only hope he's with a good family and is happy.'

Lindy's story touched Maggie deeply. It seemed that the girl had been let down on more than one occasion and Maggie wondered if there was anything she could do, other than listen, to try to make it up to her. Before their session ended, she asked the name of the social worker who was assigned to her.

'I could give you quite a list,' was the reply, but Lindy did mention the name of the last social worker she'd had and Maggie made a mental note of it.

Chapter 7
Maggie

Tears stung my eyes as I drove away from Redwood. Every time I think I've heard it all before something catches me unawares, and Lindy Baker's experience was just that something. As she described the filthy conditions of the flat which was her childhood home I could have wept openly. Okay, this rarely happens, I have a good degree of self-control but to picture a seven-year-old girl looking after her baby brother in such circumstances filled me with absolute horror. Perhaps having recently been so involved with the birth of Sue and Alan's new baby and the joy he'd brought to those around him made Lindy's situation seem that much more poignant. The woman who was her mother didn't deserve that title; the very word 'mother' in itself conveys an image of love and care, which was obviously not the case in this deeply fractured family. Joyce's words echoed in my mind, her timely reminder that it was impossible to take on all of my clients other than in a professional role. It was sensible advice but I longed to put my arms around Lindy and tell her everything would be alright, but I couldn't do that or make that kind of assurance. What I could perhaps do was to contact her social worker to ask about the possibility of tracing her brother. I could almost hear Joyce's voice saying that was not in my brief but a simple phone call surely couldn't hurt? Of course I wouldn't tell Lindy about it, as getting her hopes up would only add to her distress if it was not possible to find out where Jack was. I knew also that because he was a child, as indeed was Lindy, it would further complicate the situation. At times I've watched those television programmes which centre on reuniting lost family members but they are adults who can decide for themselves. The same with internet searches, sites such as 'Ancestry.com' and 'Genes Reunited' are ideal for adults looking into their past but I was dealing with children. Still, it was only a phone call, what harm could it do?

As there was nothing in my diary until mid-afternoon I intended to go home and have lunch with Peter. He too had little on that day and was reading the paper as I walked through the door. Getting up to greet me, he looked searchingly at my face and seeing the tell-tale signs of tears, frowned at me. I replied with an exaggerated smile and headed for the kitchen to make some lunch, only to find that my husband had beaten me to it. A tray was laid out with thick doorstep ham and salad sandwiches and buttered scones.

'How lovely!' I turned and wrapped my arms around him, leaning my head briefly on his shoulder, savouring his touch and appreciating his silence. Rarely did Peter ask about my work and on those odd occasions when he did it was in very general terms, as was the answer he received. I knew it was not because he didn't care but that he understood the confidentiality involved with counselling. After a long silent hug we moved away from each other.

'Sit down, love, and I'll make a pot of tea,' my strong silent soul-mate ordered and I happily complied, sinking into the sofa and curling my legs beneath me. Peter sat beside me and as we ate I asked about his work, a less taboo subject, and he updated me on the progress of the firm's biggest project, a nine-screen cinema complex with eating places and a multi-storey car park on the outskirts of Fenbridge. I had seen some of the plans and they were pretty impressive. Peter was now working on the final costing whilst his two partners fine-tuned the design and liaised with their client. He told me how they were progressing and that the work could begin as soon as planning permission was granted, which shouldn't be a problem as the building was generally thought to be a good use of a brownfield site which seemed to be crying out for such a development. I loved Peter's enthusiasm for his work and the passion which he and his colleagues demonstrated; surely this was one of the factors which made their small company such a success. My husband worked fewer hours than he would have liked but that was due to his health, he knew he must pace himself and of course I was always swift to remind him.

After lunch I drove back to the health centre where Carol Jacobs was due at two pm. This second meeting proved to be almost a repeat of the first one, with Carol recounting almost everything shared previously and offering very little else by way of new insights into her situation. Some past incidents of violence were picked over again with the same excuses made for Bill's behaviour. It felt as if there were three people in the room as Carol matched every nugget of information regarding the violent incidents with an excuse, generally a fault in her own actions which she obviously assumed was the reason for her husband's behaviour. Sadly this isn't uncommon, and I'd come across it often in the past. If an abused person is constantly told the abuse is their fault they eventually begin to believe it. It's almost brainwashing by instalments but completely untrue. The fault in any abusive relationship lies firmly with the abuser and I could only hope that eventually Carol would see this for herself.

Towards the end of the session Carol mentioned her father for the first time.

'He wasn't averse to slapping Mum around. Sometimes it was like walking on eggshells at home and I vowed I'd never marry a man like him... but here I am in the same situation. That often happens doesn't it, Maggie, girls marry men who are like their fathers?'

'Yes, it does but not always. What about your relationship with your father, Carol, was he violent towards you as well as your mother?'

She frowned and looked away as if seeking inspiration from the walls of the room.

'Yes, he was. When I was a little girl I thought that I must be very naughty because he often smacked me and then as a teenager we had the usual father-daughter arguments which generally ended with him striking out at me. If he got too angry and I was quick enough to see it coming I'd run upstairs and barricade the bedroom door so he couldn't get in. I suppose he then took it out on Mum or Liz, they seemed to accept it and he soon calmed down or went to the pub to get out of the house.' Carol's words seemed rather strange, she knew her father was abusive yet didn't make the same excuses for him that she made for her husband. However, that seemed to be all she wanted to share about her father and the subject was swiftly changed back to Bill. I wondered about this and hoped that at a later date she would feel able to talk in more detail about her father and any issues from her early years at home. Somewhere there was a key to unlock what was really troubling this young woman and I had a nagging feeling that there was much more to this than the abuse from Carol's husband.

By four pm I was heading back home, looking forward to a lazy evening doing nothing more stressful than watching television. We're not ones for going out much in the evening and since we lost Ben there's no incentive to walk on dark wintry nights. Things will probably change when the lighter nights and warmer weather comes, but I quite like cosy evenings in with Peter and a glass of wine. There was a programme that evening which we both wanted to see, a documentary about a breakthrough in treating multiple sclerosis patients. We sat, both transfixed by the screen as the new trials were explained and the results declared a major success. Peter's MS is the relapsing-remitting kind, the most common form which affects eighty percent of MS sufferers. The programme outlined a trial whereby patients were treated with chemotherapy. It was explained as being like rebooting a computer; stem cells were removed from the patient and replaced after chemotherapy, rather like going back to factory settings with a computer. Different MS sufferers were followed and their progress was amazing, some being able to walk after years of being in a wheelchair. We were both excited as we listened to the reports; breakthroughs like this give us hope that Peter's future might not be one of slow deterioration but the possibility of the symptoms actually decreasing. For a few moments after the television was switched off we sat in silence, both lost in our thoughts. When I did turn my face toward my husband we smiled, not needing to say anything. Peter bent to kiss me and I responded, needing the comfort of his closeness. Although the programme we had watched was full of hope for a positive future it left me feeling vulnerable, maybe because we had focussed for that hour on Peter's condition when we usually worked so hard to ignore it. He took my hand and led me to the bedroom where we quietly undressed and slipped beneath the covers of our bed. Peter's hands massaged my body; he knew all the places I liked to be touched, my shoulders and back, the base of my spine. We shifted position and kissed urgently before gently making love until we were both satisfied. Only then did we talk about our future and all the possibilities it could hold. I slept soundly afterwards, still wrapped in Peter's arms and listening to the gentle rhythm of his breathing from which I drew my comfort and strength.

We woke the next morning still on a high and greatly encouraged by the programme we'd watched the evening before. Our conversation once again focussed on the possibilities these breakthroughs could present and we were both quite animated about the future, daring to dream that Peter's illness might not disable him as much as we'd always assumed it would. Leaving for work that Friday morning, I laughed at myself for the feeling of joy bubbling up inside of me. I felt so happy that I was in danger of bursting into song and that would be worrying! Even the light drizzle outside the car couldn't spoil my mood.

The health centre where I work is adjacent to the main shopping street in Fenbridge and during my lunch break I intended to shop for a gift for baby James. At noon, I walked through the busy town centre heading for a lovely shop I'd recently discovered which was full of beautiful baby clothes and toys and aptly named 'Baby Grow'. My mind was on what gift I should buy, anticipating being presented with such adorable choices that the selection would be difficult. Turning the corner I caught sight of Carol Jacobs standing in the doorway of Fenbridge's one and only department store. She was talking to an older man who I presumed to be her husband. He had a receding hairline and was carrying too much weight for someone of his height. I stopped to watch for a few moments, curious to see this husband whom I'd heard so much about, then I chastised myself for being nosey and set off again on my mission for a gift for James.

Eventually I arrived at 'Baby Grow', enjoying the world of all things baby for a good fifteen minutes, fascinated by the beautiful clothes and toys on display. I settled on a pair of pale blue trousers with a bib front and a couple of stretchy tops to match. The trousers were made from a soft cotton fabric which I imagined would be comfortable for James to wear as well as practical. A small toy giraffe also caught my eye and ended up with my purchases for which I paid before heading back to work. I would gift wrap the presents and take them to Sue at the weekend. My mother had been itching to meet James and I could take her too, as she'd been knitting for the new arrival. By the time I returned to work, Carol Jacobs was no longer on my mind as I placed my shopping in the desk drawer and prepared for the next client.

Chapter 8
Maggie

Saturday morning dawned bright, sunny and much warmer than of late, making me feel that spring really was on its way. Peter was working for a couple of hours to finish off some costing for a minor project which he wanted to clear, so I set off to Mum's in anticipation of taking her to meet baby James. Always an early riser, my mother was ready to go as soon as I stepped through the front door. Above the fireplace was a portrait of my father with Ben at his feet, one which Peter had painted shortly before Dad died. It was always the first thing my eyes were drawn to, my father's bemused expression captured so perfectly and so typically him. The shaft of sunlight beaming on both him and Ben added almost tangible warmth to the picture and was how I liked to remember them both. The portrait was full of love and evoked so many delightful memories as well as feelings of loss; it was a bitter-sweet emotion which flowed over me each time I looked at it. Following the direction of my eyes, Mum smiled; she had told me before that the image was a great comfort to her and I know she still talked to Dad too as if he was still with us, even if only in spirit.

We set off to Sue's, me with my gifts wrapped in bright baby blue paper and Mum with a gorgeous tiny knitted jacket in pale blue. I also took small gifts for Rose and George in an effort to include them in the celebrations. James was only a week old, well, eight days to be precise but I was sure he would have grown already.

'Gosh he's filling out,' was my initial reaction to seeing him again.

'Actually he's slightly lighter than his birth weight,' Sue informed me then continued as she saw my startled expression, 'Don't worry, new babies always lose a little of their birth weight, it's perfectly natural and nothing to worry about.'
That's the trouble with never having had children of my own, I didn't know that fact but Sue and my mother did. I think I blushed a little as I reached out to take hold of James.

'If you're wondering why it's so unnaturally quiet it's because Alan's taken Rose and George to the park. They should be back any time so I'll get the kettle on while there's a chance.'

'Let me do that for you while you two catch up with your news,' Mum offered.

'Thanks, Helen, you know where everything is, don't you?' Sue was never one to insist on doing things when someone else offered. We sat on the sofa; there wasn't really much to catch up on, certainly nothing which we wouldn't want Mum to hear and we'd spoken several times on the phone over the last week.

'How are you coping?' I asked.

'Okay, I suppose, but having Alan around helps and Mum's been here most days, in fact I'm thinking of changing the locks.' Sue's pained expression made me laugh. She and Ruby had a strange love/hate relationship and often disagreed over things. I put it down to them both having similar temperaments and I knew that they really loved each other fiercely and despite my friend's regular barbed comments she would be the first to fight Ruby's corner if necessary.

'I'm a little worried about Alan going back to work,' Sue admitted, 'The morning school run might be rather hectic, it's bad enough with two to get ready, goodness knows how I'll cope with James as well.'

'Perhaps I can help? I could easily drop Rose off at school, it's just around the corner from the health centre and I can reschedule my nine o'clocks to nine-fifteen, no problem.'

'Oh could you, Maggie, that would be wonderful but only until I get into a routine. Getting George to nursery on his two days there will be easier, I can take him in any time I like.'

That's one of the things I love about Sue, she doesn't fuss and say silly things like 'Oh I couldn't possibly let you do that'. She knows I mean it and accepts graciously. What you see is what you get in the Hurst household.

Mum came through with the coffee at the same time as Alan and the children came in through the front door.

'Auntie Maggie!' Rose rushed towards me, arms wide open. I caught her with my right arm, turning slightly so that she didn't run straight into James.

'May I take him?' Mum asked Sue.

'Of course, Helen, and I'll pass round the coffee.' James was wide awake but silent, his little face contorting into some very puzzled looks, and a couple of yawns letting us know he was either tired or bored with the company.

'He's beautiful!' Mum cooed. She loves children of whatever age and I occasionally wish for her sake as well as mine that I could have given her grandchildren. Still she occasionally babysat for Sue and Alan so we could have a night out as a foursome and was delighted to do it. Alan sank down in an armchair and yawned simultaneously with his baby son.

'No need to ask if you've been sleeping well?' I smiled, and he shook his head.

'I'll be ready to get back to work for a rest!' Alan accepted the coffee from his wife and Sue began to tell him about my offer to take Rose to school.

'That's brilliant, thanks, Maggie. It'll only be until we get into some sort of routine, the school run was difficult enough with two children but with three it could be a nightmare and I'm never sure what my shifts will be.'

For me it would be a pleasure. I have taken Rose to school before on a couple of occasions and her conversation is enchanting as she anticipates her day and what work the teacher will have for her. She loves reading lessons the best and enjoys making up and writing stories too. Rose instructs me on where to stand and tells me I can go when the bell rings and the classes line up in single file in front of their teacher. It's a joy to watch her 'little schoolgirl important walk' as she joins the line, wanting to get everything just so to please her teacher. Apparently there are boys in the class who don't always do as they're told and Rose thinks that is so naughty! I was already looking forward to taking her; it would be a great start to my day too.

I took Mum home 'the scenic route' which was beside an old Victorian park which was filled with daffodils. I parked the car and we got out to see them better, a hundred-yard carpet of gloriously yellow trumpets, all facing towards the sun. It almost prompted me to recite poetry but 'A host of golden daffodils' was as much as I could remember of Wordsworth's poem. We walked a little way down the central path, surrounded by the cheerful spring flowers.

'I miss walking since we lost Ben and I'll probably be piling on the pounds too if I'm not careful.' I was finding it so much more difficult to lose weight the older I became, and each time I put on a pair of jeans the 'muffin top' reminded me of this.

'Have you thought about getting another dog?' my mother asked.

'Oh yes, it's cropped up in conversation a few times. We're probably ready to do so now, we just needed a little time to get over Ben.'

'Will you get another rescue dog?'

'Most certainly. I know pedigree dogs are beautiful but it seems such a shame to encourage breeding when there are so many lovely unwanted dogs just waiting for a home. We'll think a bit more seriously about it now the weather's picking up, so watch this space, Mum.'

Chapter 9
Maggie

Monday morning arrived far too quickly and the health centre was already packed as I walked through the door. Before reaching my room I heard a familiar voice calling my name rather loudly and turned to see Norman Longstaff waving from the waiting room. Walking over, I placed my hand on his shoulder and spoke quietly to calm him down.

'You're very early, Norman. I'm seeing someone else before you so it'll be rather a long wait, I'm afraid.'

'Don't mind, Maggie, it's warm in here and I like to look at the magazines.'

'Well okay, but you might want to go and have a coffee somewhere; it'll be over an hour.'

'Right yes, I'll do that. Coffee would be good and I'll come back at ten.' He unfolded his lanky frame, jumped up and turned towards the door, almost knocking over a lady who was just about to sit down. Watching him leave, I smiled; he was dressed as usual in baggy combat trousers with a fur-hooded parka and a baseball cap worn back to front. Being tall, extremely thin with a round head and wide grin, he put me in mind of a child's drawing of a stick man. Norman is a regular client who struggles with life at times but has a good heart which endears him to me. He has special needs and is diagnosed as somewhere on the autism spectrum, with eccentricities which include regular conspiracy theories, frequent sightings of UFO's and a fear of being poisoned by 'rampant chemicals' in the atmosphere. He also has tendencies towards obsessive compulsive disorder. When I say he's a regular client I mean that I'm able to offer him six once-a-week sessions and then wait for him to turn up again in a couple of months' time. There are restrictions on the amount of sessions we can offer NHS clients after which there needs to be a re-referral to commence another six-week block with either me or Steve Franks, the other practice counsellor. Some would say that as he rarely shows any change in his behaviour he is a drain on resources. I would disagree; knowing he will be referred again keeps Norman on an even keel. His need to pour out his thoughts and fears of life is very real and he is one of those vulnerable members of society who will always need help and support, which is fine by me if it enhances Norman's quality of life.

My first appointment was with a recently widowed lady whom I had seen only twice before. In her mid-fifties with an active lifestyle, her husband's death had come as a great shock. He too, at fifty-seven had been active and only a month before his death completed 'The Great North Run', a half marathon and was in the throes of planning his next one. Martha was devastated; her husband David looked after all the family's finances and she was left feeling totally useless and vulnerable. She told me that she didn't even know who supplied their gas and electricity and had never so much as written a cheque in their thirty-year marriage. The couple had two children, both of whom lived on the south coast with busy lives of their own. They had of course come north for the funeral but were unable to stay more than a few days. Martha felt completely lost and abandoned. Any self-confidence she once possessed had deserted her, leaving a feeling of being inept and rather stupid, neither of which were true. On her two previous visits we'd discussed completing a time-line, looking back on her life to significant periods both good and bad. Today we planned to put this down on paper and I hoped Martha was still keen to give it a go. Generally a time-line is a tool for looking back to events which in some way changed the course of life and shaped the person we are today. With Martha I hoped this exercise would not only highlight how she had coped with negative issues in the past, but validate her own worth and remind her of the strength and courage she had drawn on in years gone by. Hopefully this would enable her to face the future and build a new life as best as she could.

When Martha arrived it was with a noticeable improvement in demeanour. Her smile was more natural than polite and she had specific things to discuss, having been thinking about embarking on the time-line since we last met. I passed a pen and paper over to her and with very little assistance from me she began to note significant events from the past. She had survived the death of both parents before marrying David, suffered two miscarriages before her children came along and had at one point nursed a cousin who was seriously ill. As she recorded these events on paper I was able to point out the strength she had frequently displayed when called upon to cope with such varied occurrences. Naturally her present bereavement was the hardest thing of all, but Martha could see what I was trying to do through pointing out how she had coped with life in the past. No one was trying to tell her it was going to be easy; her marriage had been a very close one but with help she would get through her loss. Part of my job is to signpost clients to places of support for particular issues. Possibly in the next couple of sessions I would suggest events which could be beneficial and provide continuing support. I had in mind a social group run by Cruse Bereavement Care who provide an informal place to drop into, have coffee and chat to counsellors and others who are also coming to terms with the loss of a loved one.

It had been a good session and Martha left in a positive frame of mind. It's people like her who make my job so interesting and rewarding. There have been many 'Marthas' over the years and although very often I never see them again when our time together comes to an end, it's a positive thing as it means they have moved on with their lives, which is after all my ultimate aim. Norman was next on my list.

'Hi, Maggie!' He was back in the waiting room facing my door and was up and through it almost before Martha had left.

'How are you today, Norman?' I enquired, without knowing what was coming my way but as ever certain that it would be something to stretch my skills and broaden my experience of human nature.

'I'm not very happy,' Norman stated then waited for me to ask why.

'Oh, I'm sorry to hear that, is there a particular reason?'

It was almost choreographed, a ritual dance we began each session with. It was impossible to conduct a session with Norman as I would do with other clients; his expectations needed to be met so perhaps I participated a little more than I would usually like to do and empathised verbally, something again I wouldn't normally do but Norman needs this from me. He is possibly the only one of my clients who needs intervention in this way and I often find myself pointing out the bigger picture to him without belittling the issue he has raised.

'They've stopped the number forty-seven bus running on Sundays!' He looked at me with a 'what do you think of that' expression.

'Oh dear, and is that a particular problem to you?'

'No, I never use the busses on Sundays but it's wrong! How will people get to town? Not everyone can afford taxis you know.'

I nodded, hoping he would continue, which he did.

'They never think of the people who don't drive, what can they do? Busses should run every day and on time too!' Norman was becoming quite animated. This was going to be one of those instances when a little intervention would be needed.

'Can you imagine what it must be like to be a bus driver, Norman? Or even the man who makes the timetable?'

Norman held up his hand to stop me from speaking and withdrew a rather dog-eared timetable from his parka pocket. As he began thumbing through it I continued.

'They have to decide if they can afford to run the busses every day, as if not many people require a ride to town it will cost more in diesel than they will get back in fares.' My client began to rummage in the same pocket and took out a notebook.

'Say that again, Maggie,' he asked and began to scribble in the book in his tiny, almost illegible handwriting. I had seen the notebook before on several occasions. Anything which Norman hadn't thought about was recorded in there as well as an endless list of things to remember.

'That's really good, Maggie, I'd never thought about that!'

I found myself wishing that such a simple explanation could solve all of my clients' problems; we moved on from the bus timetable's deficiencies. Norman was concerned about the waste of fruit and vegetables in the local supermarket.

'I watched a programme on television about waste food and asked the manager at Asda about it. He said they did throw food away when it was out of date so

I've written to him to complain. It's shocking, Maggie, don't you agree?'

Norman offloaded his current anxieties and I listened for the remaining hour before gently letting him know our time together was up. We said goodbye and I knew he would be in the same seat in the waiting room at least an hour before his appointment time next week.

Chapter 10
Maggie

Carol Jacobs was on time and entered my office with a ghost of a smile on her lips. This was our third meeting and I was hopeful that we could really make a connection, something which didn't quite seem to be happening so far. I was pleased to see there were no more visible injuries but that wasn't to say there were none under her clothing and she didn't look too well; there were dark circles beneath her eyes and her face, devoid of make-up, looked pale. After she was seated I began by reminding her of the confidentiality clause of our meetings, then giving her my full attention I asked how she was feeling.

'Okay, it's good to get out of the house; I haven't been out since last week when I was here. Bill's decided that it's time to do the spring cleaning so I've been really busy at home.'

This didn't ring true; surely it had been Carol I'd seen in town and if it was, this was a lie, but why would she lie about something so trivial? I tried to put it out of my mind; such an unnecessary lie could destroy the trust between a counsellor and client so I decided to give her the benefit of the doubt and believe that it hadn't been her I had seen at all, or that she had simply forgotten being out that day. Carol continued,

'Bill likes the house to be clean and tidy and his mother's coming for lunch on Sunday so it'll need to be all finished by then.'

'Do you get on well with your mother-in-law?' I asked. Carol hadn't mentioned her when I'd asked about family during our first session.

'Not really, she rarely comes to our home. Bill visits her a couple of times a week and takes her shopping every Saturday. She always thought I wasn't good enough for her son so not seeing much of her suits us both.'

Carol stopped talking and sighed. She seemed to be wrestling with something, deciding what to share with me. After a few moments of silence she pulled up the sleeve of her coat and showed me her left arm. Small round blisters which appeared to be cigarette burns were on the inside of her forearm and they looked extremely painful. Tears began to fill her eyes; it was as if Carol wanted me to know about this latest injury but perhaps struggled to find the right words to explain what was happening in her life. The wounds looked freshly inflicted and untreated.

'Do you want to tell me what happened?' I asked. There was a brief silence then Carol pulled the sleeve back down and looked at me.

'I don't know what I did, Maggie, that's the frightening thing. I usually know what I've done to annoy him but he came home last night in a really dark mood about something but he doesn't talk to me about work. Then he lit a cigarette and began to complain because his meal wasn't on the table and suddenly he grabbed me by the wrists and did this... and I don't know why.'

'Carol, you don't have to stay with him. There are places to go and we can get you help and support.'

'I know, Dr Williams told me that too but Bill would only find me wherever I went.' Carol's tears were spilling down her cheeks; she looked desolate and I silently longed for her to escape the abusive life she was living.

'If you go to the police they can arrange for an order to be made to keep him away from you, it can easily be arranged and if he breaks the order he'll be arrested.' I frowned as she shook her head.

'It wouldn't make any difference; he'd find me and make life so much worse than it is now.'

It wasn't my place to try to persuade her otherwise. Having made it clear that she had options, I knew that only she could decide what to do and it looked as if she intended to do nothing at all. Carol returned to talking about more mundane matters, we were back to the spring cleaning and the meal she had to prepare for her mother-in-law. The rest of the session continued in much the same way, stunted, disjointed. Carol's mind seemed to skip from one dusty corner of her brain to another as she verbalized random facts without any visible thread to connect them. I simply listened for most of the hour, trying to follow the disjointed monologue. I was concerned about the burns on her arm and as we neared the end of our time together I asked if she would allow one of our practice nurses to dress them. She agreed and I made the phone call then directed her into one of the treatment rooms.

When Carol eventually left the surgery I knocked on Dr Williams's door to speak with him about this latest physical attack on his patient, which seemed so much more sinister than the usual hitting or punching. I feared that the abuse had taken on a more calculated and planned form and told the doctor my fears.

'She's a stubborn lass, is that one.' Tom Williams sighed. 'I don't know why she stands by him and if she's telling us about some of the things he does it makes me wonder what else there is that she doesn't tell us about.'

I could only agree but Tom seemed to feel as I did, totally helpless. We could only do what Carol would allow us to do but at the back of my mind was the fear that things might come to a head in the Jacobs household. If Carol was at the point of seeking help through counselling, it could indicate a shift in her usually passive acceptance of her domestic situation and she might at some point wish to be proactive about her position and her future. All we could do for the present was to remain in the background as support for whenever she needed us.

I left Dr William's office feeling a little frustrated, but there were other things I needed to do and my thoughts switched from Carol Jacobs to Lindy Baker. I had not as yet spoken to the social services about the whereabouts of her brother. Seeing Norman yesterday had given me an idea, and rather than ringing to speak to someone I didn't know, it might be better to start with a social worker I did know. Sarah Dent was Norman's social worker and we had met on three occasions at case conferences concerning him, to which I had been invited. Sarah struck me as being a caring professional and appeared to know Norman well. I found the number and dialled, hoping to catch her in the office and prepared to answer my questions. Her distinctive husky voice answered almost immediately and I hoped she remembered me from our previous meetings. After initial cordialities, I came out with what I wanted to know and explained the situation as succinctly as possible without revealing Lindy's identity.

'So your client has never been told where her brother is?' Sarah sounded surprised.

'That's right, I think over the years she's given up asking. I wouldn't want to criticise your colleagues but this girl seems to have been passed around not only from one foster home to another but one social worker to another as well.' I wondered if I should mention the name of the latest social worker Lindy had given me but I hesitated.

'Sadly I can believe this, Maggie, we're all snowed under with work and need to prioritise almost daily which means many of our clients don't get the attention they need or deserve. In the case of siblings, we really do try to keep them together or at least in contact with each other. If, as you say, this was a decade ago then perhaps it wasn't such an issue then as it is now. Did your client give you the name of her last social worker?' This left me with no choice but to tell her.

'Rachel Butler was the name she mentioned but there hasn't been any contact for a while.' I had already explained that my client was in a young offenders' institute.

'Ah, that explains it. Rachel has moved on to pastures new, I'm afraid. She's left the service altogether and as yet hasn't been replaced. Look, Maggie, if you'll leave this with me I'll see what I can find out but I need to have a name.'

I thought for a minute then explained that I would prefer to get my client's permission first. Sarah, who worked within the same parameters of confidentiality, understood and I told her that I'd see my client and get back to her soon. The call had given me hope that something could be done to find Lindy's brother but I would have to seek her permission, which I knew wouldn't be a problem but might unfortunately raise her hopes, something I had wished to avoid. My first thought was to ring Redwood and try to speak with Lindy but that was probably not the right way to go about it so, ringing Peter, I told him that I'd be late home as I was making a detour for an unscheduled visit to a client. My husband is wonderful, I don't mind who knows it; he asked no questions other than what I would like for dinner. Suggesting salmon, I smiled to myself, picturing him searching the freezer and then trying to work out how to defrost his find in the microwave.

Pulling up on the gravel car park, I was glad I'd rung ahead to check if it was possible to see Lindy briefly. The young woman I'd spoken to politely asked who I was and why I needed to see her without notice, but when I told her of my relationship to Lindy no problem was raised. It was four-thirty, hopefully too early for me to be disturbing a meal and it wouldn't take long to come clean to Lindy and tell her what I was trying to do.

An anxious look greeted me when I was shown into our usual counselling room. I smiled, raising my hands to indicate that nothing was wrong.

'I'm sorry to drop in on you like this, but it's nothing to worry about, please, sit down.' We both sat and I began to explain, wanting to remove that worried expression from the poor girl's face.

'Lindy, I was troubled about your lack of contact with your brother, it's not how social services work, these days at least. I've been talking to a friend of mine who's a social worker and without telling her any details I asked if anything could be done to let you know where Jack is and how he is doing.' Lindy looked stunned but remained silent, her eyes wide, 'Apparently Rachel Butler is no longer working with social services, which is probably why you've had no visits. The friend I spoke to would be happy to look into Jack's whereabouts, but I need to give her your name and I didn't want to do that without speaking to you first, so what do you think?' A huge smile invaded the girl's face. I had never seen her look so happy before, she was quite beautiful.

'Could they really let me know where he is? Will I be able to see him?'

'I honestly don't know. I didn't want to get your hopes raised but to take this any further they need to have a name. All I want today is your permission and I promise to let you know anything as soon as I do. Like all public services, social workers are stretched to the limit so I don't think this will be a priority and it could take time but I'll push as far as I can. Is this okay with you?'

'It's brilliant!' There was that lovely smile again, transforming her whole appearance.

'Can I telephone you here, Lindy? It would be much better if I could ring with any news instead of having to make the trip.'

'There is a phone, the other girls get calls all the time but I've never had any so don't know the number.'

'That's okay, I'll ask at the desk on my way out.'

It was a most satisfying end to my working day. Although I didn't want to offer false hope to Lindy, such a transformation had come over her that I felt privileged to have been the bearer of that tiny seed of hope. I would ring Sarah Dent as soon as I got home, if she had already left for the weekend I would leave a message but for now I turned the car towards home to see if the salmon was still frozen.

Chapter 11
Maggie

My mother's recent comment about another dog played on my mind for most of the week. Peter and I talked it through and both agreed that as it was now well into spring perhaps the time was right to visit the dog re-homing kennels. It was a beautiful spring Saturday, the first one in April, when we set off to Sue and Alan's house. Alan had taken a week's holiday to extend his paternity leave which I think Sue really needed; she was still very tired and James wasn't sleeping as well as her first two children had. I'd promised Rose that she could come with us when we went to choose a dog, and George too if his parents were happy about him coming. We were slightly early but not too early for Sue.

'Thank goodness you're here! They've been up since the crack of dawn, so excited about choosing a dog. You do realise that Rose thinks it's solely her decision? She's ruled George out as he's still a baby really and as you asked her to 'help' she thinks you two are incapable of deciding for yourselves. You'll also be very lucky if you come out of there with only one dog. Rose thinks you should get at least two so they'll have each other for company!'

'Ah, but will Tara want two?' I looked at my husband, 'Or Peter, he's looking rather worried!'

'We'll see!' Rose chipped into the conversation, using the words and tone her mother often did and which she always interpreted as 'yes'. Alan and Peter went to put the car seat and booster seat in our car and we were ready for our big adventure. Rose chattered all the way there, except for when she was singing and the car's gentle rhythm sent George to sleep.

I knew this could be an emotional visit for me. The older I get the more sensitive I seem to be about animals, and hearing stories of cruelty can easily reduce me to tears. I've also seriously considered becoming a vegetarian after reading an article about the treatment of sheep and cattle at an abattoir. Is this just an age thing or perhaps I'm going through the change and my hormones are playing havoc with my emotions? Whatever the reason I hoped we didn't encounter any graphic tales of the conditions their dogs had been found in, or I might be tempted to give up work and volunteer at the kennels, or to Rose's delight I might adopt half a dozen dogs! Our destination was about five miles out of Fenbridge through some beautiful countryside and winding roads with trees coming into leaf and daffodils flanking the roadside, nodding in the breeze. Rose's whoop of delight woke her brother as we arrived and pulled onto the visitor's car park. Before we left the car I reminded the children to stay close to us and not to shout too loudly in case they frightened the dogs. I needn't have worried. The barking could have drowned out any noise they could make, as excited dogs tried to attract attention with their barks and whines. This was not going to be easy! The staff had finished feeding their charges and were busy cleaning out the kennels so we were left pretty much to ourselves to look round at leisure. The kennels were spacious, each one consisting of a large outdoor area with a door through to the inside where baskets and toys were just visible through the doorway. No more than three dogs shared a kennel, with their names and details printed and hung on the outside wire mesh. Obviously this was going to take time. I estimated the number of dogs to be in the region of forty to fifty and that didn't include the puppies who were housed inside and only available to view by those who were serious about adopting one. We had decided that a puppy was out of the question for us and therefore didn't give Rose the option of seeing them as we knew she would fall in love with one or more. With George in his stroller and Rose leading the way, we began to walk round the kennels, stopping to talk to all the dogs and read the plaques attached to each cage with details about them. Sadly we had to pass over some lovely dogs as they were either not good with children or cats, and we had Tara to consider as well as our family and friends with children. But there were still plenty to choose from, and having the children with us helped to test the animals' reactions to little ones. From Jack Russells to German Shepherds, tails wagged enthusiastically as if they knew they were being considered for a new home. Most of them came to welcome us their eyes almost pleading for a stroke or a word, and it was even harder than I'd expected. Rose was taken by a small terrier but he seemed to make a constant noise, never ceasing his yapping. After forty minutes of looking around all the kennels, I was still confused. Peter had been making a list of possibilities but we were horrified to find that the list had over fifteen dogs' names on it!

'I think we should stick to one, Maggie,' Peter gently reminded me and practically I knew he was right. We walked round again, this time just concentrating on the ones on the list. Finding that some of them were quite elderly, we sadly ruled them out. Although I would love to give an older dog a home, after losing Ben we wanted to have one who would be with us for several years to come. With a final shortlist of four dogs it was time to seek out a member of staff to talk about the practicalities of our new pet. An enthusiastic young girl bearing a name badge which dubbed her as 'Angie' came to our aid, and we went into the office to sit down and discuss each dog.

'You've picked out four lovely dogs, I'm not sure I can make the decision any easier for you but I'll tell you what I can about their backgrounds.' She obviously loved her work and after asking what criteria we were looking for she began to tell us about the four dogs we liked.

'Sheba's a lovely girl; she's been with us for about six months now which is no fault of hers. When she arrived she had a few health issues and it's taken about four of those months to get her fit and well. She's about three years old and although she likes children I'm not sure how she would be with your cat. Now, Buster is an outgoing sort of dog and has been with us only a few weeks. He's two and full of energy and likes nothing more than playing fetch with a ball!'

'I'd like to play fetch with him,' Rosie said, 'He's lovely, can we get him, Aunty Maggie?'

'Well let's hear about the others first.' I pulled an excited Rose onto my knee as we listened to find out about the others.

'Jasper is a comical fellow, we haven't really much idea about his parentage but there seems to be some poodle and perhaps a bit of spaniel in him and he's a two-year-old like Buster. He's very playful and loves children and has been in a house with cats, four of them actually. His owner was an elderly lady who had to go into a care home so her dog ended up here and her cats are at the cat shelter. And then there's Lassie, she's part Border Collie and part German Shepherd and again is a dog who'll need quite a bit of exercise. All of them are house-trained and Sheba and Jasper are very good on the lead. Buster still needs a bit of training but we do run obedience classes here if you decide to take him.'

'Could we get them out of their kennels and perhaps take them for a walk?' Peter asked.

'Of course, that was what I was going to suggest next. If we take Sheba and Buster, first then come back for Jasper and Lassie?' Rose clapped her hands in delight while her brother, bored with the conversation, had again fallen asleep. We followed Angie outside again and waited while she brought Sheba and Buster. Heading for the huge field where the dogs were exercised, I took Buster's lead and as Angie kindly offered to push George, Peter took Sheba. Like all dogs they loved to be outdoors, and Buster began straining at the lead to be off.

'We'll let them off in a minute; the field's enclosed so they can't go anywhere. You see what I mean about Buster?' Angie smiled and I nodded, he was almost pulling me over.

'He'll be a lovely pet with a little training,' Angie pleaded his case. When they were let off their leads both dogs ran around the field excitedly, tails wagging and stopping only to explore a new scent. Angie had a ball and Buster showed off his ability to fetch with poor Sheba not fast enough to get there first. After about twenty minutes we walked back towards the kennels and Angie took the dogs back to their kennels then went to fetch Jasper and Lassie.

'It seems almost cruel deciding which one we want, they all deserve good homes,' Peter said.

'I know but we have to be practical.' Was that really me saying that? I'm usually the one who lets her heart rule her head but I was very conscious of Tara's needs and all the children who came to visit. Angie was soon back and again took George's pushchair while we took the dogs. Jasper walked so well on the lead, quite the opposite to Buster and he kept looking up at me as if to say, 'aren't I good?' Which he was! Peter took Lassie, who was keen to be off the lead and away. They both happily ran off but Jasper kept looking back as if to ensure that we were still there. When Angie eventually called them Jasper came immediately while Lassie ran the opposite way. Angie had to run after him, a game he thought was great fun.

Walking back to the kennels, Peter and I exchanged glances. 'Jasper,' we both said together. Angie had actually suggested that Rose held Jasper's lead on the way back and we were all impressed by how good he was with her. The suggestion had sealed it, and as he walked so well for Rose she too was in favour of taking Jasper. George woke up just as we approached the kennels and Rose proudly told him that she had chosen Jasper. I could barely look at the other dogs when we left them, feeling so guilty that we were not taking them home too.

There was paperwork to sort out, and as I'd had a dog from them before there was no problem as to our suitability, although someone would bring Jasper to us to ensure we had safe and dog-friendly accommodation. Jasper would also be checked over by a vet before he came to us so in a few days' time we would again be the proud owners of a dog. Rose chatted all the way home, telling George what he had missed even though he barely understood. She then gave her parents a blow by blow account of how she had chosen Jasper and even held him on his lead. Sue and Alan were grateful for the break; Alan would be returning to work after the weekend and I couldn't help wondering how Sue would cope. We said our goodbyes and left them to enjoy the rest of their weekend with some quality family time.

Chapter 12
Maggie

I had been right about taking Rose to school, it was the perfect way to start my day. Arriving early at Sue and Alan's house, I walked into a scene of panic over spilt milk, literally. George had decided to pour his own milk onto his Weetabix and knocked the litre bottle over the kitchen floor. Sue was on her knees with a roll of kitchen towels while George sobbed thinking he was in trouble. Rose sat at the table oblivious to the mayhem around her, eating cereal and swinging her legs in time to a song she was humming.

'Hi, Auntie Maggie, are you taking me to school today?'

'That's right but it looks as if we might have to swim.'

Rose chuckled and I lifted a sobbing George up to calm him down, singing the song which his sister had been humming. The little man soon settled and began to laugh; my singing often brings such a reaction. Sue finished the mopping up operation and flopped onto a chair.

'Hurry up, Rose, you need to brush your teeth and find your book bag. Oh, packed lunch, I've forgotten to make the sandwiches!'

'Don't worry, there's plenty of time, it's still early and I can do the sandwiches.' I was happy to help. Sue rolled her eyes,

'I've got used to having Alan around but he had an early start today. Hopefully that will mean he has an early finish too. I'm really grateful for this, Maggie.

James was up three times in the night but at least he's sleeping now. Goodness knows how I'll manage to get into some kind of routine.'

'You will, it's only been three weeks since he was born, you're doing great, Sue. I don't know anyone else who could manage three children under five as well as you do so don't be so hard on yourself. ' Although my friend kept her head down I was almost certain she'd been crying. It could of course be that her eyes were red and puffy through lack of sleep; as one who likes my sleep I could only imagine what a fractious baby could do to the nerves. With Alan off work for three weeks in all, it had given me an extra week to rearrange any early appointments and free up mornings to help Sue with the school run.

Rose skipped off to brush her teeth and I settled a now quiet George back in his high chair to have his breakfast. While Sue poured herself a cup of coffee and began to spoon Weetabix into her son's mouth, I made a sandwich for Rose, grabbed an apple and a cereal bar and put them with a bottle of juice into her 'Frozen' bag. Ten minutes later we were ready to set off and Sue was much calmer. Rose kissed her mother and little brother and we left in plenty of time to get to school. She had started in reception last September and loved it from day one. I don't think Sue ever needed to persuade her to go; she loved the company of other children, was keen to learn and thought the world revolved around her teacher who apparently knew everything. I remember asking her how the first week of school had gone and she'd replied that it was good but she still couldn't read yet. Reading was the one thing Rose had longed to be able to do. Having always loved books, she carried them round as a toddler as much as she carried her favourite doll. 'Read me a story' was probably the first sentence she strung together, and even now reading was still her preferred activity, second only to eating cake. She was somewhat disappointed that she couldn't read after the first week; it's always sad to have your expectations crushed especially if you're only five years old. The noise in the school playground reached us as soon as we got out of the car. Walking to the gate, Rose held my hand, chattering excitedly about her friends and their teacher and what they would be doing that morning. I often thought she would happily go to school seven days a week but I don't think even her wonderful teacher would wish for that. Clinging to my hand until the whistle was blown, Rose tugged at my sleeve, pulling me down to kiss me goodbye and then skipped off merrily to join the line with her classmates. I stood waving until they disappeared inside the building then reluctantly turned to go back to my car. If I hadn't gone in for therapeutic counselling I often thought I might like to have been a teacher, but we only get one chance to choose a career and counselling was something I really loved. Perhaps when I retired I could volunteer at the school to help with reading and whatever else they encouraged 'parents' to do.

Within five minutes I was pulling into the health centre car park. I could actually have walked from the school to work much quicker but with my car had to negotiate the town centre's one way system. The phone was ringing before I had chance to take off my coat.

'Hi, Maggie, it's Sarah. Just to let you know I got your message about Lindy and I'll be visiting her today. I've had a case conference cancelled last minute so thought I'd take the opportunity to go and meet her. How did she react to knowing the wheels were turning?'

'I don't think she believed it really. Lindy's an unassuming girl, sadly her life experience has taught her not to have any expectations, although it was obvious she was thrilled yet cautious to know you'd be helping her.'

'It's tragic that they were ever separated in the first place but now we can hopefully put things right. I'm up to speed with Lindy's background from the files we have and it does seem that she's fallen through the net. I'm not making excuses but it's so hard to keep on top of the increasing number of children who are being taken into care. The work load increases daily but staffing is at an all-time low, it's one of those seemingly insurmountable problems which we have to work round but I still want to look into this, Lindy's had a raw deal and deserves better. I'm rather looking forward to meeting her; from all you've told me she's not the usual sullen teenager with attitude, which sounds quite refreshing. I'll give you a ring when I've been, shall I?'

'Please, you're right, she does deserve a break and her time at Redwood will be at an end in a few months, perhaps you'll be able to talk to her about the options available when she's released?'

'Yes, I'll make this initial contact and I promise to keep her in mind for the future, we don't want to let her down again.'

Sarah seemed determined to help Lindy, which made me feel that I'd done the right thing in contacting her, and the speed with which she'd reacted was impressive. I could see them getting on well and my hope was that Lindy would find something more worthwhile to aim for instead of planning to re-offend to get back to Redwood. It had already been an eventful day and my mind wrestled with worries about Sue and trying to think of more ways to help her. Then the phone call from Sarah Dent had me wondering how she would get on with Lindy. It was difficult to concentrate on my clients' problems this morning and I had to determinedly steer my thoughts to where they should be, giving myself a mental kick to remain in the moment with the lady in front of me. The discipline worked and I found myself focussed at last, shelving my own thoughts to do the job I loved and offer the attention my client deserved.

I decided to visit Sue again during my lunch hour; seeing her looking so fraught this morning worried me, it was so unlike her. It was only a short drive and I could manage it easily in the hour and a half before I needed to be back.

'Maggie!' Sue looked surprised to find me on her doorstep. 'What are you doing here, is anything wrong?'

'No, nothing, I just thought I'd like to spend my lunch hour with you, I miss our little get-togethers at work.' I followed her down the hall to the accompanying sound of James crying in his pram.

'He's been like this all morning, I can't seem to settle him.' Sue suddenly burst into tears. I steered her to the sofa and sat with my arm around her shoulders while she cried and James howled.

'I must get him...' Sue attempted to stand but I pushed her down.

'I'll get him, you sit there for a minute or two then go and put the kettle on.' Sue wearily obeyed and I lifted James from the pram. His little chin was quivering as I lifted him to my shoulder and began to rub his back. I'm no expert with babies but I'm always willing to have a cuddle and it seemed as if Sue needed a break. She stood to go to the kitchen and during the three or four minutes she was gone James stopped crying and snuggled into my neck. Sue came in with coffee.

'I'm sorry, Maggie, you must think I'm a right idiot.'

'Why on earth would I think that?'

'Well I already have two children and here I am reduced to tears by a three-week-old baby.'

'I can see nothing wrong with that. Even I know that a crying baby can be traumatic and you'll feel worse because you already have two children, it's a lot to cope with and you have my total admiration.'

'That's the thing though, I'm not coping.' The tears began to fall again, silently this time.

'Come and sit down and have your coffee. Is James due a feed?'

'No, he's not long since had one.'

He was almost asleep so I gently laid him back in the pram and rocked it until he went over. Sitting down next to Sue, I asked her how she was really feeling.

'Stupid, incompetent, tired and miserable!' She hadn't lost the knack of getting straight to the point then.

'I'm no authority but it sounds like the baby blues, Sue. You're depressed.'

My friend put her head in her hands and cried some more. I rubbed her shoulders and waited for her to calm down again.

'Why am I depressed? I have three lovely children and a wonderful husband, it's stupid.'

'Don't forget your equally wonderful friend!'

Sue smiled.

'It's your hormones, or at least I think so and I also think you should go and see the doctor.'

'I can't go to see the doctor, I work there!'

'So if you worked in a grocery store would you never eat? Look, I can ask Tom to make a house call if that would be easier? I'm sure he won't mind and he'll be able to help.'

'Okay, you can do that thanks.' Sue gave in without a fight so I knew that she must be feeling really down, she never gives in so easily. James was softly snuffling in the pram and we had our coffee in peace before I left Sue to put her feet up and have a well-deserved rest before he woke up again.

Back at the surgery the phone rang and I was again delighted to hear Sarah Dent's voice.

'Hi, Maggie!' She sounded chirpy.

'Wow, two calls in one day, there's not a problem, is there?'

'No, it's good news, I visited Lindy this morning and I've also found out where her brother is.'

'Already, but that's great, Sarah, thank you.'

'Well don't get too excited, that was the easy part. My team leader was happy to help and I've agreed to take over Lindy's case.'

I was thrilled to hear that; Sarah would be perfect for Lindy, she already empathised with the difficult time the girl had had and I was keen to know how the morning's visit had gone.

'She was something of a surprise really.' Sarah told me when I asked, 'I expected the usual teenager with attitude and a chip on her shoulder about the bad time she's had but Lindy was nothing like that. Initially she was wary but when I mentioned your name she opened up a little. Altogether it was a great first meeting which bodes well for the future. She was naturally excited about the prospect of news about her brother but I had to caution her not to expect too much. The problem,' Sarah continued, 'is that we can't tell her where her brother is without the permission of the adoptive parents. Normally this would be a straightforward request but with Lindy being at Redwood the parents might assume she'll be a bad influence on her brother if contact is re-established.'

I could understand the predicament. Some parents would be horrified to introduce their adopted son to a sister he possibly couldn't even remember and who was presently locked away in a young offenders' institute. My heart sank as I remembered Lindy's delighted face when

I'd told her what I was trying to do. Had I given her false hope?

'What I'd like to do now that I've met Lindy is to keep in regular contact with her; she should still be having contact with a social worker anyway and it's only the change in personnel which has interrupted this. Now that I feel I know her I can go to her brother's adopted parents and put forward her case.'

'That's great, Sarah, I really appreciate you looking into this and taking Lindy onto your caseload which I know must already be heavy. I honestly think it's been the circumstances of her upbringing which have led to her being at Redwood, she deserves a second chance in life and re-establishing contact with her brother would be the best gift she could have. Can I tell her that you've found him?'

'Yes, although he wasn't really lost but I know what you mean. I'll get in touch with Jack's adoptive parents, and barring plagues, famine and other emergencies we can hopefully bring a smile to Lindy's face.' Sarah laughed and I thanked her for the trouble she'd taken then ended the call. I found the number for Redwood and rang to speak to Lindy. When I was put through to the right extension she was brought to the phone, her voice sounding distant and worried.

'It's Maggie,' I said and could almost hear her relax. This was probably the first phone call she had received during her time at Redwood. I wanted her to know that there was news but that it wasn't going to be a straightforward matter of being able to meet Jack. As I explained as best as I could and told her that Sarah Dent had found out where her brother was, she seemed to understand the problems relating to a reunion. Learning that his long-lost sister was in an offenders' institute probably wasn't the way Lindy wanted to be reintroduced to her brother either. There was around four months of Lindy's sentence left, less if she was given time off for good behaviour, and I suggested that meeting Jack could be a goal to work towards for when she was released, but stressed that it would depend very much on his new parents. Lindy took it well and as we said goodbye it struck me that a positive objective like this could be the very thing she needed to change the goal of re-offending into something much healthier and hopefully happier too.

Chapter 13

Blood pooled onto the kitchen floor as Bill lay staring up at his wife, gasping for breath. Carol couldn't make out what he was trying to say but if it was a plea for help she was pretty certain it was too late for that. It was hard to tell how long she stood, motionless, watching her husband struggling to breathe but it was probably only seconds, one or two minutes at the most whilst blood pooled over the kitchen tiles like a lustrous crimson carpet. Suddenly his eyes lost focus, sightless now forever and his chest no longer moved. He was dead and Carol had killed him, the reality of which lay before her in the silent and still, pale version of the man she had married. She could feel her own blood draining from her face, her lips tingled and for a moment she thought she might pass out. The knife was still in her hand, sticky and warm with Bill's blood. It had been a surprise how easily the knife entered her husband's body; she'd expected it would strike his ribs which would only have caused a wound and most probably not a fatal one at that, Carol had never believed she had the physical strength to actually kill him. Her hand still gripped the knife handle, almost fused to it as if it was part of her own body. Suddenly she could bear the feel of his blood no longer and dropped the knife, turning to wash her scarlet hands under the cold water from the kitchen taps. Carol was the one gasping for breath now, as dizzy and nauseous she turned back to look once again at her dead husband, then in a fog of jumbled emotions she picked up the telephone and with trembling hands dialled 999. A woman answered and with a clear, crisp voice asked which emergency service was required.

'My husband is dead. I've killed him.' Carol thought her own words sounded remote and unreal but the operator remained calm and proceeded to ask questions.

'Are you sure he is dead?' She paused for answers which Carol couldn't voice. 'Does he still have a pulse, is he breathing?' The woman decided to try simpler questions. 'What's your name? Can you tell me where you are? Is there anyone else in the house with you, a child perhaps?'

Carol listened and tried to answer although her voice was barely a whisper and sounded like some other woman; surely this was not happening to her? The crystal clear voice on the other end of the line told her that an ambulance was on its way and could she open the door but stay on the line? It was surreal; a dream perhaps from which she would wake up soon to her normal life and Bill would still be alive.

The sirens grew louder as they neared the house; the ambulance arrived first, followed almost immediately by a police car screeching to a halt outside number 34 Appleton Close and two uniformed officers jumped out and ran towards Carol's house. It was a relief for her to let these outsiders take over; they had a procedure to follow and knew what they were doing. One of the officers fiddled with a small device on his shoulder and Carol realised it was a camera. Every movement the officer made, every little thing he saw and heard would be recorded. She wondered what they would make of the mess in the house. The kitchen floor was covered with glass and broken china where plates and crystal glasses had been thrown, bar stools were overturned and of course Bill's body was sprawled where he had fallen; the whole scene would be preserved on the officer's body camera.

Carol was quickly guided out of the kitchen to allow the paramedics to do their job. One of the police officers sat with her in the lounge and they were joined a couple of minutes later by the other one with a cup of tea in one of her best china mugs. It tasted sweet. She didn't take sugar in tea but supposed it was part of the process, for shock, wasn't it? The first officer asked if she could tell him what had happened but the words wouldn't come, perhaps she was in shock? Another car door slammed outside the house and two more policemen arrived, detectives, she assumed as they were not in uniform. After speaking briefly to those already on the scene, they took over the questioning. The one who seemed to be in charge showed her a warrant card and introduced himself as Detective Sergeant Alan Hurst. Carol looked at him; he was a stocky man but not fat, in his late thirties or early forties perhaps with a balding head shaved close to his scalp as men seemed to favour these days. He had a sympathetic face and when he asked if she could tell him exactly what happened, she looked into his kind eyes and felt that he could be trusted. In quiet, halting words she began to tell him what she had done, knowing that this day would change her life forever.

More car doors slammed and people in white overalls began to come into the house. Cameras flashed and the buzz of background noise registered somewhere deep in Carol's mind. DS Hurst told her they were taking her to the police station, and as they left the house it seemed to resemble a scene from a television police drama. Cars filled the usually empty, quiet street and several neighbours stood around watching, arms folded, whispering to each other, speculating on what had happened at number 34. Yellow tape was tied across the garden path and a young uniformed policeman lifted it to allow them to pass. Carol lowered her head, not wanting to meet the inquisitive gazes of her neighbours, and allowed DS Hurst to help her into the back of the police car, beside a woman officer who didn't speak but ensured that her seat belt was securely fastened.

It wasn't clear to Carol whether the police were treating her as a suspect or a victim. They were almost too kind, considering she had readily confessed to killing Bill. At the police station she was taken to a room by the same female officer who had been in the car. The young woman took a camera from the shelf by the window and stood Carol by the wall where the morning light from the tiny window would shine on her, and took several photographs. Next the officer pressed Carol's fingers on an electronic pad to record her fingerprints; this was different to the messy print pad Carol had expected. The woman then asked her to remove all her clothing and put on the white overalls which were folded on the end of a high examination table.

'Everything?' Carol whispered.

'Yes. A doctor will be coming to see you very soon. If you have any injuries or feel unwell you'll need to tell him and he'll have some questions to ask you. It'll be better for you if you can answer everything as clearly as possible. When the doctor's finished you'll be taken to an interview room to see DS Hurst again.' The matter-of-fact way the police officer spoke to Carol was in some ways reassuring. Things were out of her hands now, even her own future would be decided by other people, yet there was a bizarre comfort in that knowledge. The doctor arrived within half an hour and entered the room where she was sitting in silence with the officer standing beside the door, guarding her... as if she had the energy to run away.

'Now then, Carol, isn't it?' The doctor's features were solemn, folds of skin sagged from his cheeks and under his eyes and he looked far too old to still be practising.

His manner could possibly be described as fatherly but as Carol had never known what a real loving father was; she couldn't judge so simply thought of him as efficient. She nodded her head and tried to focus on his words. When he asked about recent injuries she held out her left forearm, where the burn marks were still visible and would probably leave permanent scars. She mentioned her right arm and shoulder which were freshly bruised, and the doctor inspected them too. He nodded to the police woman who was still present and who took photographs of the injuries before Carol covered them up again as if ashamed of her damaged body. After asking questions to determine her state of mind, the doctor appeared to be satisfied that she was able to answer the questions which the sergeant would no doubt have in abundance. He opened the file he'd brought with him and Carol watched as he pulled out a diagram of a human form and marked it with a red pen to indicate exactly where her injuries were. She was asked if she had any objections to a sample of blood being taken as well as a mouth swab and fingernail cuttings. These were bagged separately and placed on top of her clothes, which were also now bagged and ready to be examined by the forensics team. Carol had the illusory feeling of being on a conveyer belt, being processed through the system with no say in what happened next. It was nothing more than she expected, as when that knife plunged into her husband's body she knew that her whole future was in jeopardy and in that one violent moment she had forfeited the right to make any future decisions for herself.

Alan Hurst sighed. He could have done without an unlawful killing on his first day back after paternity leave. *Nothing like being thrown in at the deep end*, he thought, as the instructions were issued to sct up the major incident room to investigate the killing of William Jacobs.

'Welcome back!' his DC, Colin Brownlow smiled at him. 'I think they've taken your suspect to the interview room.'

'Thanks, and what a welcome this is,' Alan replied and as his colleague headed out of the room he called, 'Don't disappear. I want you in on this one.'

DC Brownlow turned back.

'Surely it's an open and shut case? The wife's confessed so we lock her up, right?'

'And you know better than that, Colin, due process in all cases. Someone else could easily have done it and the wife could be covering for him or her. It doesn't feel like the usual domestic gone too far to me.' A PC came past Alan's desk and handed him a file.

'The doc says she's good to go but he thinks you should look at his initial findings first.'

Alan took the file and opened it. The words 'Evidence of Abuse' stood out and after scanning the page quickly he passed it to DC Brownlow who read the salient points and gave a low whistle.

'The worm turned, or so it seems. Cigarette burns, the bastard! Okay, Alan, ready when you are.'

Chapter 14

Sarah Dent was more than a little impressed with Lindy. The girl had been polite and was visibly keeping her excitement under control although this was probably the best news she had ever received, which in itself was so sad. Lindy had missed out on any kind of childhood; she'd taken on responsibility for her brother when she should have been nursing dolls, not a real baby. Her mother readily gave up both children and then tragically they had been separated. Surely Jack had come out of this better than his sister, with a permanent home and two parents who loved him unconditionally, Sarah hoped as she drove to Leeds to meet them. Naturally there had been questions when she made the initial contact with Jack's adoptive parents, questions which Sarah would prefer to address in person rather than on the telephone, so she made light of her visit speaking vaguely about an issue from Jack's past but nothing to worry about. She tried to make it sound like a routine visit but suspected that Mrs Simpson read more into it than that.

Gemma and Ben Simpson waited anxiously to meet this social worker, worried even though she'd told them not to be, perhaps even more so because she'd told them not to be. Sarah followed instructions from her sat nav and arrived promptly at 79 Poplar Avenue, which nestled in the middle of a delightful leafy suburb of Leeds. She was late enough to have avoided rush hour traffic but early enough to accept the coffee which Gemma Simpson offered. Gemma was a tall thin lady, perhaps in her mid-forties, Sarah thought, with a wide mouth pressed into a thin line. She carefully set down a tray of coffee and biscuits. Ben Simpson was of a similar age, over six feet in height with a body that suggested he worked out regularly or possibly ran. The room they occupied was comfortably furnished and warmed by the spring sunlight streaming through the bay window. On the walls were photographs of the family, some of the couple alone when they were much younger but mostly with a boy whom Sarah assumed to be Jack. Other photos were displayed on the top of a piano which stood at the end of the room, again family groups and several of Jack, the unmistakable yearly school photographs in which he was posed but smiling naturally. There was certainly a resemblance to Lindy, the hair colour and the set of his eyes were exactly like his sister's.

'How old is Jack now?' Sarah tried to ease into a rapport to get this couple onside.

'He's nearly eleven but can you just tell us why you're here?' Gemma Simpson needed to know, the pleasantries were clearly short and obviously over. Ben took his wife's hand as if preparing her for a shock.

'Well actually, I hope my news will be good news for Jack. I don't know if you were made aware when you adopted Jack that he had an older sister?' There, it was out. The couple exchanged glances and Ben took the lead.

'I seem to remember something being said about a sibling but it was a long time ago,' he said. Sarah nodded; she thought they would have been made aware of Lindy; it would be most unusual for them not to be.

'She's seventeen now, Lindy's her name and she would very much like to have some kind of contact with Jack.'

'Why now? If she's not bothered about him for all these years why would she want to be part of his life now?' Gemma's words couldn't disguise the anger she felt. Sarah understood that this woman would feel somewhat threatened, after all Jack was their only child and they wouldn't welcome any disruption to their comfortable lives.

'When you adopted Jack, Lindy was only seven years old and sadly her path through life hasn't been as easy or as fortunate as Jack's. She's never known a stable family life and through no fault of her own she's been passed from one foster home to another. There have also been changes in her social workers through the years and although Lindy has periodically asked for news of Jack, she's somehow never managed to find out anything other than that he was adopted into a good home.' Sarah hoped the Simpsons would feel a little compassion for Lindy. They exchanged glances, then Gemma spoke.

'Jack doesn't know he has a sister and we think it might unsettle him to find out now. He'll be moving to secondary school in September, which will be a big change for him to cope with without his past resurrecting itself.'

'I understand that, and Jack's certainly lucky to have you as parents but having a biological sister is a fact, one that will not go away. Perhaps he even has distant memories of her; they were very close as Lindy was his main care giver even though she was so young herself,' Sarah appealed to them, knowing how important this was to Lindy.

'He has no memories of that time!' Gemma spoke sharply, causing even her husband to look at her with surprise. He squeezed her hand and said,

'I'm sorry, but it's a difficult age for Jack and he's doing so well at school that we wouldn't want him to be unsettled by this girl coming into his life.'

'Yes, I do understand but perhaps you could think about it for a few days and we could meet to discuss it again? Lindy would be delighted just to know how he's getting on. We could maybe begin by them exchanging letters and photographs and see how things go from there.'

Ben Simpson nodded thoughtfully as if this might be acceptable, but his wife wasn't so sure.

'I don't think that would be appropriate. Jack's a sensitive child and something like this could upset him. Anyway, where is this girl now and what's she doing, is she still at school?'

It was the question Sarah had dreaded but she needed to be truthful.

'As I said, Lindy hasn't had the chances in life that Jack's had. She's been in several different foster homes and sadly is currently in a young offenders' institute although she'll be released soon.'

'A young offenders' institute?' Gemma almost shouted, 'And you want her to have contact with Jack? I think it's time for you to leave.'

'It's not as bad as it sounds, Mrs Simpson. Lindy was living rough on the streets for a while and the only way she could get food was by shoplifting. It's a minor crime and she's more a victim of circumstance than any kind of criminal.'

'If she broke the law, she's a criminal and that settles it. There'll be no contact between this girl and our son and that's final!'

'Darling, don't be so hasty we don't know the circumstances...' Ben tried to reason with his wife but her mind was made up.

'No. I'm sorry you've had a wasted journey, Miss Dent, but I think this meeting's over. You can tell this girl that Jack is happy and well but that is all, he doesn't need a sister.' Gemma rose to her feet, leaving Sarah no alternative but to do the same. She thanked the Simpsons for listening to her and offered a card with her details on in case they changed their minds. Gemma made no move to take it so Ben stepped forward and took the card as he opened the door for Sarah to leave.

The drive home was a time to reflect for Sarah and she wondered if she could have handled the meeting differently. The more she thought about it, the more she became convinced that the Simpsons had known her reason for coming. After admitting that they knew Jack had a sister they had probably worked out why a social worker was visiting about an 'issue from Jack's past'; what else could it be? And had Sarah been naive in expecting them to have some sympathy for Lindy? Perhaps she had, and she was disappointed for Lindy's sake. She'd hoped to be driving away from Leeds with at least some grain of hope for Lindy, a photograph or a promise that she could visit when she left Redwood. But there was nothing and Sarah would have the unenviable task of visiting her to tell her that she wouldn't be seeing Jack or even hearing from him. Sarah decided to leave it for a few days on the off-chance that Gemma and Ben Simpson would change their minds but in reality there seemed to be very little hope of that happening. It appeared that the only way of reuniting the siblings was to wait until Jack was eighteen when social services could approach him directly, and sadly that was all that Sarah could offer to Lindy.

Chapter 15

By early afternoon Alan felt as if he had never been off work. He'd begun the day positively enough, answering questions about the latest member of the Hurst family and readily showing pictures of James to all who showed an interest. He hadn't even had his first cup of coffee of the day, nor finished perusing the mountain of paperwork which had built up on his desk, before the call came in about the stabbing. Now he had the doctor's initial findings and the okay to begin questioning the victim's wife who, it seemed more than likely, was the one who had killed him.

Carol Jacobs looked small and scared when Alan and DC Colin Brownlow entered the interview room. Colin's comment earlier about it being an open and shut case could prove to be right but as with every other fatality, this investigation would be carried out with as much vigour as all suspicious deaths. Alan was designated SIO with DC Brownlow and DC Russell assisting. Tony Russell was already gathering the team and setting up the incident room next to the staff canteen; an excellent place to be based, Alan thought, as his body craved the coffee he would normally have had by that time of day. They were fairly certain that the deceased was William Jacobs, Carol's husband but it was still necessary to have the body formally identified. The scene of crime team would still be gathering all the evidence they could find at the house and the body would be on its way to the morgue to await the post mortem, which in this case would be fast-tracked. The detectives needed to find out as much as possible from their suspect, and as they sat opposite her, Alan offered coffee which she declined with a frightened shake of her head. He then began to ask the same open-ended questions he had asked at the scene of the crime.

'Can you tell me exactly what happened this morning, Carol?' he began.

'Am I under arrest? Should I have a solicitor with me?' Her voice was quiet.

'No, you're not under arrest at this time, we're simply trying to establish what happened but if you feel you need a solicitor we can arrange it?'

She again shook her head.

'We're taping this interview, Carol, so would you mind speaking clearly for the tape?' He pointed to the machine on the table.

'No, I don't want a solicitor,' she said.

'So, about this morning, what happened?'

'I killed Bill.' Carol was visibly shivering although there were beads of sweat on her top lip and the room if anything was too warm. Her hands were clasped in her lap, the knuckles showing white, and she flinched at any noise from outside the room no matter how distant.

'How did you kill him?' Alan asked.

'The knife, you saw the knife?'

Alan nodded. 'Tell me exactly how it happened.'

Carol began rocking backwards and forwards in the chair; her eyes were wide but there were no tears. She focussed on a spot on the table, a coffee cup stain, as if that would inspire her to speak, to explain.

'Bill was mad at me, he gets angry sometimes but he doesn't mean to hurt me.'

'And did he hurt you this morning?'

'Yes.'

Alan stifled a sigh; it was going to be a long day, and getting information was like pulling teeth but he had to tread carefully. He couldn't appear to put words into her mouth or direct her thinking in any way. Deciding to change the topic for the moment he asked,

'Is there anyone we can contact to identify the body, Carol?'

'What do you mean, it's Bill, you know it's him!' She sounded upset.

'Yes but there has to be an official identification, a relative or close friend perhaps?'

'There's only his mother.'

'That would be fine; can you give us her name and address?' As she reeled off the information, DC Brownlow scribbled it down then left the room to pass it on.

'Is there anyone you would like us to call for you?'

'No, no one.'

In the incident room Colin Brownlow gave the address to Tony Russell.

'Right,' Tony said, 'The body should be at the morgue now so I'll send someone out to inform her and ask her to come in. Do we know if she's elderly or infirm at all?'

'No, nothing. It's like trying to get blood out of a stone with this one; she's either in shock or a damned good actor. Have you started the house to house yet?'

'A team's on its way as we speak, they're all up to speed with what little we know but as the houses up there are all detached and most of them have tree-lined drives we'll probably draw a blank. It's not the sort of area where you find a couple of curtain-twitchers ready to dish the dirt. SOCO's have brought in the first bags of evidence. Lap tops, his and her mobile phones, the contents of a desk, bills and the like, it all looks pretty routine so far.'

'Good stuff. Is anyone running background checks yet?'

'Yes, Della's doing that now. The electoral role shows only two people living at the address. She's looking into any history either of them might have with us.'

Colin returned to the interview room, where it seemed he hadn't missed much. The investigation was moving swiftly but Carol Jacobs was struggling to answer even the simplest question. Alan nodded to Colin as he sat down, an indication for him to take over the questioning.

'How long have you been married?' DC Brownlow tried a different line of questioning, leaving the day's events to delve into the lives of the Jacobses. Carol looked surprised by the change but answered immediately, looking more focussed. Very slowly the two detectives began to build a picture of the dynamics of her marriage. It was only when they asked about the events of the day that their suspect became confused again. After two hours they decided to give her a rest and she was taken by a female officer to the custody suite, where she was given coffee and sandwiches.

Alan was beginning to wonder if she really was competent enough to answer questions. As he made his way to the incident room he told Colin to get the duty doctor to take another look at her. DC Russell had made more progress than he had.

'Mrs Jacobs's maiden name was Stewart. She has a mother and sister, both living in Fenbridge; do you want me to go to see them today?'

'Yes, and I think I'll come with you. Colin can have another crack at Carol Jacobs in an hour or so and we'll try having a female officer in on it too. Is Della free?'

'She is. I think she's come to a standstill with the background checks and it'll be good experience to sit in on the interview. I'll tell her and then we can get off to the mother and sister, shall we?'

Alan nodded then moved to the corner of the room, took out his phone and rang Sue.

'Sorry, love, but I've got a suspicious death on my hands. I'm on my way to see relatives before I can get away, are you going to be okay?' He really did feel bad about being late home on the first day he'd left Sue to cope alone.

'Do I have a choice?' Sue sounded more weary than sarcastic.

'Look, when I've done this interview I'll call it a day. How about I bring a take-away in with me?'

'If you want to eat that's probably a good idea. Sorry to sound so grumpy, I'm just tired. Good luck with the visit.'

Alan left instructions with Colin Brownlow to have another go at Carol Jacobs and have Della sit in with him. They would keep her overnight and make some decisions as to whether to charge her tomorrow; they had twenty-four hours to hold her without charge and the superintendent could authorise another twelve after that if necessary. He was glad the case had come in during the morning, as had it happened now there would have been no way he would have got home that night and an all-nighter wasn't something which appealed to him at all; his new baby son could more than likely provide him with as many all-nighters as he could possibly want.

Chapter 16

On the way to visit Carol Jacobs's family, Alan took a phone call from Colin Brownlow to say that William Jacobs's mother had formally identified the body. The elderly lady had naturally been extremely upset and a uniformed officer was taking her home. Alan had DC Della Johnson in mind to act as family liaison officer and asked that after she had interviewed Carol Jacobs with Colin, Della could visit the old lady and take up duties as the FLO. Colin suggested that he accompany her to informally interview Mrs Jacobs to help them build a broader picture of the Jacobses' marriage rather than relying solely on Carol's version. Alan agreed, realising that his colleagues would be working overtime, and grateful for their diligence and commitment to duty. As for him and Tony Russell, they would have to see how their interview went and it could be late by the time they finished for the day too. It was so important to move quickly in a case of unlawful homicide and the first day could easily be a twelve- or fourteen-hour shift.

The council house where Carol Jacobs's family lived was a far cry from the exclusive address which was her current home. Alan reckoned they were post-war houses, built for returning soldiers to settle down with their sweethearts and start a family. The Stewarts' front door had seen better days and the windows looked well past renovation and were crying out for replacement. An overturned dustbin spilled its rotting contents onto the small forecourt, and children played in the road hardly bothering to avoid the parked cars. Alan expected his own car would be at risk, one of the minor hazards of the job. It was five-thirty pm and if either Carol's mother or sister worked, hopefully they would have finished for the day. They were in luck and the door was opened by a young woman who could only be their suspect's sister. She was taller than Carol, scrawny in build with mousey hair curtaining a long face with deep set eyes and a pointed chin. If Alan had to guess he would say Liz Stewart was younger than her sister but it was difficult to tell. Showing their ID, they asked if they could go in to talk to her and her mother. The front door opened directly into the square living room where Mrs Stewart sat and eyed them with suspicion as her daughter introduced them. A strong smell of fried food filled the small room; fried eggs and bacon Alan thought, or heart attack on a plate as Sue would call it.

'What's wrong?' Joan Stewart asked rather anxiously. Her age too was difficult to guess and Alan was useless at ages anyway. She was plumper than either daughter with tightly curled grey hair framing a ruddy face and a cigarette between her fingers. Pulling a cardigan tighter around her chest, she eyed both detectives as if they were from another planet.

'We'd like to talk to you about your daughter, Carol.'

'Why, what's happened?'

Alan began to explain that William Jacobs had been killed that morning and that Carol was helping them to piece together what had happened.

'So we're not talking about a heart attack here and you want to know if Carol is capable of killing him?' Joan Stewart was very perceptive and correctly read the back-story of Alan's carefully chosen words. Liz Stewart, Carol's sister, remained silent, looking anxiously from her mother to the detectives.

'The cause of death has yet to be confirmed but it is being treated as suspicious. What we'd really like to do is build up a picture of your daughter's marriage and her relationship with you and any friends or other close relatives.'

'We don't have a relationship with Carol. She ditched us when she married Bill, not good enough for her then, were we, Liz?' Liz nodded in agreement.

'So when was the last time you saw your daughter, Mrs Stewart?' Tony asked.

'Must be about four years now, when she married the poor sod. We got an invitation to the wedding but she hardly spoke two words to us. He was her ticket out of here and she never looked back, not even to say goodbye.'

'And there's been no other contact, phone calls, letters, anything at all?'

'No, not even a Christmas card.'

'We tried to contact her.' Liz Stewart had found her tongue. 'We sent a birthday card and tried to ring but she'd changed her number. It was quite clear that she wanted nothing more to do with us.'

'Is there a reason for that, a particular argument maybe?' Alan asked. Liz looked as though she was about to answer but her mother cut her off.

'No, nothing, she got too big for her boots when she met William Jacobs and we became an embarrassment to her. Now you didn't really come to ask about our relationship, did you? As I said before, you want to know if we think she could kill him, don't you?'

'We're here for any kind of information you can give us. If you think your daughter could be violent then yes, we do want to know, and what about her early life, what kind of child was she, did she get on well at school? Anything you can tell us would be useful. As I said, we're just gathering information at this stage.'

'She was very bright at school.' Liz entered the conversation again. 'The teachers said she should go to university but she was more interested in boys and after her GCSEs she took a job in the supermarket for pocket money.'

'Aye and I never saw a penny of it. She expected me to keep her while she spent everything she had on clothes and make-up. When William Jacobs came along she thought her dreams had come true. Having money certainly made up for him being so much older than her and having nothing in the looks department.' Joan Stewart was obviously bitter about her daughter's rejection of her family but sadly they had nothing to contribute other than a sketchy picture of the adolescent Carol.

'And yourselves, could you tell us where you work, Mrs Stewart, Elizabeth?'

'What's that got to do with anything? Think we killed the poor sod now, do you?' The older lady wasn't about to make their job any easier.

'As I said, we're just building a picture of Carol's life and as you are her closest family it will help to have some knowledge of your family.'

'Mum's retired and I work at the bookies down the precinct,' Liz answered, ignoring the reproachful look her mother flashed in her direction. There was little more to be gained for the time being, so Alan and Tony thanked them for their help and left feeling no wiser at all.

'They didn't ask how Carol, was did they,' Tony observed.

'No and they showed very little curiosity as to how William Jacobs died either. I think they're just totally disinterested in what happens to Carol or they're playing their cards close to their chest. Perhaps Liz might have been more forthcoming if her mother hadn't been there and it might be worth paying her a visit at the bookies. Time will tell, I suppose, but now I'd like to pop back to the station to see if Colin and Della have got anything new from our suspect. You can knock off now if you like, we've probably done as much as we can for today. We'll start again with fresh eyes tomorrow and hopefully get more out of Carol once she's had a night to consider today's events.'

As they drove back to the station where Tony had left his car, they discussed first impressions of the case.

'It's likely we'll be looking at a manslaughter charge,' Alan began. 'If there's a history of violence it could even be self-defence and a suspended sentence. Carol certainly appears shocked by her own actions and has the injuries to attest to the physical abuse.'

'I'd like to get an understanding of their finances. Seeing her background, she certainly appears to have landed on her feet with Jacobs, unless of course the abuse has been throughout their marriage. We need to see a will or any insurance policies they might have too. Perhaps her mother's right and she only married him for money and if that's the case the violence probably came as quite a shock,' Tony added.

'Well tomorrow we'll start digging into their finances and get any medical records we can. A bit of digging into Carol's history wouldn't come amiss either; the family aren't going to give much away so we could be looking at old school friends or even teachers, you never know what might turn up.'

DC Colin Brownlow was leaving the station with Della Johnson as Alan pulled into the car park.

'We didn't get chance to interview her again.' Colin sounded disappointed. 'The doctor had another look at her and she apparently broke down so he's given her a sedative and said she's to get some rest. Della settled her in the custody suite and hopefully she'll be okay to interview again tomorrow. We're on our way to see Mrs Jacobs senior now.'

'Great, she gets a good night's sleep, and we're left with too many questions and not enough answers. See what you can get from Mrs Jacobs then call it a night. We'll need an early start in the morning. Did you update the superintendent?'

'Yes. He's happy to give us another twelve hours if we don't get to charge her within the first twenty-four. She might feel more like talking in the morning. Oh and I've put her on suicide watch, just in case.'

'Good, you've done well. Ring me at home if your visit turns up any surprises, otherwise keep it short and get home for some rest, it's probably going to be a long day tomorrow.'

It was seven forty-five when Alan finally got home. Rose and George were both in bed and Sue was sitting feeding James in the lounge. Toys were strewn across the floor and the children's clothes left a trail to their bedrooms. Looking at Sue, he didn't have to ask what kind of day she'd had, her face said it all. Suddenly she burst into tears. Alan sat down beside her and encircled both her and James in his arms.

'Hey, what's all this about? Things getting on top of you, love?' His gentle tone and the strength of his arms was exactly what she needed, and she leaned into his body until the crying ceased. Alan took James and the bottle and began to feed his son.

'Tell me about it?' he asked.

'Oh I'm sorry, I'm just being silly. Rose and George have been so good but I can't seem to get on top of everything. I feel exhausted all the time and I'm sure James can sense it, he's not settling for long at all between feeds and I hate it that I've resorted to the bottle so soon, I managed to feed Rose and George for at least six months.'

'Well this little fellow seems happy on the bottle and at least we know how much he's getting, and I can do my bit too if he's bottle-fed. So what is it that you have to get on top of that's so important?' Alan squeezed her hand.

'Your dinner?' she replied.

'Oh, that! Well it just so happens that I remembered to call in for take-away, Chinese all right for you?'

Sue smiled, and Alan finished feeding James then took him up to settle him into his cot while Sue warmed up their meal. He looked in on the other two, kissing their sleeping heads and regretting not having been home to help with bedtime. This homicide had come at a bad time; Sue was usually so good at keeping the plates spinning but was obviously feeling the pressure. Perhaps he could suggest they asked Ruby to come and stay for a few days... but would that make things any better for Sue? He doubted it, knowing how they sometimes clashed. What he really needed was to wrap this case up quickly which hopefully he could do; things seemed to be cut and dried and barring any surprises they could have all the loose ends tied up by the weekend.

Chapter 17
Maggie

Sue looked exhausted when I arrived to pick up Rose. Being so used to her cheery smile and witty comments, I was rather concerned, this was so unlike my friend.

'What kind of night did you have?' If James had been up several times that would explain Sue's weariness.

'Okay, I suppose. He wanted feeding at midnight and again at three, then he was up and wide awake at six. With Alan back at work I didn't like to ask him to take a turn at feeding, he had a long day yesterday and was tired himself. I've given up on trying to breastfeed him, I don't seem to have the energy to keep trying and at least I can tell how much he's getting when I bottle-feed.'

'Well, after you drop George off at nursery, take the opportunity to sleep when James does. I had a word with Tom Williams and he's going to call in early this afternoon.'

'Thanks, Maggie, what would we do without you? I don't seem able to sleep very soundly at all; I suppose I'm always listening for the next cry. When he does have me up in the night I find it hard to get back to sleep. Sorry to moan, I must have been spoilt with Rose and George, they were such good sleepers.'

'True but you only had two children then; with three it's bound to be harder and I'm sure Alan wouldn't mind doing the odd feed in the night, he'll get used to working again and it'll be the weekend before you know it.'

'I don't know if he'll get the weekend off, he picked up a suspicious death yesterday and I know what it's like when he's on a homicide case.'

'Well I have the weekend off so I can always take them off your hands for a few hours?'

'You're an angel, Maggie but you've already done so much.'

'You're joking, it'll be a treat for me and I bet Mum would be round pretty quickly if she knew I had children in the house.'

I left a rather sombre Sue, wishing there was more I could do to help. Rose skipped at my side, excited about getting to school. I would happily keep this up for as long as it was needed, it was a joy to be in my goddaughter's company and if it helped my friend, all the better.

My first client that morning was Carol Jacobs, who I felt I was still getting to know. At times she appeared to give out mixed messages and I was unsure of what she really felt about her marriage or what she wanted from our counselling sessions. She'd been very honest about the violence her husband inflicted on her and certainly wanted me to know about it, but she always took the blame herself, saying that she had failed to do what he wanted, and continually making excuses for him. It made me wonder if there was more that Carol wasn't disclosing. It wasn't unusual for a client to verbalise one type of abuse, often the physical kind, when the real problem could be psychological or even sexual abuse, both of which could be consciously designed to shame and humiliate the victim and therefore were more difficult to talk about or even to understand. Perhaps with time and when Carol felt she could trust me she would open up more, and when specific problems were admitted and understood we could begin to address them.

Nine-thirty came and went with no sign of Carol. I left the office and went to reception to see if there was a message from her cancelling the appointment, although messages were usually relayed as soon as they were received. There was nothing, but Laura the practice manager waved me over.

'Can you pop in to see Dr Williams, Maggie? He said it was urgent.'

I knocked on Tom Williams's door. He was behind his desk with the morning paper in front of him, which he spun round so that I could see the headlines.

'Local businessman murdered!'

The picture underneath the caption was of a rather nice detached house in an area I didn't recognise.

'It's Bill Jacobs,' he said.

I gasped, stunned.

'The report says a twenty-four-year-old woman is helping them with their enquiries.' Tom's expression was grave as I took in the meaning of his words.

'Surely not Carol?'

Tom nodded. 'I didn't think things were that bad but it seems she's reached her breaking point.'

'Now I know why she hasn't shown for her appointment this morning. Does it mention Carol by name?'

'No but it sounds highly likely that it's her, the age is right and they don't mention any break-in or that they are looking for anyone else. You've spent more time with her than I have, Maggie, does this surprise you?'

'Yes, absolutely! We've only had three sessions and she's not been the easiest client to work with. Her thoughts skip around and therefore what she shares is very disjointed. The abuse has always been central to her thinking and she certainly doesn't hide it, yet at the same time she makes excuses for her husband and generally blames herself for whatever befalls her. Some of the things she's told me indicate a degree of psychological abuse too, the isolation, withholding money, the usual signs but Carol seems to be of the opinion that this is natural behaviour in a marriage. I sensed a degree of uneasiness in her situation but I certainly didn't think she was so traumatised that she would kill him.'

'That about sums up what I've learned about the situation too. It could be that the physical abuse went too far and she cracked. We'll not know for certain until the police charge her or someone else. This is still supposition, Maggie, even though it seems likely.'

It was only when I got to my own office that I connected Carol's case with what Sue had told me about Alan's involvement in a homicide. Surely it was the same case; Fenbridge was too small to have two suspicious deaths running simultaneously, thank goodness. Tom had given me the newspaper and I settled down to read the full report. It was sketchy and didn't actually say much. The police hadn't officially released the dead man's name but neighbours had speculated on events from what they had witnessed and readily told the press who lived in the house. The house itself rather surprised me. Appleton Close wasn't an address I knew and I hadn't given much thought to Carol's material circumstances before now. She had told me she didn't need to work and that her husband had a good job, but looking at the photograph in the paper it was apparent that they were quite wealthy. I read the article a second time, picking up nothing new. The thought that the police may want to see me suddenly dawned on me. The confidentiality clause was rarely tested in this way, but I didn't think there was anything I could tell them which would actually help other than the evidence of abuse. Perhaps I was racing ahead of myself, Carol might not be the 'woman' who was helping the police but I had a depressing feeling that she was. If the police began to look at her as the perpetrator, then Tom would most likely get a request for her medical records, which would have to include the sparse notes I'd made concerning my time with Carol.

Chapter 18

Early the next morning when Alan arrived at the police station, he was informed that Carol Jacobs had requested a solicitor. The duty sergeant had already made the phone call and they were expecting the solicitor at nine am. Alan made his way to the incident room, grabbing a coffee on the way, and found most of his team already at work. The early editions of the local and one or two national newspapers were spread on the table and Alan's heart sank when he saw the word 'murder' on the front page of the local rag. The information they'd given to the press described the incident as a suspicious death, but like a game of Chinese whispers it had been distorted and sensationalised and they had used the word 'murdered' when in fact there was nothing the press actually knew and it was all supposition on their part. True, they had covered themselves in the body of the article by saying it was a possible murder but the headline is what most people see and believe.

It was time for the team to plan their day, and Alan laid out what he wanted doing and what was to take priority. Technically there were two crime scenes; the Jacobses' house and Carol Jacobs herself, whose clothing alone could tell a story from the patterns of blood spatter on each item. The SOCO's had resumed their search of Appleton Close but would most likely be finished in a couple of hours and Carol's clothing and DNA samples were already being processed by the forensic team. The gathering of evidence was ready to shift from the physical to third parties. Colin gave a summary of his visit to Mrs Jacobs senior, which hadn't given them any more than they already knew. The old lady was obviously upset, William had been her only child and she was quick to condemn her daughter-in-law although most of her comments were spiteful thoughts on Carol's character rather than any facts which might prove useful. Della had called for Mrs Jacobs's doctor and stayed with her until he arrived. She would be going back there later to take up duties as the FLO and try to gain more helpful information on her son's marriage.

'Before you go, Della, I'd like you in on the interview with me; perhaps a woman might help Carol to open up more so can you take the lead?' Alan asked. Della smiled, glad of the experience; she had only recently been promoted to DC and as this was her first suspicious death, she was keen to learn.

'Did the house-to-house throw up anything useful, Tony?'

'Nothing so far. One man was returning from walking his dog at roughly the same time we got the 999 call and said the street was quiet. If his timing's right it seems that a third person is unlikely, anyone fleeing the scene would have been noticed and one or two women said their husbands were leaving for work at that time too. We're going back to speak to them later today.

'Colin, I want you to look into William Jacobs's finances. The papers from his desk are a good place to start. I want to know how much he was worth, who benefits in his will, any insurance policies, you know the drill. We also need to know more about his business, financial stability, any enemies, that sort of thing. Tony, take someone from uniform to the school Carol attended as a girl. Find out as much as you can, close friends, enemies, any trouble she might have been in, what her teachers thought of her and the family. It's not that many years since she left, surely someone will remember her.'

After the briefing Alan and Della headed for the interview room. They had been informed that a solicitor had arrived and been ensconced with his client for the last fifteen minutes. As they entered the room, Carol Jacobs looked up. She was pale but somewhat calmer than the previous day. Alan surmised that she'd probably had more sleep than he had. After introductions—the solicitor was a Mr Jeremy Albright, a rather unfortunate name in the circumstances, Alan thought—Della began by reminding Carol of the tape recorder.

'Did you manage to get any sleep?' she began slowly, attempting to get their suspect on side.

'A little,' was the whispered reply.

'We're still trying to piece together the events of yesterday. I know we've probably asked some of these questions already but do you think you could tell us again exactly what happened?'

The solicitor gave Carol a brief nod and she took a deep breath which seemed to catch in her throat, and began.

'I was in the kitchen making breakfast when Bill came in. He began shouting, wanting to know why I'd slept on the couch. He was angry and coming towards me; I knew he was going to hurt me again and I couldn't take any more. The knife was in the block on the worktop and I picked it up, just to frighten him a little, to keep him away from me, you know? But he kept coming, saying awful things about how useless I was and the names he called me were horrible. The next thing I knew the knife was in his chest and there was blood everywhere. I didn't know what to do so I dialled 999.' Her voice trailed off almost to a whisper and she lowered her head, staring at her hands in her lap, palms facing upwards as if she could still see the blood on them.

'And all this happened in the kitchen?' Della wanted to clarify the exact location.

'Yes, it did.'

'There was glass and crockery on the kitchen floor, Carol. How did that get there?' Della wanted to keep her focussed. After a slight hesitation, Carol frowned as if trying to remember.

'That was from the night before, we'd argued and Bill started throwing things.'

'What was the argument about?'

'I honestly don't know. He came home from work in a bad mood and started drinking, then he didn't like the casserole I'd made for dinner and he just lost it. He grabbed my shoulder and dragged me from the table and...' She was crying softly now, the memories painful.

'And what, Carol? Can you tell me what happened next?' Silence filled the room. 'Take your time, I know it must be difficult but anything you can tell us will help us to understand the events leading up to your husband's death.' Della's voice was soft and even.

'He....he forced himself on me.' Tears were falling then. Carol looked almost ashamed to have told them.

'Do you mean sexually? I know it's hard but we need you to be specific. Did he force you to have sexual intercourse with him?'

'Yes.'

'And afterwards?'

'He...Bill drank for most of the evening and I stayed in the kitchen. When he went to bed I slept on the couch. I didn't think he'd notice, he always slept so soundly when he'd been drinking but he did and that's when he came at me again.'

'You're doing really well. Could you tell us more about the stabbing? I know it's hard for you to think about it but how many times did you stab him?'

'Just the once, I think.'

'And whereabouts on his body was that?'

'His chest, I think, there was such a lot of blood, it was everywhere.'

'Did you have the knife in your right hand or left?'

'The right.' Carol's tears were streaming now and her solicitor indicated it was time for a break.

'You've been very helpful, thank you. We're going to leave you now for a little while and send in some coffee. You can have a talk to your solicitor and we'll come back shortly.' Della switched off the tape recorder and she and Alan left the room.

'Good job, Della, you handled that well,' Alan praised the DC. 'It's looking more likely that we have a manslaughter case on our hands. Do you think she's telling the truth?'

'Yes, I think so.' Della looked pensive. Alan offered his opinion,

'The only thing that troubles me about this morning's interview is the broken glass on the floor. If Carol's as afraid of her husband as she says surely she would have cleaned the mess up after he'd gone to bed.'

'But if she was at breaking point she wouldn't be thinking straight. I know he was her husband but he'd just raped her, she would be in shock and not thinking logically, surely?'

'That could explain it. Ask her about it when we go back in but for now grab yourself a coffee and get some sent into the interview room. I'm going to update the superintendent; I think we're ready to charge her.'

The superintendent agreed that there was sufficient evidence and with a valid confession they could charge Carol Jacobs with manslaughter. Thirty minutes later,

Alan and Della returned to the interview room. They only had another two or three questions, the first one being about the breakages from the evening before the killing.

'Did you not think to clear the broken glass up, Carol?' Della asked.

'What?' She looked confused.

'The glass, you told us Bill had thrown things on the floor. Did you not want to sweep it up before you went to sleep?'

'No, I wasn't thinking straight, I was scared and tired, I just sat in the kitchen and didn't move.'

In the presence of her solicitor, Della then charged Carol with the manslaughter of her husband. Before the solicitor left they asked if she would give permission for them to obtain her medical records to help with the investigation. The solicitor nodded to his client and she signed the forms Alan had brought with him.

'Will I have to stay in prison?' she asked.

'Mr Albright can apply for bail and we have no objection to that as the charge is manslaughter not murder. By the end of today your house should be released and you can go back there unless you'd prefer to stay elsewhere, your mother's house perhaps?' Alan asked.

'No, I'd like to go home.' The decision took no thinking about.

'The CPS will want you to see a doctor, a psychiatrist for an assessment. It's routine in cases like this, as I'm sure your solicitor will advise you. When you're cleared for release we'll need to know where you are at all times, so please remain in Fenbridge so we can contact you if we need to.' Alan and Della left to continue with the investigation. Carol's solicitor would set the wheels in motion for bail and no doubt enlighten her as to what to expect as the case progressed. While he would prepare her for a custodial sentence, he would almost certainly be working on a self defence strategy in the hope of a suspended sentence.

Chapter 19
Maggie

I was still feeling stunned by the day's events later in the afternoon, when Laura the practice manager told me that Alan was waiting to see me. My immediate reaction was one of relief that it was him rather than any other police officer. He had spoken to Tom Williams first, catching him before he left for his rounds. I was anxious as to what he might ask and how much I could tell him without breaching Carol's confidence, but my worries were unfounded as Alan showed me a signed consent form from my client giving him permission to see any notes I'd made and to ask about our meetings. I'd already drunk three cups of coffee, a bad decision, and my nerves were jangling. I really should change to decaf. As I poured Alan a cup, we settled in the easy chairs to have the kind of awkward conversation which I was unused to having.

'Carol has admitted stabbing her husband and for the moment it appears that that is what happened and we've charged her with manslaughter. She was happy to give permission for us to speak to you and Dr Williams, and the doctor's detailed the recent physical injuries she's suffered so I wondered if you could shed more light on her state of mind.'

'I've only seen her three times so our relationship is really still a work in progress. I can give you a copy of the few notes I took after each of her visits although I doubt they'll be of much help.'

'At this point anything you can tell me will be helpful and I'd appreciate your opinion of Carol too. Do you think she was capable of stabbing her husband?' Alan didn't pussyfoot around.

'Wow, that's a big question. Our sessions have certainly been focussed on her marriage and the considerable violence she suffered, which she was quite open about. I think that anyone who has been treated in such a way would have the propensity to kill if they felt in danger, but if you're asking whether she was capable of planning to kill him, then I simply don't know. Do you think she did plan it?'

'We don't rule anything out, Maggie, and it's still early in the investigation. Did she talk about her life before she married Jacobs or her relationship with her family?'

'No, she claimed to have no contact with her mother and sister and I believe her father is dead. Her mother-in-law obviously saw her son but only occasionally visited their house, so there was no close relationship there either. Carol did share that her father physically abused her, her sister and mother, but she was reluctant to talk about it except to say she'd always vowed never to marry a man like him but sadly it seems she did. Carol appears to have no friends, as Bill didn't like her socialising when he was at work and kept control of their finances too so she rarely had money to spend on herself.'

'And do you think she was being truthful about her situation?'

'I begin at the point of belief in all my clients, Alan, and I had no reason to doubt what she was telling me. I saw the evidence on her body.'

'Is it true, Maggie, that girls who've lived in an abusive household often marry men who abuse them?'

'Obviously not always but yes, many do, it's funny but she asked me that same question. I wanted to explore Carol's relationship with her father in more detail to see if her negative feelings for him could possibly have been transferred to Bill. With her father being dead she's no longer able to target these emotions at him and Bill was conveniently on hand.'

'So do you think she hated Bill so much she would actually intend to kill him?'

'Oh, Alan, no, that's not what I'm saying, I was just thinking aloud and it was a possibility I would have liked to explore with Carol. Do you remember Matthew West?' I asked, knowing that like me Alan could never forget. Matthew had been a client of mine during his recovery from a particularly vicious attack. He seemed to be making progress and moved on from our counselling sessions only to return a few months later.

'His experience had soured most of his relationships, and in need of closeness and comfort he directed his feelings towards me with a desire to begin a relationship. Transference is the inappropriate and unconscious redirection of feelings which can just as easily manifest itself with love or hate.' Alan and I were both silent for a moment. Sadly Matthew killed himself in a horrendous incident of dousing himself with petrol and setting it alight. The image still haunts me at times as I torture myself with the 'what ifs' of the situation when generally I am an advocate of banishing the 'what ifs' and 'if onlys' of life.

'I hope you don't still blame yourself for that, Maggie? You did everything you could to help that boy and have absolutely no reason to feel guilty.'

I smiled; it was easy to accept academically that there was nothing I could do but I still wondered if perhaps I could have handled him differently. But we were talking about Carol Jacobs now and I returned my thoughts to her.

'There was perhaps one incident when I felt Carol wasn't being truthful, but it was something trivial which didn't really matter.'

'What was that?'

'Nothing significant, just that she told me she hadn't been out of the house since our last meeting yet I'd seen her the day before with her husband in the town centre, but I could have been mistaken.' I felt as if I was betraying Carol by telling Alan this.

'Right, so she wasn't above telling a lie?'

'I could have been mistaken; it might have been someone else entirely or she may have forgotten that trip out.' Perhaps I shouldn't have mentioned it but it was too late.

'What happens to Carol now? Will she be released?' I was wondering if she might want to continue her counselling.

'Yes, by the end of the day she'll be released on bail on the condition that she doesn't leave Fenbridge.'

'And what if she wants to come back for more counselling?' I really hadn't a clue what I would do in that situation.

'We'd rather she didn't. Counselling can change the way people remember things, which can be confusing for them and difficult for us to have more than one version of events. Of course I can't stop her coming back but if she shares anything relevant to our investigation you'd be obliged to tell us, you'd need to make this clear to Carol.'

'Yes, of course.' There was little more help I could give Alan and after asking me to keep him updated if I saw or heard from Carol again, he left, leaving me unsure of whether I wanted this client to come back or not.

Chapter 20

DC Tony Russell pulled into the drive of Fenbridge Academy, a purpose-built secondary school on the outskirts of the town.

'I used to come here many moons ago,' PC Martin Smith admitted as they made their way to the office. 'Couldn't wait to leave, I'll never understand why people insist schooldays are the best days of your life, they certainly weren't for me.'

'Can't say mine were either, come to think of it but they have it much easier these days. Too much free time and not enough discipline if you ask me.' Tony rang the bell on the desk and a secretary's head appeared through the glass partition.

'Can I help?'
Both officers showed their warrant cards and Tony asked if they could see the head teacher. A buzzer released the door into the school and they were shown into a waiting area while the secretary went to see if the head teacher was available. Five minutes later they were seated in Mr Wilson's cosy office and offered coffee, which they gratefully accepted.

'I'm afraid I've only been here for the last four years so the name means nothing to me,' the headmaster told them. 'I'll get Patricia to pull any records we might have and there are a couple of teachers who've been around forever, I could ask them to speak to you if that would help?'

'That would be great, thanks.'

'It's morning break in ten minutes, I'll get them to speak to you then and you can use my office.' He pushed a buzzer and asked for someone to send the message to Mr Robbins and Mrs Carter, the teachers he'd mentioned.

'I remember the family, there were two girls and Carol was the elder, a bright student but she wasted her talents. Hit adolescence and went completely off track, such a shame really,' Mrs Carter told them.

'Was there anything in particular you can remember or just a lack of interest in her studies?' Tony asked.

'She did seem more interested in the boys than her exams and we caught her smoking on school premises more than once but it seemed as if she was marking time during her last year, keen to get out into the adult world, sad really, a waste of potential.'

'Mr Robbins, can you remember anything at all about Carol?'

'My memory isn't as good as Julie's but it must be what, eight or nine years ago now?'

'That's right, what subject did you have Carol for?' Tony asked.

'Oh, I'm the PE teacher, she played hockey and tennis if I remember correctly, like all fifth-year girls do.'

'Did she excel in sport?'

'I honestly can't remember, she would only have been with me for two periods a week.'

'Elizabeth, her sister, was a different kettle of fish. She was never any trouble but simply didn't have the brains Carol was gifted with,' Mrs Carter added.

'Do you remember the family at all; they lived on Hargreaves Terrace?'

'Yes, of course! Now you come to mention it I remember Carol's father dying, it was about the time she took her GCSE's, some kind of accident I think.' Again it was Julie Carter who had the clearer memory.

The secretary entered the office and passed a thin file to Mr Wilson. He looked it over before telling them they had very little information to offer.

'I'm afraid the file doesn't tell us anything much, just her address and examination results. After Carol left we had one request for a reference for a job in a supermarket, then nothing further at all.' The headmaster seemed to think the visit was over; a bell was ringing in the corridor outside and presumably he wanted his staff to get back to their pupils.

'Thank you for your help.' Tony addressed the headmaster then turned to the two teachers. 'If you do remember anything else please give us a ring.'

The visit had proved rather fruitless and the pair made their way back to the station.

In the incident room Alan was studying a document; he looked up and waved Tony over to him.

'It's the autopsy report. A single wound, deep and delivered from a right-handed person and the knife we took from the house has been confirmed as the one which killed him. It somehow bypassed the ribs and pierced the heart, a lucky or unlucky blow depending on what she intended.'

Tony's eyebrows rose. 'You're not thinking this was premeditated, are you? We've charged her with manslaughter now, are you changing your mind?'

'I'm not entirely sure. She's plausible and certainly carries the evidence of physical abuse but there's a little niggle in my mind, something I can't quite grasp. The other thing the autopsy shows is a few minor cuts to Jacobs's head and face, obviously not from the glass on the floor. He fell on his back so cuts on his face seem somewhat incongruous as according to Carol he'd thrown the glass the night before.' Alan had the crime scene photographs spread on the desk in front of him and Tony looked more closely, trying to follow Alan's thinking.

'Does it really matter when the glass was thrown? Carol was confused, who wouldn't be and you always tell me that a crime scene that's too straightforward is probably contrived.'

'Goodness, Tony, I didn't think you ever listened to what I say!' Alan laughed but remained perplexed, unable to visualise exactly what had happened in the Jacobses' house that morning. Colin Brownlow approached the pair.

'I'm just off to Jacobs's office. Apparently he was a genius with technology and invented an online security system about twelve years ago which turned out to be a licence to print money. Over the years it seems he's refined the software and it's a global best seller, he must be worth millions. I also found a copy of his will, dated four years ago shortly after his marriage to Carol. She inherits everything; no other beneficiaries, not even his mother or the local cat's home.'

'No one expects to die before a parent. I certainly wouldn't think to include my mother in my will,' Tony said.

'Yes you're right, nothing suspicious there then. Is the original with a solicitor?' Alan asked.

'It is, a local firm, Black and Sugden in Post House Lane. Mr Black is the executor of the will.'

'Good, when you've been to Jacobs's office call there to find out if another will's been made since then or a codicil with any significant changes.' Alan was pleased with how the investigation was coming together, although he had learned over the years never to take anything for granted; the unexpected could always be around the next corner waiting to surprise you.

Colin was at Jacobs's office within half an hour. It was a modern exclusive new build with high ceilings and bright lighting. The soft furnishings were actually comfortable and the coffee he was offered fresh and strong. The spacious room was divided by full length glass partitions, one third of the space obviously for the managing director with a plush leather chair noticeably empty and a large black glass desk, more for style than functionality Colin thought. The remaining two thirds of the floor space held desks for the four other people who worked with Jacobs; his deputy, a rather geeky looking man in his late thirties whose over-large glasses constantly slipped down his nose requiring correction every minute or so; two other men who were cloistered deep in conversation in a corner by the coffee machine and a younger, red-eyed woman who looked like a frightened rabbit. Colin began with the deputy, whose name was Terry Sutherland.

'It was such a shock!' Sutherland began. 'We knew nothing when we turned up for work yesterday. Bill's always here first and unlocks the office so I knew something was wrong when he wasn't here. Then we couldn't reach him on his phone and eventually when I tried the landline a police officer answered and told me it wasn't possible to speak to either him or his wife. We needed to know what to do.... still do really, as I suppose she's in charge now.'

'I don't think she'll be of much help and shouldn't be involved in the business until our inquiries are over,' Colin told him. 'If you're the deputy perhaps you should take charge until things settle down. Do you have work to do, commitments to fulfil?'

'Well yes, but in the long term what will happen?'

'I'm afraid I can't tell you that, perhaps the company solicitor would be the one to consult. Could you tell me exactly what you do here?'

'It's all about online security. Bill built the company up from nothing by selling a great product. He is, sorry, he was constantly updating it to stay on the top of the game.' Terry's brief description wasn't of much help.

'So what role do you all have here and is this the full workforce?' Colin gestured to where the other three workers were trying to look uninterested in their conversation.

'Yes, this is it. Harry is our hacker, he spends his time trying to hack into the systems, and if he succeeds Bill or I will modify the security to close up the loopholes he finds. I'm also the bookkeeper and Mick and Pam work in sales generating new markets and keeping regular customers happy. We also have several programmers who we outsource to when we need the extra help. They're self-employed and work only on a part time basis during our busy times.'

'So it's a fairly small operation then?' Colin asked, wondering how on earth something so small could generate such a huge turnover.

'Comparatively yes, I suppose it is,' Terry answered.

'What was Mr Jacobs like to work for?'

'Great, he was an easy going sort of man and as long as things were running smoothly he was happy.'

'Did you socialise together at all?' Colin hoped this visit was going to be worth his time.

'Not really. Bill was a private sort of person. He was generous to us all, good bonuses at Christmas and he paid for us all to go to a posh restaurant for Christmas too but he didn't join us.'

'So you didn't meet his wife, Carol?' This wasn't what Colin expected from such a small team, he thought they would go out for drinks together, celebrate new business, that sort of thing but it didn't look as if that was the case.

'No, never. He kept his home and office life totally separate,' Terry replied.

'What about competitors; was there any close competition for business or any rivalry at all?'

'In this market competitors could be at the other side of the world, in fact many of them are. Bill was content to make our product the best he could and we ensured we updated our systems and offered them to our clients which in turn brought loyalty from them. So really competition was never an issue.'

Colin spoke to the other staff but gained very little information from them either. Bill Jacobs seemed to be the ideal boss and they all liked him. Before he left, Colin told Terry Sutherland the name of Jacobs's solicitor. It would be his unenviable task to decide what would happen to the business.

Chapter 21
Maggie

The drive to Redwood was welcome especially as the sun was shining, giving a much brighter outlook than the weather we'd had of late. I tried to imagine what Lindy's face would have looked like when she met Sarah and knew that someone else was on her side and looking out for her interests. I was sure the pair would get on and briefly wondered how much thought went into pairing up social workers to clients, or was it just a matter of dishing out names like bus tickets, first come first served? When Lindy walked into our little stark room there was a light behind her eyes which I'd never noticed before and a smile on her face. I grinned back at her and we settled down to discuss Sarah's visit and the possibilities it could hold.

'Thanks ever so much for doing this, Maggie, I can't believe that I might get to see Jack!'

'It's certainly good news but please don't get your hopes up too much. I haven't heard from Sarah but I know she'll do her best. It's really up to Jack's adoptive parents. They may decide not to let him see you and if that's the case you know that Sarah won't be able to tell you where he is, don't you?'

'Yes, I know but it's certainly brightened up my week and I know you didn't have to do it so I really am grateful.' Lindy was such a sensible girl; I hoped this worked out well for her; she deserved a break and a chance of happiness. I asked what she would like to talk about, hoping that it wouldn't all be about Jack and their possible reunion but it wasn't; Lindy said she'd been thinking about her years in foster care and would I mind if we talked about that.

'That would be fine, you can talk about whatever you want to, it's your hour, remember?'

She nodded and began.

'The children's home we went to after we were taken into care was okay, especially for the few weeks that Jack was there with me. They let me spend time with him when he came out of hospital but it was only for three or four weeks, he was too young to be in there so they put him in foster care and later he was adopted. I'd dreamed that perhaps the couple who adopted him would have taken me too but it soon became clear that wasn't going to happen, and I quickly learned that most couples who adopt want a baby or at least a child under two. When Jack left I cried myself to sleep most nights, trying to be quiet so as not to disturb the other girls in the dorm. Being the youngest there wasn't easy and I was frightened of the older children, one in particular who took a dislike to me and called me names, he hit me too when he could get away with it... when no one was looking.'

'Didn't you tell the staff what was happening?' I asked when Lindy paused.

'There was no point; he would have only made life even more difficult.'

Sadly that was probably true; bullying is never a straightforward issue to deal with.

'I remember being so happy when they told me I was being considered for foster care and I was to meet a couple who wanted to foster a little girl. They were nice people and their home was like something from a magazine. I'd never seen anything like it before, all cream carpets and white walls. After a couple of visits I went to stay for a weekend, which was so strange, they didn't know what to say to me and I didn't know what to say to them! We watched a lot of children's videos that weekend and went for aimless walks in the park. It wasn't their fault, they'd never been around children before and I wasn't the easiest child to deal with, I was scared of my own shadow at that time. When I was asked later if I'd enjoyed myself and would I like to live with them I said yes. It was a better prospect than staying in the home and being bullied and so I moved in with them. They didn't mistreat me or anything but were always telling me not to touch things and be careful to keep things tidy. I did my best and although I was there for a few years it never felt like a home. When I was due to go to secondary school they decided they didn't want to foster any more. She'd become pregnant by then and I was in the way, they said they'd never wanted an older child anyway.'

I listened to Lindy's words, hardly able to believe them but instinctively I knew they were true. How could a couple keep a child for so long without bonding and then just send her back again when she was of an age they didn't want? It was beyond me. She continued the story.

'I often wonder if they did it for the money, they were very materialistic and enjoyed their holidays abroad.'

'Did you travel anywhere with them?' I asked.

'No, I went into respite care when they needed a holiday, they didn't want me hanging around with them all the time. The next foster parents I lived with were an older couple. Their house wasn't as nice but they were okay and we seemed to get along. They were very strict but that was something I didn't mind, at least I knew what I could and couldn't do and it felt as if they cared enough to make those rules for me, you know?'

I nodded, wondering why this placement had gone wrong.

'I'd have happily stayed there but they decided to retire and so I had to go. I hadn't realised that fostering was just a job for them. The next two foster homes I was sent to were okay but they both wanted a baby and only took me to show willing to the social workers. When they were offered a baby, in both cases, I was surplus to requirements and moved on again.'

Lindy paused, silently reflecting on her past life. I was astounded; yes she hadn't been mistreated by any of these foster carers but surely they must have known what it would do to a child emotionally if they simply sent her back when caring for her became inconvenient. If Lindy was a disruptive child I could maybe understand but I couldn't imagine her being difficult in any way. Yes, she was probably withdrawn and not easy to reach but basically she was a good child, one who would be easy to love.

'It was the last foster home I went to that made me run away. At first it seemed okay, they were a couple with no children of their own but they had fostered others in the past, preferring to have only one child at a time. The wife was scared of her husband, I worked that out pretty quickly and she encouraged me to be good and not 'upset the apple cart' as she put it. After a few weeks the husband began to get a bit physical, you know? He started touching me, at first just rubbing my arm or stroking my head but it soon turned into more and when I tried to stop him he shouted and called me ungrateful, telling me I should do what I was told. He began coming into my room at night, touching me again and telling me to be a 'good girl' for him. One night he came into the bathroom while I was in the bath, they didn't have a lock on the door but I always made plenty of noise so that they would know when I was in. He didn't go out but sat on the toilet seat and watched me. I tried to cover myself up but he only laughed. I managed to grab a towel and draped it over me as I got out the bath, but he pulled it from me and I ran to my bedroom, so ashamed and embarrassed. I was fifteen by then, old enough to know that this was wrong and so I decided to tell his wife. It was difficult to explain but I think she actually knew what was happening before I said anything. She began to shout that I should be grateful for such a good home and then suddenly she grabbed me by the hair and got a pair of scissors from the drawer. Shouting that it was all my fault for being too pretty, she cut off my ponytail and threw it into the bin. I'd always had long hair which I usually tied back but I've kept it short ever since that day. I remember running crying to my room, wondering if it really was my fault and if there was something bad inside me which made people dislike me. It was hours before I dared go downstairs again but when I did they just acted as if nothing had happened. That was the night I ran away... and the last time I cried.

'Living on the streets wasn't a great life and I often felt scared, but at least there was no one making my decisions for me without asking what I wanted.'

Lindy's story trailed off and I wondered if she had shared any of this with Sarah Dent. I had a lump in my throat by then and for the second time I left Redwood fighting back my own tears. How could such an agreeable child as Lindy not find a loving home, a forever home? For a girl who had missed so much schooling she was very bright and had so much potential but would it ever be realised? I must admit that at times I heard the voice of my supervisor, Joyce, reminding me not to get emotionally involved. Of course she was right but I could still hope things would work out well for Lindy; if anyone deserved a break it was her. She wasn't the sort of girl who asked much of life or indeed expected it and the one thing which would really make her happy was to be reunited with her brother Jack. Even that was fraught with problems; his adoptive parents might be reluctant to allow her to see him and even Jack himself might not have any memories of an older sister. This in itself was sad, that he didn't know there was someone who really loved him and had done her very best to keep him safe in such dire circumstances. I found myself longing to hear from Sarah. She had kept her word and rung me after her first meeting with Lindy but I'd missed the call and only heard the message she'd left. From the message it was clear that Sarah had connected well with Lindy and would try her best for her, for which I was grateful. Perhaps in a few days I could give her a ring to see if there were any developments.

Chapter 22

Alan hated going to work and leaving Sue in the state she was in. He'd never seen his wife cry so much and it was distressing for him and the children. Knowing Maggie would be arriving soon to take Rose to school made things a little easier, and he'd persuaded Sue to let him ring her mother last night and Ruby would be coming round to help look after James and George. Once again he regretted the timing of the Jacobs case but it was looking as if it might all come together soon and then he wouldn't have to work quite so many hours to keep on top of it. It sometimes surprised him how things did come together so swiftly in such cases and hopefully this too would soon be wrapped up and in the hands of the CPS.

Alan woke the children and got them dressed, leaving Sue in bed to have a few more minutes' sleep, and he was giving them breakfast when Maggie arrived.

'You're early, Maggie.' He smiled at her.

'Yes, I thought maybe I could help get the children ready but it looks as if you're managing just fine!'

'Thanks, but if you don't mind I'll get away now that you're here and hopefully I'll be able to get home a little earlier tonight. Sorry to put on you like this, Sue's still in bed and James is sleeping at last! Ruby will be here shortly so can I leave you to hold the fort until then?'

'Of course you can, that's why I'm here.'

Alan kissed the children before leaving and closed the door quietly behind him. Maggie sat at the table in between Rose and George and began to help George spoon cereal into his mouth rather than onto the floor.

'Mummy's tired again, Auntie Maggie,' Rose said with a sigh.

'I know, sweetheart, it's only because she worked so hard to have baby James and he's awake through the night, keeping Mummy awake too. But he's getting bigger all the time and soon Mummy will feel like herself again.'

Rose seemed happy with the explanation and Maggie turned the subject to their visit to the kennels to choose Jasper.

'He'll be coming to live with us in a couple of days then you can come round and help me settle him in,' she suggested.

'Will he cry at night like James does?'

'No, I don't think so, Jasper's a grown up dog not a puppy so he should sleep through the night. He has a basket at the bottom of our bed so we'll be nearby if he wakes.'

'Is that where Ben slept?'

'Yes, Rose, it is.' The doorbell sounded and Maggie went to let Ruby in, hoping it hadn't awakened Sue.

'Hi, Grandma, have you come to help Mummy?'

'I have, and to get a kiss from you before Auntie Maggie takes you off to school!' Rose ran to give her grandma a hug then went to brush her teeth.

'Is she any better?' Ruby asked, nodding her head towards the stairs.

'I don't think so. She's still in bed and James is asleep, she'll be glad you're here.'

Ruby raised an eyebrow, which I pretended not to see as I began to make Rose's packed lunch. Sue appeared at the kitchen door.

'Hey, you, you're supposed to be having a lie in!' I said.

'The doorbell woke me.' Suddenly there was a cry from upstairs and Sue looked as if her world had just collapsed.

'Don't worry, I'll get him, that's what I'm here for.' Ruby began to climb the stairs.

'I didn't want Alan to ring her but he insisted,' Sue confided.

'Well I think he was right. Let her take control for today, she'll love it and you could do with the rest. So how are you feeling?'

'Awful! Dr Williams prescribed some antidepressants. It makes me feel like a fraud, I've never been depressed in my life so why now when I have everything going for me?'

'If you had flu you wouldn't beat yourself up about it and this is an illness too. It's all down to hormones so don't be so hard on yourself. If you let us all help you now you'll soon get over this and one day we'll look back on it and laugh.'

Sue gave me a 'that's what she thinks' look and Rose came skipping back into the kitchen.

'Aw, Mummy, I thought you were having a lie in. Let me pour you some coffee.'

We both looked at her, startled, Rose had never poured coffee in her life but her concern for Sue was touching. When I eventually took her to school, Ruby had the day organised and was busy getting the boys ready for a morning in the park.

When Alan entered the incident room with a mug of coffee in his hand, Colin Brownlow walked purposefully towards him.

'The DI wants to see us with an update.'

'When?'

'An hour ago.'

'Oh hell. Have there been any developments overnight?'

'No, nothing. I think maybe we've covered all the bases.'

'Come on then, let's get it over with.' Alan left his coffee on the desk, hoping it would still be warm when he came back, and they made their way to the DI's office.

'Come in, have a seat. How far have we got with the Jacobs case?' The inspector was straight to the point and as always using 'we' when he really meant 'you'. If the case was going badly he'd soon revert to 'you'.

'It's coming together nicely, considering this is only the start of the third day,' Alan replied.

'And you're certain now that there was no third party involved?'

'Absolutely, the house-to-house gave us a good picture of the street at the time and according to at least three witnesses the street was deserted other than themselves, and there's also no evidence inside the house to show that there was anyone else there except William and Carol Jacobs.'

'So now that you've charged the wife we can move on to other things?'

'There're a few more avenues I'd like to explore first, if that's okay with you?'

'Like what, it's pretty straightforward, isn't it? What makes you think the investigation merits more time?'

'One or two things really; firstly the money involved. It seems that Jacobs was worth a few million which conveniently all goes to the wife. Secondly, I think her mother and sister know more than they're letting on and I intended to speak to the sister today at her place of work, see if she's any more forthcoming without her mother there. And after speaking to Mrs Jacobs's counsellor yesterday it seems that she's not above telling lies. I know it doesn't amount to much but put these little niggles altogether and I think the case warrants a little more time, sir.'

'Okay, Alan, as you said it's only been a couple of days. Stay on it for the rest of the week to see where it gets you and keep me up to speed, will you?' The inspector turned to look at a file on his desk, the sign for Alan and Colin to leave. Outside Colin was keen to know what Alan had learned from the counsellor.

'It's nothing really, Maggie thinks she caught her out in a lie but it was a trivial thing and she could have been mistaken. But I do feel there's more to this than a straightforward domestic turned bad. From the information we've had about Carol Jacobs, she doesn't endear herself to those around her. I know this could be due to the fact that Jacobs isolated her but we've yet to find anyone to speak up for her, not even her own mother. Now, Colin, how's Della getting on with Mrs Jacobs senior, any luck there?'

'She's in the incident room updating her notes before she goes back to the old lady's. We could have a word, see how it's going?'

Della was signing off her computer and about to leave the station.

'Morning, Della,' Alan greeted her, 'Have you got anything interesting which might shed more light on our case?'

'Well if we take Mrs Jacobs's word as true, Carol is the most vicious wife that ever walked the earth. She's got a real downer on her daughter-in-law, says she was only ever after the money and is of the opinion that it was cold-blooded murder.'

'Wow, she's either one perceptive lady or the stereotypical mother-in-law from hell. What's your opinion, Della?'

'Somewhere in between, I expect. Mrs Jacobs doesn't have any facts to back up her allegations; she strikes me as a bitter old lady whose only child left her to marry when she wanted him to stay at home. One thing which is interesting is that the couple met through a dating site. I had wondered how they met, with the age difference and everything, I couldn't see them frequenting the same places, clubs, pubs or whatever, so this sort of makes sense.'

'Interesting, I could see William Jacobs using a dating agency to find companionship and possibly to get away from an overbearing mother but I'd like to know what Carol's reasons were for doing the same. A young reasonably good looking woman shouldn't have to resort to a dating agency, should she?'

'That's what I thought,' Della agreed.

'Look, before you go back to Mrs Jacobs's house will you call in to see Carol? See if you can get her chatting about how they met and find out how she feels about her mother-in-law,' Alan asked. Della beamed, she was enjoying her involvement in this case and Alan was becoming impressed with her intuition; he'd really like her take on Carol Jacobs and perhaps she'd get more from her woman to woman.

'Right, I'm off then!' Della wasted no more time, she was on a mission.

'And you and I, Colin, are off to the betting shop!'

Chapter 23

Della stared up at number 34 Appleton Close which was a much grander house than she'd expected. She would love to look round the inside but wasn't there for a tour, she'd have to close her mouth and pretend being in such lovely houses was an everyday event. It took several minutes for the door to be answered. Della rang the bell three times before finally being greeted by a bleary-eyed Carol, still in her dressing gown even though it was nine-thirty am. She frowned at Della before standing aside to let her in.

'I'm not sleeping well so I took a pill,' she explained, leading the way to the lounge. Della marvelled at the quality furnishings and took a seat on the luxurious cream sofa, so far removed from her own battered sofa which was always covered in cat hair from her pet ginger tom. Carol offered coffee saying she could do with some herself and Della accepted, taking the chance to follow into the kitchen and have a sneaky look round there too. It lived up to her expectations; sleek modern fittings lined the sides of an enormous space with an island in the middle and one of those huge American fridges which, Della thought, would fill her tiny kitchen if she could ever afford such a thing. She'd need more than one promotion to be able to buy a house and contents like this. On her way to Appleton Close Della had decided to play the friendly role. When she'd interviewed Carol on the day of the killing, (was it really only three days ago?) her manner had been naturally gentle and considerate; after all here was a woman who'd been abused by her husband to the point of defending herself with one of those expensive kitchen knives which sat in a block on the grey marble worktop. Della was surprised that Carol wanted to return home when she was bailed but now, having seen the house she wondered who would not want to return here.

'It must be distressing for you after what happened here. Would you not sleep better staying with friends or family?' she asked, already knowing the answer.

'There's no one really. My mother and sister don't speak to me and Bill made sure I had no friends. Besides it's familiar, I need somewhere that's familiar at the moment.'

Della could understand that but wanted to probe deeper.

'What about Bill's mother?' Again Della knew the answer but was interested to hear Carol's opinion of her mother-in-law.

'She's never forgiven me for taking her precious son away from her. She hardly ever came here and on the odd occasion she deigned to come it was like preparing for a state visit. There's no way she would want to help me now... and that suits me fine.'

They carried their coffee (the real deal from one of those very expensive machines) into the lounge and as they sat opposite each other Della asked,

'How did you and Bill meet? He was so much older and if you don't mind me saying he was no oil painting.' It was perhaps an unprofessional approach but she was trying to get Carol on side, woman to woman, and her words brought a smile to Carol's face.

'You're not the first to comment on that but it was quite romantic really. We met on an internet dating site.'

'Really?' Della feigned surprise.

'Yes. It wasn't his looks that attracted me; he came over as gentle and caring. At the time I thought it was sweet that he lived at home with his mother and looked after her. I didn't really find out what a battle-axe she was until after we were married.'

'And how long was it before you married?'

'Just three months. I thought he was so romantic, sending me flowers and buying little gifts. Now I understand what they say about marrying in haste, I didn't get to know the real Bill until it was too late!' Carol's eyes filled up and she rummaged for a tissue in her dressing gown pocket. Della gave her a few moments before continuing.

'Why did you stay with him when he began to be violent?'

'He threatened me, told me that if I ever tried to leave him he'd find me and make me sorry. I knew he meant it, he always carried out his threats.'

'Were there no good times?'

'Very few, and virtually none after we were married. I wasn't allowed to go out to work, he said he would provide for me, which he did but just sometimes I would have liked to go out with friends They stopped asking of course, thought I was too stuck up now that I'd married well, and I really missed the banter and the fun of a night out with the girls. Bill and I did go shopping together occasionally, he liked to choose my clothes and he was always very generous, but he wouldn't let me have money of my own, only for the housekeeping and then I had to keep receipts for everything I bought.' Carol reached down to put her cup on the coffee table and Della noticed the scars on her arms from the cigarette burns. She mentally cursed Bill Jacobs; anyone who treated a woman in that way deserved all he got. The thought shocked her and the realization that she was feeling sorry for Carol hit her hard. Yes, she was trying to befriend her but only as a tactic to get to the truth.

'What's going to happen to me?' Carol looked hopefully at Della.

'Well when we're finished investigating the case will be turned over to the CPS who decide what the charge will be and then a court date will be set, which will be a good few months away. Because of the circumstances you'll probably be able to remain out on bail but will have to report to the station regularly. Surely your solicitor has told you all this?'

'He probably did but I don't remember. Everything's a blur at the moment. I can hardly believe that Bill is actually dead, and worse still that I killed him. I didn't mean to do it, he was coming at me and I was scared after the burns and everything and how he was the night before. The knife was the nearest thing I could use as a weapon, I didn't want him to hurt me again!' Her eyes filled up again and Della spoke soothingly.

'If you just tell the truth like you have now it won't be so bad. We can't turn the clock back, and although it might not seem it at times, we're here to help you sort this out. Bill was a bully, his behaviour was inexcusable. Having said that, you do realise that what you did was also wrong and it won't go away overnight.'

Carol nodded as she wept silently. Perhaps Della wouldn't learn anything new here; could she even trust her own judgement? She finished her coffee and after a few more questions thanked Carol and left.

Alan and Colin Brownlow made their way to the betting shop where Liz Stewart worked, arriving at about nine-forty am. Betting shops were not somewhere which either of them frequented so they were unsure if it was usual to have only two men in the shop, both intently focussed on a large television screen which dominated one wall. Liz was behind a counter, shielded from the main area by a plexi-glass screen. She saw them as they came in, and as they approached she spoke to a colleague then let herself out from behind the counter to talk to them. Alan introduced Colin then they moved to a corner away from both the television and the counter to give a measure of privacy.

'What's going on with Carol?' Liz asked.

'She's been charged with manslaughter but is out on bail,' Alan answered. Liz frowned, looking as if she was concerned about her sister, which was more than her mother had been.

'She's back at home, maybe you'd like to visit her, I should think she could do with a friend just now.'
Liz simply nodded.

'We used to be close at one time you know, the two of us united against the parents, that sort of teenage thing. I don't know if she'd welcome seeing me now. Anyway, why are you here?'

'Just a few more routine questions; perhaps you've thought of something which might be able to help us build a picture of Carol and Bill's marriage?' Alan looked directly at Liz who turned away from the eye contact. He continued, 'When we spoke at your mother's house and asked about any particular argument which made Carol cut you off, you seemed as if you wanted to say something on the matter but didn't get the chance?' The girl looked back at Alan, her face betraying the conflict she was wrestling with.

'What happened then surely has no bearing on Bill's death... does it?' she asked. Colin replied,

'Anything you can tell us could help us piece together what happened that morning and in the months leading up to it. Something which may seem unrelated to you may prove relevant when compared with the other evidence we're gathering.'

'What was it that you were you thinking of when I asked that question?' Alan was sure there was something but Liz was taking her time, undecided whether to speak to them or not. She eventually decided to talk.

'There was something going on around the time before Carol was due to sit her GCSE's but I didn't really know what. Being the youngest, although only by a year, they kept me in the dark most of the time but Carol and Dad were arguing much more than usual. I remember one night when she barricaded the door to our bedroom, pulling furniture behind it because she was frightened that Dad was going to thrash her.'

'Did he make a habit of thrashing her?'

'Yes, he thought nothing of giving us a slap if he felt we deserved it but generally he picked on Mum more than us. Mind you, Mum was never slow in whacking us with a slipper when she felt in the mood, we sometimes had to run from her as well.'

'So you think there was something going on but you didn't know what?' Alan paraphrased.

'That's right. She began to cause trouble at school too, bunking off occasionally and arguing with the teachers. I remember her being particularly obnoxious to the PE teacher, Mr Robbins. When I was in the changing rooms once I overheard her almost shouting at him although I couldn't make out what they were saying. Carol hated games, thought she was too old to have to run around the field in her gym kit. I thought she would get sent to the head teacher after that but nothing happened. Mr Robbins was known as a bit soft and most of his classes took advantage of his inexperience so Carol wasn't the only one. I shouldn't think any of the teachers actually enjoyed having her in their class, which was a shame really as Carol was the one with the brains, she could have gone far.'

'When did this happen, Liz?'

'Shortly before Dad died, I think, and when he was gone Carol only got worse, bossing me and Mum about and then leaving school so suddenly.'

'How did your father die, Liz?' Alan asked.

'In an accident, he fell down the stairs and broke his neck. By the time we found him he'd been dead for most of the day.'

Alan wanted to return the conversation to Carol and Bill.

'What did you think when your sister married William Jacobs?'

'I was shocked, we didn't even know she was seeing anyone, she announced one day out of the blue that they were getting married. She'd never brought him home, I think she was ashamed of us and where we lived, so the first time we met him was at the wedding. The boys round here were just kids as far as Carol was concerned, she was bored with them and wanted someone more sophisticated, which is why she went on that dating site. Carol did tell me about that but only after announcing that she and Bill were getting married. If I'm honest I think she only married him to get out of here; he was her knight in shining armour rescuing her from this dull life. The money would have made him attractive too, she boasted that Bill had money and she always did like to spend big, did our Carol. Then after the wedding she cut us off and we never saw her again.'

It wasn't relevant to their investigation but Alan asked,

'Why do you stay here, Liz? Did you not have the same dreams as Carol, to get away from this life like she did?'

'That's easier said than done. Carol was the one with the brains and the looks, it came naturally to her and I was always in the shadows. With this job I don't think I'll ever be able to afford anything better than staying at home with Mum.'

Alan and Colin left the betting shop and returned to the incident room. The picture they were now getting of the young Carol Jacobs seemed to have another facet to it. She hadn't been the sort of teenager who simply took what her father meted out without complaint; she had spirit and fought back before making what now appeared to be a conscious decision to look for a man who could give her what she really wanted, but it didn't seem to have worked out as well as she'd expected. Could it be that William Jacobs had knocked all the spirit out of his wife?

Chapter 24
Maggie

With yesterday's events still dancing through my mind, it was again not easy and something of an effort to focus on the present day's work. I had two clients that morning and both were interesting cases which would need my full attention. First was Norman Longstaff, who I knew had been waiting in the surgery for an hour before his appointment time. If he could manage to arrive exactly an hour before each session I wondered why he couldn't just be on time, but that was Norman, he needed routine in his life to be comfortable, which included always being early. I'd actually been quite looking forward to seeing him. He was very likeable and sometimes his take on life, although naive, was refreshing and I often wondered if I got more out of our time together than he did. His smile was huge as he almost sprinted into my room.

'I've got a job, Maggie!' he beamed.

'That's great, Norman, congratulations!' He plonked himself down making the chair creak and I sat too, eager to hear about his good fortune.

'It's in the Oxfam shop, three days a week and I start tomorrow.' His face beamed with pride. Norman had had jobs before, usually on some kind of scheme where he could gain experience and basic training for a small wage, and they were nearly always temporary.

'How do you feel about it?' His face told me he was pleased but I suspected there was more to it than that.

'I'm excited but there'll be a lot of work to do. I went in yesterday for a look round and the shop needs reorganising. The racks are too full and I think I'd like to colour co-ordinate the clothes, all the blue ones together and all the red ones. What do you think, Maggie?'

This was a difficult question. If any other client directly asked for my opinion I'd tell them it's not about me and try to lead them gently to making the decision for themselves. Norman, however, was a special case. With previous jobs he'd started with the same enthusiasm as he was displaying now but had very soon tried to change the way the employer wanted the job doing, which obviously didn't go down too well. I thought it prudent to advise caution in the hope that this was a job he could keep and enjoy.

'It sounds a reasonable idea, Norman, but perhaps you should wait until you've been there a while before you start suggesting changes.'

'Oh but if you could see it, it's a mess, not at all tidy and I know I could make it better!'

'I'm sure you can too, you always have great ideas but think about the people who work there already; many of them are volunteers and they wouldn't want someone new coming in and telling them they've got it all wrong. How would you feel if someone did that to you?'

'But they have got it wrong, Maggie!' He looked hurt, wounded; to Norman this was a black and white issue, they were wrong and he was right, his condition made it very hard for him to empathise and see things from another person's point of view.

'Perhaps they have but there's a manager and probably a deputy manager who work there and they will have decided to display the goods the way they are now. It could be that they're organised by size, I always like that in a shop as you don't have to look at everything to find the size you want. You wouldn't want to upset them, would you, Norman?'

'Well no, I don't like upsetting people.'

'I know you don't, so perhaps if you do things the way they ask you when you start tomorrow and maybe in a few weeks' time you could share your ideas with the manager.'

'Do you think that will be better?' He looked crestfallen.

'I do, Norman. Just enjoy being there and try to do what they ask of you and I'm sure you'll be a great help. You're good at keeping things in order and you're pleasant to people too, which is really important when working in a shop.'

'You're right, I am good at those things and I will enjoy it.' I had a mental vision of Norman standing outside the Oxfam shop an hour before it opened, which made me smile. Norman's visits were always stimulating and so fast paced that at times I struggled to keep up with his train of thought. As we talked some more and the hour passed, he seemed ready to leave to prepare for his first day at work and I said a little prayer that all would work out well for him.

In preparation for my next client it had been necessary for me to do some homework. On several occasions I'd helped clients with various phobias, from spiders to fire, to flying and in each case had used techniques based on Cognitive Behavioural Therapy, (CBT). CBT changes the way a client thinks about the phobia and its object which, together with practical therapy, can make them feel less anxious. Gradual exposure to the object of fear, also called desensitisation or exposure therapy, is what I'd been using with Sylvia. Her fear was of snakes, a common well-documented fear with its own unmemorable name, ophidiophobia. In previous sessions I had begun with reading a factual passage about snakes then asking Sylvia to read it aloud too. It was a relatively easy beginning and she managed to read the passage without hyperventilating or feeling nauseous. This might not seem much to occupy a full hour but she also talked about how the fear had begun and how it had impacted on her life over the years. During that first session she also began to trust me, something which is essential for a successful relationship. I liked Sylvia, a woman of about my own age who had never needed to address her phobia until recently due to her eldest daughter moving to Australia to live. Naturally Sylvia wanted to visit but her fear of snakes seriously hampered any plans to travel to a country where she might come into contact with them. My aim was to introduce Sylvia to snakes gradually, in a safe, supportive environment.

For her second visit I had sought out pictures of snakes and looked up the type of snakes she might encounter in Australia. Many of the common varieties there are venomous, which led me to conclude that some measure of fear or respect for snakes can be healthy! The King Brown snake, Brown snake, Tiger snake and Red Bellied Black snakes are probably the most common ones to be found in Australia and they are all venomous, some more deadly than others. I'd managed to find photographs of each of these varieties, courtesy of the internet, and hoped that Sylvia would be able to cope with seeing them. We began our session by talking over the last week and discussing snakes in general, something which would normally send her running from the room. Once I felt she was comfortable with our conversation I asked permission to show her some pictures. It again had gone well and today we were meeting for the third time when we would recap all the work we'd done previously and I would introduce some video footage of live snakes. Sylvia was calm as we went back over familiar ground and she even picked up the photographs to study them close up. In preparation for the next step I described the video I was about to show and when she felt ready I turned it on, swinging my laptop around for her to see. Initially Sylvia flinched; the colours were vivid and the sounds rather unsettling. I moved to switch it off but she stopped me, saying that she was fine and wanted to watch it. Afterwards we discussed where to go from there. She had coped remarkably well, and next week I planned to combine everything we had done, reading and talking about snakes, seeing still photographs and watching the video again. I asked Sylvia if this was acceptable and she agreed, then asked where we would go from there. Ideally if we lived near a zoo I would have suggested a field trip to the reptile house. As this was impractical the local pet shop would have to suffice. I'd used the pet shop before for similar reasons and the owner was a very kind, understanding man who was always willing to help. We would visit together, taking it slowly and initially just looking at the snakes in their tanks. Afterwards we would leave the shop to have a break before going back to actually handle one of them. Of course if we didn't get that far we could leave it for another week or even cut out the handling of a snake altogether. We can all get through life without such an experience, and the aim was to familiarise Sylvia with snakes so that her reaction to one would be acceptable rather than extreme. Before she left we went over exactly what we would do next time until I was confident that she was in control of her fears. In many cases phobias are not always completely banished, but success is when a client feels confident to manage those fears and Sylvia was well on the way to doing just that.

Chapter 25

Sarah Dent was procrastinating. She knew she should tell Maggie about her visit to the Simpsons in Leeds but it was going to dash Maggie's hopes and more importantly, disappoint Lindy Baker. It had been a difficult meeting and Sarah wondered if she could have handled it better. The main problem seemed to lie with Mrs Simpson, who was certainly the more aggressive of the two. Perhaps she felt threatened by the thought of a blood relative making a sudden reappearance into Jack's life. From the way the couple reacted it seemed to Sarah that they knew what her visit concerned. It wouldn't, of course, take much of a leap to work it out. Sarah had told them she wanted to talk to them concerning something from Jack's past and they admitted to having known he had a sister, so two and two would be easy enough to guess. She did wonder if she dare approach the father again on his own but that would be difficult as she had no idea where he worked and could hardly ring their home to find out. One thing she did know was that she was going to try again. She would give it time; two or three weeks maybe, and then call at the house without prior notice as she was certain Mrs Simpson would refuse to meet her again if she rang beforehand. If she didn't get past the doorstep then so be it but for Lindy's sake she felt compelled to give it one more go. The next step for now, however, was to speak to Maggie and tell her what had happened and also to Lindy, a visit which would not be easy. As she contemplated the time scale of when to do this, her telephone rang.

'Mrs Dent?' a male voice asked.

'Yes, can I help you?'

'It's Ben Simpson here. You came to see my wife and me the other day?'

'Yes of course, how are you, Mr Simpson?' Sarah was suddenly ultra-polite, uncertain why he should be ringing and wondering if it might be to enforce the fact that they wanted no contact with Lindy whatsoever or even to register an official complaint about the way she pushed the issue.

'Gemma and I have been thinking over what you told us. We're not too happy about Jack's sister being in an institution but we thought perhaps we could let her have a couple of photos of him just to let her know he's okay.'

'That's wonderful, Mr Simpson! Lindy will be so pleased. Are you going to tell Jack about her?'

'No, not at this stage.' Sarah was disappointed but at least they were conceding this much.

'Gemma needs time to get used to the idea, it's a big step and we're concerned about how this could affect Jack. All I can promise for now is that we'll send some photos, is that okay by you?'

'Yes, thank you, it will be a great comfort to Lindy; she genuinely wants to know that her brother is well and happy. I have met Lindy myself and will continue my involvement in the future and I can tell you that she's a lovely girl, both intelligent and caring and if they were ever to meet in the future we could arrange supervision or...'

'Ms Dent, I'm only offering to send photos. Gemma needs time to consider any kind of visit.' Ben Simpson cut Sarah off and she realised she was getting ahead of herself.

'Yes of course, and I'm very grateful.'

'I think perhaps Jack does have vague memories of a sister. When he first came to us his speech was very limited even for his age and he often said something which sounded like 'Lindy'. When he woke in the night that was the name he shouted. Gemma found it quite distressing at first as naturally she wanted him to call for her. He only had a vocabulary of five or six words and gradually as he learned more words he stopped shouting 'Lindy' and began to use Mummy and Daddy. It probably doesn't sound such a big deal to you but we'd been trying for a baby for several years and when we decided to adopt Jack was our dream come true. He's very much our son and we want to protect him for as long as we can.' Ben Simpson sounded so sincere.

'Can I ask what made you change your mind?' There was a pause and Sarah thought she was pushing it again when she heard him draw in a deep breath and say,

'I told Gemma something which she didn't know, which no one knows. When I was a teenager I was caught shoplifting too. I was lucky and got away with only a caution but I could have ended up like Lindy, it was only the fact that I came from a respectable and loving home that made the difference. It's been a shock to my wife but we'll weather it and hopefully she may agree to meet Lindy at some time in the future.'

'Thank you so much for sharing that with me, I appreciate your honesty. Lindy will be delighted to see some photographs and I'll look forward to receiving them.' The call ended and Sarah almost jumped from her chair in joy. Now she could ring Maggie with something positive, admittedly not as much as they'd hoped but it was a good start. Then she would wait for the photos to arrive and hot-foot it to see Lindy. The phone call had made her day.

Sarah rang Maggie's number, which was answered almost immediately, and Sarah began to relate her visit.

'I came away with nothing; they were almost hostile to my very presence, particularly the mother. It was as we expected and the big thing was the fact that Lindy's at Redwood. I could understand but I really think the mother would have raised objections anyway, she seems overprotective of Jack and probably feels threatened by an older sister who might claim her son's affections.'

'That's understandable; perhaps the fact that Lindy's in Redwood was a convenient peg to hang their objections on. I'm glad they've thought some more about it though and decided at least to send photographs, Lindy will be delighted.'

Sarah didn't of course disclose the reason Ben had given as to why they'd had a change of heart but it was good news, certainly for Lindy.

'Do you want to ring her, Sarah?' Maggie asked.

'I'd like to but I hope she won't be disappointed that she can't see Jack.'

'I'm sure she won't, she's a very down to earth girl and has few expectations from life. She'll look forward to seeing the photos and will be grateful for that. It's much more than she's had over the past few years. I'll be seeing her again in a couple of days, so you can be the one to ring with the good news.' Maggie put the phone down and anticipated the smile on Lindy's face when she knew that contact had been established, and even though it wasn't the best news she was convinced it would be welcomed by her young client.

Chapter 26

In the light of the morning's discussion with Liz Stewart, Alan felt that another trip to Carol's school was warranted but first he called Tony Russell to ask him to go over his opinions on the teachers he had met.

'We spoke to two teachers who remembered Carol, a Mrs Carter and Mr Robbins, the PE teacher. He didn't remember much at all so Mrs Carter did most of the talking.'

'Were they the only ones who were there during Carol's time?'

'Probably not but it was the middle of the morning's lessons and we didn't think speaking to every teacher that knew her would give us any more insight into this case.'

'That's fine but I think a little more digging might be necessary now.'

'Do you want me to go back, boss?'

'No, I'll do it myself, I'd like to get a feel for the place, see if anyone's remembered anything new since your visit, it's bound to have been the hot topic of conversation in the staff room.'

Alan rang the head teacher next, hoping to be able to go when school finished and more of the teaching staff would be available.

'I shouldn't think there's anything more that they can tell you than the last time your men came.' Mr Wilson obviously thought Alan was wasting his time.

'I thought if I came at the end of lessons it would cause less disruption for you and perhaps you could find out how many more of your teachers remember the Stewart family.' Alan wasn't going to back down.

'Very well. Last period finishes at three forty-five. I'll get Patricia to find out who was here then and ask them to stay behind to talk to you.'

At three forty-five precisely, Alan and PC Martin Smith were shown into Mr Wilson's office where Mrs Carter was waiting. The PC had jumped at the chance to go back to his old school and Mrs Carter smiled at him.

'It's Martin Smith, isn't it? I thought I knew you last time you were here.' Martin blushed but replied politely, and the two had a quiet conversation while they waited for others to join them. Slowly another six teachers arrived and finally the PE teacher, Mr Robbins, who looked as if he'd just stepped from the shower. The ever-efficient Patricia declared that these were all of the teachers who taught at the school when Carol Stewart attended and Alan thanked her for her help.

'I'm sure you will all have heard about Carol Jacobs's husband, although you'll remember her as Carol Stewart. My colleague spoke to a couple of you a few days ago to see what you remembered about the girl and her family. Now I'd like you to cast your minds back to her last few months here and tell me anything you can remember. We're interested in the time that Carol's father died too, surely that would have impacted on Carol and her sister.'

'Wasn't he the one who fell down the stairs? Sorry, I'm Jim Green, history teacher.'

'Yes, Mr Green, he fell and broke his neck and the girls found him when they got home from school.'

'Terrible shock for them, I took the fifth formers at that time and Carol was in my class. A bit of a moody girl as I remember, always wanting to be somewhere else rather than in school but then I think many of us were like that as teenagers!'

'Thank you, Mr Green, can anyone concur with that?'

'Yes, that sounds like the girl I remember. I took her for mathematics which she obviously hated, she never handed her homework in on time, work which she could easily understand. It was such a shame seeing her wasting time like that but there have been many like her since and always will be, I'm afraid.'

'And your name is?' Martin was taking notes.

'Oh sorry, Charles Bird, mathematics.'

'Did the girls have much time off school when their father died, and can any of you tell us how it affected them?'

'They stayed off until after the funeral. I'm Mary Emerson, I was Elizabeth's form tutor at the time. I remember her being very quiet and withdrawn after the accident but she did come round, and quite quickly too. I think Elizabeth was always in her sister's shadow, it was true that she wasn't as clever as Carol but she had other qualities and certainly didn't cause as much trouble. I didn't have much to do with Carol but we all cut her a bit of slack when her father died, it was a difficult time for them.'

'Thank you, Mrs Emerson. Does anyone else remember anything about Carol or the family?'

'Shouldn't speak ill of the dead I know but the father was a nasty piece of work. Mrs Stewart sported the occasional bruise when she came into school for any reason, and listening to local gossip people had him pegged as a drinker too. The girls might even have felt relief when he died, Mary, that's why she came round pretty quickly. Sid Turnbull, English teacher, by the way.'

The questioning had almost turned into a discussion, which Alan didn't stop. Martin was taking notes and they both listened carefully to each contribution about the Stewart family. The only one who didn't join in fully was Mr Robbins. When Alan thought they had exhausted all avenues, he thanked the teachers and they began to leave.

'Mr Robbins.' Alan stopped the PE teacher from leaving. Judging by his still youthful appearance it must have been very early in his career when he taught Carol Jacobs. 'I wonder if I could have a quick word?'
Robbins sat down again and waited for his colleagues to leave the room.

'We've been told of a particular occasion when you and Carol Stewart seemed to be having quite a heated argument; this would be around the time just before her father died.'

'I rather think there would have been more than one incident, I had many arguments with Carol and other pupils like her.'

'Did you not think to report her to the head teacher or discipline her in any other way?' Alan asked. Robbins actually blushed.

'It was my first job as a teacher, I was young and inexperienced and Carol was feisty to say the least. I didn't want to go running to the head every time I had a problem with a pupil, he'd think I couldn't hack it as a teacher!' It sounded plausible. Alan remembered one or two teachers from his own school days who were 'soft' and taken advantage of by the pupils.

'So you don't remember a specific incident as standing out from the others?'

'No, sorry, but I don't.'
Alan thanked him then with PC Smith left the school. In the car Martin was thoughtful and eventually asked Alan,

'Did you ever do that thing at school where you chose the pupil most likely to succeed in your class?'

'Not that I can remember, why, did you?'

'Yes, Trevor Wright got voted in by nearly everyone, about ninety percent of the class I think.'

'And did he succeed; is he at the top of his tree?'

'No, I nicked him about a year ago for drunk driving!'

Alan dropped Martin back at the station and went in briefly to see if Della was there with anything new to report on Carol Jacobs. He found her at her computer.

'How did the visit to Appleton Close go, Della?'

The DC looked up and smiled. 'I enjoyed the house viewing, what a lovely place, I didn't expect Carol would be living in a house as grand as that.'

'That's all down to her husband, you should see Carol's childhood home, chalk and cheese doesn't cut it. So how's our girl holding up?'

'Well she was in bed when I arrived, not sleeping well apparently, which isn't any big surprise but she made coffee and we chatted about things. I saw those marks on her arm; it almost makes you think Jacobs got what he deserved.'

Alan raised his brow in surprise and Della instantly realised she shouldn't have said that and tried to save face.

'Sorry, sir, I didn't really mean that but any man who can do that to a woman who he's supposed to love is a total bastard. Carol's been through a lot and she's confused but nothing new came out of the visit. I don't really know if she fully understands the enormity of what she's done, she seems to be getting by on automatic pilot and is taking sleeping pills, which possibly confuse her even more.'

Alan thanked Della then said he was calling it a day. He knew Sue would be anxious for him to get home quickly so that Ruby would leave. Her mother's presence was a debatable blessing; she was certainly dependable but was perhaps the one person Sue didn't want helping her out.

'Ah, so you're home at a reasonable time, are you?' Ruby greeted him as he walked down the hall. 'Your wife's lying down, she seems totally unable to pull herself together but I've put a pot roast in the oven which will be ready in an hour or so. I'll get off now that you're here, it's bridge night tonight.'

Alan sighed, understanding why Ruby grated on Sue; she was well meaning but liked everyone to know that she was capable which would only serve to make her daughter feel even more inadequate.

'Thanks, Ruby, we do appreciate your help. Are you able to come tomorrow?'

'Yes, I'll be here in time to take George to nursery, it is his day tomorrow, isn't it?'

'It is, thanks again and bye for now.' Alan closed the door behind her and turned to find Sue coming down the stairs.

'Hey, I thought you were sleeping?'

'I did have a little nap but I've been hiding from Mum for the last half hour, she's driving me nuts.'

'I know, love, but we need her at the moment and she needs to be needed if that doesn't sound too confusing! It's just her attitude that's hard to put up with, she has a good heart really.'

'Yes, yes I know that, but I just don't feel in the mood to cope with her. If only she wasn't such a know it all! Her mantra when I was a child was 'I told you so' and I'm just waiting for her to say that now then I'll probably explode... and it will be messy!' Sue went into the kitchen to check on the meal for which Ruby had left specific instructions, as if her daughter was incapable of timing the cooking. Alan went upstairs to the children's play-room from where much laughter and squealing emanated. He found Rose and George playing in their tent; his daughter had made pretend tea and was happily spooning water into George's mouth, Alan only hoped she had got it from the tap and not from the toilet bowl which she had been known to do in the past.

'Good day at school, Rosie Rose?' he asked.

'Yes, Daddy, I got a sticker for good spelling, I got them all right!'

'Clever girl, you'll be teaching the teachers next.' A sticker for his daughter was the equivalent of an Olympic medal; she thrived on them and coveted any which went to other pupils.

'Don't be silly, Daddy! Have a cup of tea?' She passed him a tiny plastic tea-up half full of water which he pretended to drink then smacked his lips.

'Mmn, you make a lovely cup of tea, Rosie Rose!' She laughed and Alan left them to their game and crept quietly into their bedroom to see James in his cot. He was wide awake, gurgling to himself, so Alan picked him up and took him downstairs.

'Hey, little boy, are you not sleepy anymore?' Sue stroked James', head.

'He knows his Daddy's home, don't you, James?' Alan sat down with his baby son on his knee and began to sing *Row, Row, Row your Boat* completely off key. It made Sue smile.

'Feeling better today?' he asked hopefully.

'Now that you're home yes, I think the tablets Tom prescribed are beginning to kick in. It's nice to have you home early too instead of you coming in when I'm at the point of wanting to go to bed.'

'I know, love, this case has come at a bad time for us but I did have three weeks off.'

'Yes and you spoiled me. I don't know where I'd be without you...and Maggie... and okay, even Mum!' Sue snuggled up beside Alan and James; she really was feeling more like herself and would hopefully soon be able to cope with her family and not be so dependent on other people.

Chapter 27

Lindy's phone call from Sarah Dent brought both good and bad news, but typically the social worker put a positive spin on her contact with Jack's new family, and the thought of receiving some photographs of her brother was at least something to look forward to. From what Sarah said Jack was in a good, loving home and doing well at school, which was more than she'd known since they were separated and Lindy was genuinely pleased for him. If Jack's new parents never agreed to let them meet she would only have herself to blame and understood why they would assume her to be a bad influence. Had the roles been reversed she would have thought so too. It was something to talk over with Maggie on her next visit, visits which she now looked forward to. Perhaps they could explore finding some kind of job when her sentence was over too; she could now see the stupidity of her original plan to re-offend in the hope of being sent back to Redwood. If there was even the remotest chance of seeing Jack again she would need to stay out of trouble with the police.

Lindy derived great satisfaction from the lessons available at Redwood and surprised herself at how much she enjoyed studying, and anticipating the approaching English GCSE exam brought a strange mixture of both excitement and dread. She was also taking a computer course, which would hopefully prove useful when looking for a job. Reading the set books for the English course was a delight, and she was a frequent visitor to the library where she also read many of the novels from the well-stocked shelves. Sally and a few of the other girls teased her about the number of books she read but they took Lindy into other worlds and through their pages she travelled to exotic places, meeting interesting people even if they were only fictitious. Reading was also helping with her spelling, and the tutor encouraged the whole group to read as widely as possible, something which was certainly no hardship, and she devoured as many books as possible in her free time. Sitting for hours at the little table in the room she shared with Sally, Lindy became lost in the plot of her current novel and eager to finish it in order to begin another. Books had never featured much in her life before and she had only vague memories of the 'Janet and John' stories from which she had learned to read. Often now she was so engrossed in an exciting plot that Sally needed to remind her to go for meals, but Lindy loved reading and knew this would be something she would continue when released. It made her wonder about the possibility of finding a job in a library but again her time in Redwood would probably go against her.

Something else Lindy would miss about Redwood was Tracey and baby Sam. She had formed a bond with the little boy and although cautioning herself not to get too close, it proved impossible. His little face was so beautiful and the smiles he was now readily bestowing were captivating. Sam reminded her so much of Jack when he was tiny and Lindy couldn't help wondering what kind of life this little boy would have. Tracey was okay but really hadn't a clue when it came to caring for her son, often because she was simply too lazy to make the effort. Most nights it was Lindy who bathed and settled him into his cot while Tracey spent the time in the recreation room or catching up on the soaps on television. Lindy didn't mind, in fact she enjoyed caring for Sam but wished that his mother showed a little more interest in him. At least with the situation as it was there would be support from social services when Tracey left Redwood, and hopefully they would keep a close watch on Sam to ensure his safety; not that Lindy was over-enamoured with social services but hopefully they would have a better experience than she'd had.

Maggie had taken Rose to school before travelling to Redwood with much on her mind. Knowing that Carol Jacobs was released on bail, each time the phone rang she jumped, half expecting it to be Carol but so far she hadn't been in touch although it was feasible that she would want to pick up the counselling sessions again; after all they had only met three times and if anyone had issues to work through it was Carol Jacobs. Maggie was unsure of what to do if the call did come. It wouldn't be easy but as long as her client understood that the confidentiality clause had changed and accepted it, then Maggie could see no reason for refusing to continue. Also on her mind was Sue and Alan's predicament and she wished there was more she could do to help. Taking Rose to school was a delight and Maggie would happily keep doing so for as long as it was necessary, although Sue was beginning to seem a little more like herself of late which was certainly good to see. For Alan the homicide case landed on his desk at a difficult time, and although no one knew how much longer he'd be working on it Sue would certainly be relieved when it finished and his hours became more predictable. Maggie still found it difficult to believe that Carol had actually stabbed her husband; perhaps she should have seen it coming but would never have anticipated such an incredible scenario in a million years. After only three sessions her knowledge of Carol was superficial; they hadn't reached that point of any in-depth work and it was still very early in their relationship.

It was such a beautiful morning, with a cloudless blue sky allowing the warm sun to pervade the atmosphere and burn off the earlier ground frost. Maggie would have enjoyed the drive much more if her mind wasn't whirling with so many thoughts. Arriving at Redwood, the familiar crunch of gravel and a cloud of dust was a reminder of where she was, pulling her thoughts back to Lindy and wondering how she'd taken Sarah's news. The smile on the girl's face on entering the room brought an almost audible sigh from Maggie's lips; hopefully Lindy was looking at the glass half full rather than half empty, which proved to be the case. The first thing she wanted to talk about was Jack.

'I can't wait to see some photos, although I'll probably not recognise him; he must have changed so much.'

'Are you okay with there being no face to face contact for now?' Maggie tentatively asked.

'I'm disappointed but can understand it. The fact that I'm in here puts me at a disadvantage to begin with and I'd probably feel the same if I was in their position. Does Jack even know he has a sister?'

'I'm not sure, you might be better asking Sarah about that.' Maggie was delighted with Lindy's attitude, it showed a maturity beyond her years.

'Do you think I'll be able to see him when he's eighteen? I know it's a long way off but he'll be an adult then, won't he, and able to make his own decisions?'

'Yes but any contact will still have to go through social services who will liaise with Jack directly and then the decision will be his.' She knew that to someone Lindy's age seven or eight years seemed a lifetime away.

'So I'll just have to be content with photographs until then.'

Maggie smiled and nodded, knowing that Sarah would be trying her best to build a relationship with the

Simpson family and hoping that when they got used to the idea of Jack having a sister they might change their minds, but neither she nor Sarah would tell Lindy that. Perhaps after her release from Redwood, Sarah would try to approach the couple again but that too was in the future and for now Maggie wanted to steer the discussion to other subjects and remain in the present.

'What kind of week has it been?' she asked.

'Quite good, I'm revising for English GCSE now as the exams begin in a couple of weeks.'

'And do you feel confident?'

'In some ways, yes, I know all the set books and have tried to think of every possible question on them but I think my spelling might let me down and I don't know if bad spelling will lose marks or not.'

'Perhaps your tutor can tell you that, but with a couple of weeks left to revise there's still time to work on your spelling too. Then it won't be much longer until your release. Have you thought any more about that?'
Lindy smiled, 'Yes, I have and in the light of hopefully seeing Jack at some time in the future I'd like to try and get a job or even train for a career. The biggest problem though is that when employers learn I've been in here they won't be interested.'

'Maybe that's something else you could discuss with Sarah. She's had experience of finding work for young people and there may be some kind of scheme where you can gain work experience and have a chance to prove yourself to a prospective employer.'

'That would be good. Sarah did say there was a hostel for me to go to when I'm released so I'll ask about work experience too. Wanting to get sent back here when I leave wasn't much of an ambition, was it? But since you and Sarah have begun to visit I feel so much more positive, and even if I can't see Jack until he's older at least there's a contact through Sarah who might be able to keep me informed as to how he's doing.'

Maggie was so relieved to hear Lindy sounding so upbeat and was glad she'd made the call to Sarah Dent that day. Even though seeing Jack was most likely going to be put on hold for the time being, Lindy remained hopeful and was thinking more positively about the future than she'd anticipated or expected when they first met. When their hour was over, Lindy stood and spontaneously hugged Maggie before leaving the room with a smile on her face. Maggie was left thinking about what a lovely girl she was, with so much potential. Perhaps if she'd had a better start in life she wouldn't be in Redwood. But hopefully now that Sarah was involved the future would be a brighter place and in some measure make up for the tragic past the girl had known.

Chapter 28

To Alan's dismay the national newspapers were now showing more than a passing interest in the Jacobs case, even printing a photograph of the couple on their wedding day, goodness knows where they'd got that one from. What had been only a small column inside the papers had now become front page news. One pesky wasp had suddenly become a swarm. The press office were receiving constant requests for updates and when there was little to give them they embellished the facts and built it into some kind of drama, with Carol as the heroine unable to take any more abuse from a cruel husband. The wave of sympathy both locally and now nationally didn't help the police investigation. Alan knew that Carol had been approached by some papers for her side of the story and hoped she hadn't spoken to any of them as he'd asked, but they were getting their information from somewhere. It was always more difficult to investigate a case when there was so much public sympathy for the person they were investigating. The press had decided that Carol was the victim here and support for her was coming from many sources. Alan read an interview, published in one of the national papers, with a spokesperson from an organisation called WADA, 'Women Against Domestic Abuse' which read;

'Although WADA obviously cannot condone killing, we fully support Carol Jacobs in this case. Mrs Jacobs was driven to such drastic measures by what she had suffered from years of living with an abusive husband. It is a clear case of self-defence against a man who was frequently violent and perpetrated regular vicious attacks

on his wife. Carol Jacobs is the victim here and we will put our full weight behind getting justice for her. She has already served a sentence trapped in a violent relationship and suffering the mental and physical torment which such a relationship brings. In this case we would hope to see a suspended sentence; this poor woman needs support and understanding, not locking away.'

Alan knew that this type of publicity would make his job even harder. In the local press the same morning the headline read *'Local Businessman, Wife Beater.'* It seemed that Bill Jacobs's character was being sullied and Alan couldn't help hoping that Mrs Jacobs senior would not see this. The case was a big event in Fenbridge, a peaceful little market town where crime figures were low, and perhaps for this very reason it was receiving unprecedented press coverage. He put the newspaper down with a heavy sigh, knowing that there would be pressure from above to wrap this case up swiftly. As the team was assembling in the incident room, Alan was poring over the evidence they had gathered. In front of him were photographs of the Jacobses' house, both with the body in situ and after it was removed, and several more shots of the kitchen where the stabbing had taken place. Carol Jacobs had been photographed wearing her clothing before it was taken to forensics for analysis, and there was an image of her clothing after it was bagged and marked by the examiners to show the pattern of blood spatter. This, with the wound itself enabled them to tell at what angle the knife went into Jacobs's body. A table at the back of the room was groaning under the weight of paper recording the results of house-to-house enquiries, as well as copies of all interviews with Carol, her family, the school she attended and the staff at William Jacobs's place of work. Jacobs's computer and the contents of his desk were stacked on another table with the results of the team's digging into his financial affairs and copies of his will from Black & Sugden.

Alan gathered the team around and set about brainstorming the case from the very beginning.

'Right, what exactly have we got? A 999 call from the wife followed by a confession, the most damning evidence of all. Her fingerprints all over the knife making it seem a cut and dried case. No fingerprints found in the house at all other than Mr and Mrs Jacobs themselves. This fits in with what she told us about never having visitors and also goes a long way to ruling out a third person being involved. Evidence from the house-to house-confirms that the Jacobses were a quiet couple and no one remembers ever seeing visitors at the house. The blood spatter on Mrs Jacobs's clothes confirms that she was the one to actually stab him.

'We've charged her with manslaughter and as things stand at the moment this will stick, and if the court decides to be lenient it looks as if she'll get off with a suspended sentence. We appear to be almost at the stage of wrapping it all up. Della, I'd like you to come with me to see Carol Jacobs one more time and, Colin, could you get on to forensics and see if they've had anything new crop up? Tony, we've had the usual number of crank phone calls mainly due to our friends at the press, could you sift through them again and see if you can find anything that's actually relevant to the case? It's been over a week now, and all being well I think we might sign this off by the end of the day.'

Alan and Della arrived at Appleton Close at ten am and were eventually let in and offered coffee, which they both declined. The purpose of their visit was to once again go over every minute of the morning when Carol Jacobs stabbed her husband, but first Alan wanted to check that she was not the one who was talking to the press.

'No, you asked me not to so I've said nothing,' Carol confirmed. 'They've been knocking on the door but I just didn't answer and when they phone I've been cutting them off.'

'Good. When the press pick up on a story like this they can be persistent and often people tell them things just to get rid of them.' Alan spoke as if his words were a question but Carol again denied that she had spoken to anyone from the press.

'But you've read some of the papers?'

'Yes.' Carol hung her head and spoke quietly, 'The reports are better than I'd expected and the support expressed has gone in some measure towards helping me come to terms with what I've done. I've felt terrible about it, taking a life is horrendous and I just wish I could turn the clock back. It's like some dreadful nightmare but it isn't, it's real.'

Della was nodding sympathetically while Alan decided to get down to business.

'I know we've gone over this several times but we need to be absolutely sure that the sequence of events that morning is accurate. So I'd like you to cast your mind back to the night before and tell us exactly what transpired between you and your husband.' He nodded to Della to begin taking notes and Carol wearily began to tell her story again.

Chapter 29
Maggie

The phone call I had dreaded came after the weekend. My thoughts were still happily on my home, which now had its new addition, and Peter and I had spent the weekend settling him in. Jasper is a lovely boy, playful and affectionate and always wanting our approval which we give him in spades. At one point Peter accidentally stood on the poor little chap's tail and he jumped up with a yelp. Peter immediately fussed him to say sorry and Jasper wagged his tail with no malice at all, licking his face, eager to please and giving such unconditional affection. Tara was wary of this interloper but was already showing signs of coming round and had only hissed at Jasper once and then instantly retreated to hide under the bed. I hadn't realised how much we were missing Ben until Jasper arrived to fill that dog-shaped void. Making my way to work that morning, I almost envied Peter, who was working from home and able to spend time with our pets. When I called at Sue's to take Rose to school the little girl was full of questions about Jasper, bouncing up and down with energy and wanting to know when she could come and see him.

'Well tomorrow I have the afternoon off,' I told her, enjoying the look of expectation on her little face, 'so I thought if it was okay with Mummy I would pick you up from school and then you and George could come to our house for tea. Afterwards we can take him out for a walk, how does that sound?'

Rose grinned, 'Awesome!' was the instant answer and she raised her fist to 'fist bump' me. I'd only just got used to high fives but Rose had moved on to cooler things. Sue smiled at me.

'You've been such a help, Maggie, I don't know what we'd have done without you!'

We left for school and I watched Rose running in, excitedly telling her best friend that she was going to help Auntie Maggie with her new dog tomorrow. I smiled and continued on my way to work, where in the first ten minutes the phone rang.

'Maggie, it's Carol.' She waited for my reaction. Her next visit had been scheduled for that morning but I'd assumed she wouldn't come and was anticipating catching up on other things.

'Hello, Carol, how are you?' It struck me as a silly question when the poor woman was facing a charge of manslaughter after stabbing her husband and her whole world must be in turmoil, but I'd actually said those words, an automatic response, I suppose.

'Can I still come to see you?' she asked.

'If you feel you can and you want to, then yes of course.'

'I don't suppose it would be possible for you to visit me instead, would it?'

I thought for only a moment before recklessly saying yes again. She gave me the address which now I already knew and I told her I'd set off immediately. As I put on my coat which I'd only just taken off, images of Peter, Joyce Pattison, Tom Williams and Alan flashed into my mind. Each of them would caution me not to go, which was perhaps why I wasn't going to tell them. Instead I wrote Carol's name and address on a piece of paper and sealed it in an envelope. On the front I wrote, *Maggie. Should be back by 11.30am.* On my way out I gave the envelope to Laura, the practice manager who was working a spell on reception. Having had similar notes before Laura knew why I was leaving it and also to open the letter if I was not back by eleven-thirty am.

Number 34 Appleton Close was impressive, a quiet street of rather exclusive individually designed houses all with immaculately manicured front gardens. I rang the bell and Carol answered immediately. Stepping aside to let me in, she offered coffee which I refused; it's one of those situations where it is best to keep things on a professional footing, and drinking coffee together introduced an element of familiarity or even friendship. I was there to be Carol's counsellor not her friend, though goodness knows she could probably do with one. We took seats in the lounge, a pleasant spacious room, tastefully and expensively furnished with a large picture window letting in the morning sun.

'I'm sure it's difficult to know where to start, Carol, but as always this hour is for you to use as you wish. I should, however, tell you that the confidentiality issue has changed since you agreed to allow the police to see your medical records.' I thought it best to point this out at the beginning and then waited for her to collect her thoughts.

'Yes, I understand that but there's nothing to hide so giving permission was never an issue. It's been a tough week and I'm scared about what will happen now. My life's a mess, Maggie.' There were tears in her eyes; no doubt she had shed oceans of tears over the last few days. I nodded, keeping my attention focussed on her face. She looked so young and vulnerable and quite out of place in the perfect room which I thought looked more suited to an older, professional couple.

'What did the police tell you?' It was a natural question for her to ask.

'That you had stabbed your husband and he was dead.' Dead is such a hard word to say, two vowels squeezed between two consonants leaving absolutely no room for compassion to be expressed in speaking it. Fat tears began to roll down her cheeks; she sniffed and rummaged in her pocket for a tissue.

'I didn't mean to kill him, Maggie, but he was wild, out of control. The night before we'd had a huge row, I don't know why really but he was drinking and he didn't like the meal I'd made...' Her voice cracked, it was difficult to get the words out.

'Take your time, Carol, there's no hurry.' I waited until she regained some composure.

'He raped me! On the kitchen floor... he began to throw things around and then...' Another silence filled the room and I waited again.

'After he went to bed I stayed downstairs and slept on the couch. Bill came down the next morning and was furious...he shouted and was coming towards me! I don't remember picking the knife up but I must have because the next thing I knew I'd stabbed him with it. If he hadn't kept coming at me like that and he was so angry...' Carol's head dropped into her hands and she sobbed openly. Moving to sit next to her on the sofa, I put my arm around her shoulders and could feel her pain; she had done something which could never be undone and would be with her for the rest of her life. She turned her head onto my shoulder and cried bitterly. After two or three minutes she sat upright again and began to pull herself together.

'It was horrible at the police station. I had to take off all my clothes and be examined by a doctor before the detectives began to ask questions, the same questions they'd asked here before we left. I tried to tell them what had happened but it was hard, I was so confused. I wish it was me that was dead, not Bill!' Carol stood up.

'Sorry, Maggie, I need a glass of water.' She moved into the kitchen at the other side of the hall and as I watched her go I tried to imagine what it must feel like to actually kill someone. I pictured her husband's body on the floor; it must have been in the kitchen, had it been in here the carpet would have been ruined and how could she come back here afterwards? Carol returned with her water.

'What have I done, Maggie? What will happen to me? I didn't intend to kill him; I just didn't want him touching me again!'

'What happens next is really up to the police and the CPS, but I do know that they're fair. Their role is to see justice done but they take everything into consideration. Has your solicitor explained the process to you?'

'Yes, but I don't think I was taking it in.'

'Then perhaps you need to speak to him again. It's his job to represent you and let the appropriate bodies know why this happened, and your circumstances before the event.' I didn't really want to give advice, I wasn't qualified to do it either, but Carol seemed unsure of what would happen and her solicitor was the best person to ask.

'Have you got anyone who can come and stay with you, or somewhere else you could go perhaps?'

'No, there's no one. Bill made sure I had no friends and he isolated me from my family. I don't mind staying here except the newspaper reporters keep calling or ringing, it's like being a prisoner in my own home but perhaps that's something I'd better get used to.'

It wasn't clear whether Carol was anticipating a custodial sentence but surely she'd seen the support she was receiving in the press. It seemed more than likely she would get a suspended sentence, it hadn't been a planned attack, she was simply defending herself.

'Again your solicitor is the best person to advise you about what might happen, why don't you give him a ring?' I wasn't going to be drawn into speculation which wouldn't help at all and would simply amount to empty platitudes. Carol took another sip of water.

'It was awful living with Bill but I never meant to kill him.' That was the third time she'd said it. 'I should have got to know him better before we married but I was so keen to get away from home that I got carried away planning a beautiful wedding and not having to think about the cost. Bill was so generous then but he changed almost immediately after we married and started hitting me after only a couple of weeks. At first he would apologise afterwards and be gentle and caring, but pretty soon the beatings became more frequent and he made no pretence of being sorry. I should have left him then but I had nowhere to go. Things had been difficult with Mum and Liz, and I knew I'd get no help from them so I stayed with Bill, always hoping things would get better.'

'Do you think your mother and sister would be more supportive now that they know what you've been through?'

'No, I'd be too ashamed to go to them now and they'd only say I got what I deserved. I've repeated the pattern, haven't I?' Carol looked at me for an answer.

'What pattern do you mean?'

'The cycle of abuse, I married a man like my father, a bully; isn't it often the case, Maggie?'

'It does happen, yes, but patterns of behaviour can be changed.'

'When I was little I used to look up to my dad, which every little girl should be able to do but as I grew older and saw what he was really like I began to hate him and was glad when he died. Do you think that's awful of me?'

'No, I don't think anything like that at all. None of us can help our feelings and to respect someone, that person must be deserving of our respect.' A picture of my own wonderful father flashed through my mind, if ever there was a perfect dad it was him and I still missed him so much.

'I'm not sorry that Bill's dead either. Does that make me a bad person?'

'As I said, we can't help our feelings and you didn't act on feelings, you acted on a self-preservation instinct, you were protecting yourself, Carol.' This was the most open Carol had been with me and as we talked some more she went far back into her childhood and managed to verbalise some of the angst she still harboured even now. If only we could have connected sooner, things might have worked out differently.

After an hour I had to leave to get back to the surgery promptly so no one would worry about me. I hoped Carol might decide to take a step of faith and contact her family but somehow I didn't think she would.

Chapter 30

Carol Jacobs was to have one more visitor that day, when totally out of the blue her sister Liz arrived late in the afternoon. Carol's face must have reflected her surprise; the sisters hadn't seen each other for over four years.

'Well, can I come in?' Liz asked. Carol remained silent but opened the door to allow her sister in. Eventually she collected her thoughts enough to speak.

'Why are you here?'

'To see if you're all right and if I can help in any way. You must feel pretty lonely at the moment, how are you coping?'

'I'm doing okay. What makes you think you can help anyway?' Carol frowned.

'I was thinking of company for you, someone on your side? I'm offering an olive branch here, Carol. We used to be close and I thought you might need your family after all that's happened.' Liz was making a genuine offer of friendship in spite of all that had transpired in their past.

'I'm surprised you've bothered.' Carol's words were spoken harshly and laced with sarcasm.

'I wasn't the one to cut off contact though, was I? You decided to have nothing more to do with us once you found your rich husband, were we not good enough for you then?' Liz sounded as bitter as her sister, which wasn't what she intended; her visit had been altruistic and her offer of help genuine.

'Look, Carol, I'm here to see if you need company. For all I know you may have dozens of wonderful friends and some of Bill's family too but I would imagine after what happened any of his family or friends won't want to know you anymore. You did kill the poor bloke, didn't you?'

'Only in self-defence! He abused me, I'm the victim here, not Bill... look!' She pulled up the sleeve of her jumper to show Liz the cigarette burns.

'Painful.' Her sister had the good grace to wince. 'But I'm surprised you let him get away with it. You were never one to be bullied as I remember; in fact it was usually you doing the bullying.'

'That's when we were kids at school, you don't know what my life has been like since then! Bill scared me; I've been living with a monster. As well as the beatings he kept me short of money and wouldn't let me go out alone. It was him who stopped me from seeing you, he didn't want to know anyone from my past.' Carol blurted all this out, trying to convince her sister. Liz looked at her, really looked as if trying to read what was in her mind before deciding to believe what she'd said. A few moments of silence were broken when Liz asked,

'So you haven't made me an auntie then?'

'No, it was bad enough living with Bill without having a baby to look after!'

Liz wasn't at all surprised; her sister was always too wrapped up in herself to want to have children.

'Well don't you want to know how Mum is, or what I've been doing with myself these last few years?' She didn't want to get into her sister's life with her husband; Carol's words were difficult enough to believe.

'Of course, how is Mum and yourself too? Come through to the kitchen and I'll make coffee.' She was suddenly friendly and Liz followed her into the bespoke kitchen, silently admiring the house which would now belong entirely to her sister. Carol boiled the water, using the activity of coffee-making to decide exactly why

Liz was there. Had her mother sent her to snoop or was she genuine? Last time they were together Liz was little more than a child going through that awful gawky teenage stage. Was she really offering an olive branch or was there something else, curiosity perhaps or simply snooping? It was difficult to tell although her sister had always been an uncomplicated girl, unless she'd changed in the last four years.

'So what are you doing now? Still living with Mum?'

'I've got a job at the bookies in the precinct and yes, I'm still living with Mum.'

Carol smiled.

'What?'

'Nothing.'

'Then why the grin?'

'Just that you haven't changed, have you? No ambition, no dreams or aspirations.'

'And look where dreams and aspirations have got you!' Liz countered.

'Ah but when all this is over I'll have much more than you could ever imagine.'

'I presume you're talking about money but that's not everything is it? Where are all your friends?'

'You know nothing about my life; I might have dozens of friends for all you know!' Carol was angry; what right had her sister to make a sudden appearance and sit in judgement? 'You're just jealous because I've done so well for myself and you haven't and I presume there's no boyfriend,' she continued, spitting the words out; what right had Liz to comment on her life?

'Do you seriously think I'm jealous? Of what, being charged with murder, killing your own husband?' Liz couldn't believe what she was hearing.

'It wasn't murder, it was manslaughter and because it was self-defence I'll probably only get a suspended sentence.' Carol sounded smug and Liz was beginning to wish she'd never come.

'I haven't come here to argue with you, we're not kids anymore and you're in trouble. You're my sister and I wanted to help.' Liz's conciliatory tone did nothing to calm Carol down.

'Well I don't need your help; I have everything I need here!' Her hand swept around in an arc to indicate the fabulous kitchen and what Liz didn't doubt was a fabulous house from top to bottom.

'And I hope it's worth it all, a dead husband and no doubt his family grieving which obviously you're not. I'm sorry to have disturbed your perfect little life. I'll leave you in peace to continue playing house in your ideal home!' Liz turned to go. When she reached the door she looked back and said,

'It was just the same with Dad, wasn't it? He wouldn't give you all you asked for; did Bill refuse you something too?'

'It's nothing like it was with Dad and just be careful what you say about that!' Carol retorted.

'You expected me to help you then but you obviously don't need me now, you've got it all planned out, haven't you? Well goodbye, Carol, I hope you enjoy your lonely little life!' Liz walked out the door leaving her sister angry and reflecting on what damage Liz could do if she put her mind to it.

Chapter 31

After their visit to Carol, which had thrown up nothing new, Alan went back to the incident room while Della made her way to Mrs Jacobs senior to see how she was faring. It was Alan's intention to gather the last strands of the investigation together that day before going to see the DI and then let the wheels of justice run their course. His work would be mostly done then until the trial of course, but that was a long time into the future and meanwhile he could work more reasonable hours and hopefully spend more time at home with Sue and the children. On entering the incident room he noticed Tony and Colin huddled together, looking rather serious.

'Anything wrong?' he asked as he approached them.

'A couple of things, Alan,' Tony answered. 'I've been looking at the phone calls like you asked, most of which were the usual crackpot ones, all followed up of course and without results but there's one that came in early this morning which hadn't been passed on until the last half hour. It's from a Pamela Clark who was keen to talk to the officer in charge of the investigation. The desk constable who answered wrote down her number but no message, she didn't say what she wanted to talk to you about and unfortunately he didn't ask.'

'So who is she?'

'She works for Bill Jacobs, or rather she did. I met her briefly when I visited his office, she didn't appear to have anything to help then and was still rather tearful so perhaps something's come to mind now,' Colin answered.

'Right, let's ring her back and go out to see her.'

'I've rung already, she's at work and I told her someone would be there as soon as possible.'

'Good, so what are we waiting for, come on, Colin.'

'There's something else,' Tony said. 'I spoke to forensics and they've brought up something which could be nothing but I thought you might want to know.'

'Which is?'

'The broken glass and crockery from the floor; most of it was fragmented but from the larger pieces they managed to lift some prints. Twenty-three pieces in all were big enough to find fingerprints and partials and they all matched Carol Jacobs.'

'And Carol told us her husband had thrown the glass... I think we need another little chat to Mrs Jacobs. Right, Tony, Colin and I will go to see Pamela Clark and I'd like you to take a uniformed officer and bring Carol Jacobs in. She might have to wait a while until we're back but I think it might be time to put a little pressure on her and see what she has to say about this.'

In the car DC Colin Brownlow gave Alan the rundown regarding the dynamics of William Jacobs's business and reminded him of the four staff members and their respective roles.

'I spoke mainly with Terry Sutherland, Jacobs's right-hand man, a nice bloke who I felt sorry for. He hadn't a clue what should be done about the business so I suggested Jacobs's solicitor might be the one to turn to. This Pamela Clark was too shocked to be of any help so I'm interested to see why she wants to talk now.' They parked the car and Colin led the way into the ultra-modern office where all four staff members were busy at their desks. Terry stood first and went to talk to the two officers but when they explained that they were there to see Pamela he showed them into William Jacobs's office where Pamela joined them. She acknowledged the officers with a weak smile and thanked them for coming, then her eyes strayed to the empty desk in the middle of the large open space. She obviously hadn't come to terms with her employer's death and seemed somewhat nervous.

'Are you comfortable here or is there somewhere else we could go?' Alan asked.

'No, this is fine, thank you.' Pamela sat on one of the easy chairs in the corner of the office and the two detectives took their place on the matching leather sofa.

'So why did you want to see us Pamela?' Alan began.

'It's the newspapers. I couldn't believe what they were writing about Bill, it's just not true, any of it and it's so unfair when he can't defend himself.'

'What particular allegations upset you?' Colin asked.

'They claimed that he beat his wife, that she's led such a terrible life with him because of his violence but Bill was one of the most gentle people I've ever known, it's just not true!' The colour was rising in Pamela's face and her arms were wrapped tightly around her body as if protecting herself.

'But these allegations have come from his wife. None of us ever really knows what goes on in a marriage, many abusers are like Jekyll and Hide and seem to have two completely different personas depending on where they are or who they're with.' Alan spoke softly, this woman was obviously distressed.

'I know that but I also know, sorry knew, Bill. I began to work with him in the early days of the business and I've watched him work his way up through a very competitive market. In his business dealings Bill was always a gentleman and scrupulously honest, I think that's why our customers have stayed with us, they recognised his integrity. I knew him before he married that girl too. She flattered him and wormed her way into becoming his wife. We met at their wedding and there was something perplexing about her even then, she acted as if she owned Bill but when he came back to work after their honeymoon he was already regretting the marriage.'

'Pamela, I can understand that it's been upsetting to see the bad publicity Mr. Jacobs has received but what you've told us is really just your opinion. Did your employer actually tell you any of this?'

'Yes, he did!' Pamela looked quite defiant and both Colin and Alan raised their eyebrows.

'Can you tell us what exactly he said and when?'

'Perhaps I should tell you about my relationship with Bill first. When I came to work for him I was married, unhappily so but married nevertheless. Bill and I were attracted to each other, something which we eventually acknowledged and if he'd asked me I would gladly have left my husband for him but he didn't ask. He believed in the sanctity of marriage and would never have come between us but we were still friends and I suppose I was his confidant. We spent most of our lunch hours together, just here in the office and we talked. There was never anything improper about our relationship, we were simply friends. It was something of a surprise when he told me he was getting married, he said he'd found a girl he felt he could love. He wanted companionship and the chance to have a family while he was still young enough. Possibly he also wanted an escape from his mother who dominated him and tried to live his life for him. She was furious at his plans and tried everything possible to dissuade him from marrying Carol but the wedding went ahead. It didn't change our friendship and at first Bill was loyal to his wife; there were times when I knew something was troubling him but he never said a word against her until recently.'

A tap on the office door interrupted Pamela as Terry brought in a tray of coffee and biscuits. They thanked him and Pamela began to pour the welcome scalding liquid as she continued her story.

'About three or four months ago Bill confided in me that all was not well at home. It was difficult for him to do this but I think he was almost at breaking point and in the security of our friendship he felt able to talk to me. Carol was the one abusing him! And not only physically, she made his life unbearable, always demanding more money, a better car; to her Bill just seemed to be a cash machine and she was obsessed with money. The physical abuse was more of an embarrassment to him, he held her off when she became violent and in no way retaliated, the very thought appalled him. I noticed the odd bruise on occasions but I don't think anyone else did. Then there were the arguments about having a family. Bill was quite a bit older than Carol and desperately wanted children; he'd have been a great dad. Before their wedding she'd talked happily enough about having children and he believed that she wanted them as much as he did, in fact Bill thought they were trying for a family until he found a packet of her birth control pills. It was all a cruel lie and Carol had no intention of having a child. I think that bothered him more than anything, Bill was turned forty and could see his dreams of a family slipping away from him. She'd married him under false pretences and he became a broken man.' Pamela had said her piece, and turned away blinking back tears.

'Pamela, you've been extraordinarily brave to tell us this and very loyal to Bill but there's really very little we can use. You said that Bill couldn't defend himself from the allegations in the press but the same is true of what you've told us. Bill can't verify what you're saying and in a court of law it would pretty much be your word against Carol's and as I said before, no one really knows what goes on in other people's marriages.'

'So you don't believe me?' Pamela looked horrified; having poured out her feelings it looked as if it had all been in vain.

'No, I'm not saying that at all but we deal in facts and hard evidence and nothing which you've said gives us that, but we will certainly take your words into consideration during our investigations. Is there a chance that any of your colleagues was party to these conversations with Bill?'

'Sadly no, they usually go out at lunch time but even when they were in they wouldn't have been able to hear from out there.'

'I'm so sorry, Pamela. If you do think of anything else which would help us in any way will you ring me?'

'Yes of course.'

A very dejected-looking Pamela returned to her desk and Alan and Colin left. In the car on the way back to the station Alan asked,

'Well what did you think of all that?'

'If it's true it turns our investigation on its head, doesn't it?

'But do you believe her?'

'Yes, I think I do. Pamela's got nothing to gain by making this up and she's a much more credible witness than Carol, what she said sounds reasonable enough to me. What about you, Alan?'

'I believe her too. There's always been something about Carol that I was uncertain about. With the picture we got from her old school it seems she wasn't a very nice character even then and as for cutting off her family, she's always said it was Bill who made her do it but her mother and sister seem to think otherwise. Well she should be at the station waiting for us now and I wonder what she'll say when we tell her that we've heard a different version of her marriage. And I'd like to hear what she has to say about the fingerprints on the broken glass too. This should prove interesting.'

Chapter 32

Carol Jacobs was more than a little annoyed at being dragged to the police station again; she would much rather they visited her at home, as she felt more comfortable on home ground. The room she was taken to this time was even smaller and stuffier than the last one she'd been in. After declining to have her solicitor present, assuming this was just another trivial repetition of the same questions answered dozens of times already, the amount of time she was kept waiting was beginning to unnerve her. After forty minutes Della Johnson entered the room with two cups of coffee, one of which she gave to Carol.

'Sorry to keep you waiting but DS Hurst is tied up with some new evidence; he'll be with us shortly.' Della smiled and took the seat opposite the other woman.

'What new evidence?' Carol frowned, 'Surely there's nothing more to look into, it's been so intense for the last week.'

'I know but we need to be absolutely clear on all the facts before we can pass the case on to the CPS.' Della wasn't entirely sure what Alan was doing but Tony had updated her on the forensic report into the fragments of glass and Colin had quickly summarised the conversation with Pamela Clark. It looked as if Alan's wish to wrap this case up by the end of the day wasn't going to happen. Five minutes later Alan entered the room.

'Sorry to keep you waiting, Carol, it's been a busy afternoon.' He took the seat next to Della and switched the tape recorder on. After giving the date and time he named the persons present then began.

'Carol, about the broken glass and crockery on the kitchen floor, could you tell me exactly when was it thrown?'

'I told you, it was the night before, Bill was in one of his rages and he threw anything he could get his hands on.'

'And are you sure that it was Bill who threw it?'

'Yes, of course I'm sure but we've gone over this before.'

'I know,' Alan agreed 'But my problem is that when forensics examined the pieces the only fingerprints on any of the fragments belong to you and not to your husband, who you said threw them.' Carol's face blanched and her eyes darted to the corner of the room but she remained silent.

'Can you explain this to us?' Alan asked.

'Perhaps I threw something too, it's all a blur now and I can't remember the exact sequence of events. Bill threw things... and then he raped me!' Carol began to cry but Alan wasn't finished.

'But if you had both thrown things then surely we would have found fingerprints from both you and your husband, wouldn't you think?'

'Well maybe there were, surely you can't get fingerprints from all the pieces?'

'We found prints on twenty-three separate pieces and they all belonged to you.' Alan looked directly at her but Carol had nothing to say and wouldn't meet his gaze so he continued,

'We've also had some new information from someone who knew your husband and told us that Bill confided in them that he was the one being physically abused, not you.'

Carol's face took on a hardened expression and her eyes flashed.

'Who told you that?' she demanded.

'A friend of your husband's, someone he felt able to share his thoughts with.'

'I want my solicitor,' Carol said, folding her arms and sitting back in the chair. It was obvious she wasn't going to engage further with them so Alan switched off the tape and stood to leave the room.

'We'll ring him for you and continue when he arrives.'

'Wait a minute, you can't keep me here, I want to go home, it's getting late.'

'I know what the time is and we'd all like to go home but there seem to be a few details to clear up first. We'll make that call and come back when your solicitor arrives.' Alan and Della both left the room at six-twenty pm and Alan asked Della to call the solicitor while he rang Sue to apologise for again being late home. Standing in the corridor outside the incident room for a little privacy, he spoke to his wife.

'I'm sorry, love, I'd really hoped to be home by now but a couple of things have come up and I'm waiting for a solicitor before I can finish this interview.' Sue was fine about it, she'd had a relatively good day and the children were already bathed and ready for bed. Rose came on the line and Alan said goodnight to her and promised to go into her room when he got home to kiss her goodnight. With another apology to Sue, he put his phone away and went into the incident room where Tony and Colin were still working.

'This case just gets better and better!' Colin had a broad grin on his face. 'Liz Stewart is in interview room six, she wants to see you.' As Alan turned to go out of the room Della was coming in.

'The solicitor's on his way, he didn't appreciate having his evening meal disturbed but should be here in about half an hour.'

'Could have been longer, I suppose. Come with me, Della, we have Liz Stewart in room six, I wonder what she wants.'

The two officers entered the room where Carol's sister sat anxiously biting her fingernails. Liz had wrestled with her conscience since leaving her sister's home that afternoon. She walked slowly to the police station and even walked once around the block when she got there, uncertain of what to do. In the end she made one of those silly deals with herself and decided to ask for DS Hurst and if he wasn't there she would go home and forget all about it. When the desk sergeant said that DS Hurst was still in the station Liz nearly bottled out and ran, but she'd made the deal so would stay to talk to him.

'Hello, Liz.' Alan sounded friendly. 'This is DC Della Johnson, how can we help you?'

'I went to see Carol this afternoon...' The girl was nervous and couldn't seem to find her words. Della smiled at her and said,

'That was kind of you; she could probably do with a friend at the moment.'

'Well you wouldn't have thought so. We ended up arguing and I left feeling decidedly unwelcome. It appears that even though Carol's husband is dead she still doesn't want to know her family.'

'And what is it you wanted to tell us, Liz?' Alan tried his best to sound patient but he would much rather be at home with his family, even though the investigation was beginning to move at speed and in a different direction than it had done previously.

'It's something from the past, something I did wrong. Would I be in trouble if I'd lied to the police in the past?' It was obvious that she was in two minds about whether to talk to them or not.

'It depends what it was but telling the truth is always the better option.'

'It was when Dad died. The police interviewed us all and asked when Carol and I left the house that morning. We did leave together like we said but Carol had forgotten her homework and went back to get it. She didn't tell the policeman at the time and I kept quiet and just agreed that we'd walked to school together as usual.' There, she had said it, that ugly lie of omission which had risen up to trouble her on many occasions since. She knew what she was implying and by the expression of the police officers' faces they knew too. Alan looked directly into her eyes and asked,

'Liz, are you suggesting that your sister might have had something to do with your father's death?'

'I suppose so, yes. We never really talked about it afterwards but it was always there. Carol told the police that we left home together at about eight-forty and I simply didn't contradict her.'

Alan sat at his computer and pulled up the information on Frank Stewart's accident from eight years previously. The report's conclusion was accidental death; it was assumed that he either tripped on loose carpet at the top of the stairs or simply overbalanced, possibly due to a hangover as he was a known heavy drinker. His elder daughter had called it in when she and her sister arrived home from school and the autopsy suggested that he had been dead for between six and seven hours when he was found. The fall had broken his neck and severed the spinal cord, death would have been instantaneous. The usual investigations within the family had found nothing to give cause for concern. His wife Joan had left for work at eight that morning while Frank was still in bed, and both of his daughters left for school at eight-forty by which time Frank was up and in the bathroom. There was no mention of Carol going back to the house for any reason. The girls arrived home first and found their father's body, and Carol rang 999. The coroner returned a verdict of accidental death and the case was closed.

What should have been a straightforward case now gave Alan an uncomfortable feeling in his gut, one which he knew meant he would have to look into Frank Stewart's case again before wrapping up the William Jacobs investigation. As the inspector had long since gone home Alan decided that as this was still only another line of enquiry and not a new development as such, he could introduce the historic accident with Carol and see what her reaction would be and then take it to the DI in the morning. It seemed that Carol Jacobs had been close to two deaths in her short life; her father's, which was assumed to be an accident and now her husband's, which had at first appeared to be self-defence but was now looking like something else. Alan scribbled on his notepad, trying to make sense of what they now knew.

a) Re. Frank Stewart, Carol had lied to the police about when she left the house and her sister had not contradicted her.

b) Re. William Jacobs, Carol admitted fatally stabbing him but claimed it was self-defence.

c) Pamela Clark provided a different insight into the Jacobses' relationship than the one Carol had led them to believe.

d) Carol's fingerprints were all over the broken glass which she claimed her husband had thrown.

e) Maggie Sayer had caught Carol out in an unnecessary lie, one which perhaps gave a different perspective on the 'abused wife' whom she was claiming to be.

Each one of these on their own would be insignificant and could probably be explained away as an oversight, but drawing them all together they became something more and Carol became something other than the innocent victim of a violent husband.

Della appeared in the door of the incident room,

'Mr Albright has arrived, Alan, we're good to go!' She was keen to get on with the interview but first Alan wanted to show her the notes he'd been making. Della's mouth dropped open as she read the list.

'This should be interesting!' she smiled as they made their way to again interview Carol Jacobs.

Mr Albright looked particularly stern, and as soon as Della had switched on the tape and recited the names of those present he made his complaint.

'My client came here voluntarily at your request and it appears that you have kept her waiting around, unaware of why you need to interview her yet again and I would like it recording that I object to this treatment. Mrs Jacobs is still in a fragile state after recent unfortunate events. Could this interview not have been conducted in her home and during office hours?'

'Thank you, Mr Albright, your comments have been noted. I'm sure we would all like to be in a position where this incident is cleared up but new information has been coming in and we need to clarify a few more things with Mrs Jacobs.' Alan smiled across the table. Albright sat back in his chair with his lips pursed and directed his angry gaze to the table.

'Carol,' Alan began. 'We were talking about the thrown glass and crockery, have you had anymore thoughts on this while you've been waiting?'

'No, I possibly did throw some of it, the events are jumbled up, it was such a horrible time.'

'Okay we'll leave that for now.' Alan noted that her solicitor didn't ask what that was all about so presumably she'd told him about the latest fingerprint evidence.

'And then there's your husband's friend with whom he shared information. They allege that he told them you were the one who abused Bill.'

'That's preposterous!' Mr Albright sat forward, engaged again in the proceedings. 'You've seen the bruises and the horrific burn marks on my client's arm and you say she was the one doing the abusing?'

'No, I'm not saying it, I'm just repeating what this witness told us but we can move on from that if you wish.'

'Yes, I do wish.' The solicitor was emphatic.

'Carol, why did you lie to the police on the day your father died?' Alan's voice was even, but he was curious to see her reaction to this change of focus. As he watched her face turned red, with anger or distress he couldn't tell. She remained quiet, and her solicitor looked at her as if he'd never seen her before then tackled Alan again.

'Not only are you distressing my client with repeated questions about this case, you're now taking her back to another distressing incident!'

Carol suddenly burst into tears. Della stood and grabbed a box of tissues to pass to her and poured a glass of water for her. She held a wad of tissues to her face and continued to sob quite violently. Mr Albright fussed over her but it became evident that she could not continue.

'We'll take a break now and send in some coffee. Shall we recommence in fifteen minutes?' Alan offered.

'No, we'll finish now for the night. Mrs Jacobs is obviously in no state to answer any more questions, in fact I think she may need to see a doctor.' The solicitor's face reflected his anger.

There was little else to do but suspend the interview for the evening, and Alan told the solicitor to be at the station with his client by nine o'clock the next morning. Mr Albright made a big fuss about leading his client out and Alan and Della watched, frustrated.

'I rather enjoyed that.' Della smiled.

'Yes, me too. I think I expected that to happen, she doesn't want to answer questions without being prepared. I'd like to be a fly on the wall at number 34 Appleton Close tonight. Anyway, let's get off home, we'll see you bright and early tomorrow, Della, and hopefully continue this interview.'

Chapter 33
Maggie

Jasper and the warmer spring weather gave both Peter and me the incentive to go out walking more often. Our little dog was settling in brilliantly and his tail never stopped wagging; even when he was asleep it thumped on the floor as if he was dreaming happy dreams. It was a warm evening and after taking Rose and George back home after their promised visit for tea, we ventured out with Jasper again. The children had been so excited to play with the dog and he had been gentle and accommodating, only occasionally sneaking off to hide in Peter's study for a sleep. As we again walked our dog, he kept looking up at us almost every minute, wagging his tail as if seeking our approval.

'Good boy, Jasper!' I must have spoken those words at least twenty times. 'He looks as if he's smiling at us, Peter.'

'I should think he is, he's certainly got his feet well under the table as well as the rest of him!' But Peter had to agree that adopting Jasper was one of our better ideas, the little fellow seemed to complete our family and even Tara was beginning to come round after her initial aloofness.

'I wondered if we could fit in a few days at the cottage in Scotland now that the weather's picking up. Could you free up some time in your diary?' my husband asked, and I took no persuading.

'I'd like that, perhaps Mum would like to come too and I'm sure Jasper will enjoy the walks in the countryside, it was certainly Ben's idea of heaven. It had crossed my mind to offer the cottage to Sue and Alan for a few days before she goes back to work, they could do with a break and it would do them both good.' The cottage had been Mum and Dad's retirement home where they had lived for several years before Dad became ill. It was in a pretty little village in the border region, so not too far to travel for a few days. Mum had gifted the cottage to me after Dad died, which meant that she too could visit the place where they had lived so contentedly during their last years together. I was more than happy to let friends use it too; it needed people in it to give it that lived-in feeling which was evident whenever we went. It seems silly but I often feel that a house has a personality, and our little bungalow always feels welcoming when we go to visit as if it appreciates the company. I could easily arrange my diary to free up a long weekend and I knew Mum wouldn't need asking twice.

As Jasper continued to seek our approval, I couldn't help but marvel at how faithful dogs can be and how unconditional their love and loyalty are. This reminded me of an article I'd read recently which I shared with Peter.

'There's been an experiment in the US where prisoners were given a dog to live with them in their cells and to look after. The dogs, all from a nearby animal sanctuary, and the prisoners quickly formed a bond which proved beneficial to both parties. The inmates had sole responsibility for caring for their pet which strengthened the bond between them, and the young men in those prisons, many of whom were from difficult backgrounds, felt loved for the first time in their lives. They went on to become more responsible members of the community on release.' Peter listened as I rambled on, saying how this should be introduced into our prisons and detention centres. I really had Redwood in mind, thinking how much Lindy would love Jasper if only I could take him to visit.

'You could always suggest it to someone in authority at Redwood; they might take the idea on board,' Peter encouraged. He knew that I was visiting a client at Redwood but didn't know any other details. I smiled; even if I ever got to speak to the warden in charge, he would most likely think I was mad although I could cite many instances where a pet proved to be more therapeutic than several hours of counselling.

We completed our circular walk which was just long enough to exercise Jasper and not tire ourselves out, and went back into the house to settle down for the evening. Peter had an hour in his study to finish off an estimate he was working on and I began to flick through the day's paper to see if there was anything worth watching on television.

The following morning my first client was Lindy Baker. I'd grown to love these visits, as the drive to Redwood was a pleasant, peaceful one which gave me time to reflect and take in the stunning scenery. I've always felt so blessed to live in North Yorkshire, particularly now when summer is just around the corner and the rich hues of green blanket the hills and moors. Lindy was such a likeable girl, naive in many ways yet worldly-wise in others and a pleasure to work with. I intended to suggest that our future meetings be more than a week apart as they were at present. The reasoning behind this was twofold, initially it would wean Lindy off weekly counselling and hopefully she would become more self-reliant. Secondly, if we made the sessions less frequent I could probably see her right up until she was due to be released, which would enable me to support her through the coming exams and help to prepare her for the outside world. I was certainly more positive about her future since knowing that Sarah Dent was in the background, and Sarah had talked about a halfway house where she could live after her release and which would hopefully help her to become independent and look for a job. Admittedly I worried about Lindy and feared for her future. Considering her history she was generally a very well-balanced girl, not bitter about her past and having few expectations of help or material gain, and in spite of missing so much formal education she came over as intelligent and keen to learn. My young client had shared with me how much being able to read meant to her whilst at Redwood; access to books is something we take for granted and it was sad to think that for her books had never been readily available. Through this newfound passion for reading she was educating herself about a world of which she had so little knowledge. Also to her credit, she was polite, honest and completely unassuming. You might have guessed that I'd grown very fond of this girl and was therefore concerned about her future.

'What's your week been like?' I asked when we were seated in our usual little room.

'Really busy! I've been doing as much revising as I can but little Sam's been full of cold and Tracey doesn't know what to do for him. I've spent quite a bit of time with him while Tracey's been catching up on the sleep she's missed when he's been up most of the night. He seems to be over the worst now, which is just as well as the exams are getting nearer.'

'Do you feel well prepared for them?'

'Yes, I think so. I'll be glad when they're over but then I'll only worry about the results.' Lindy said this with a smile on her lips. I'd noticed an envelope in her hand when she came in and the smile broadened as she opened it to show me the contents.

'Sarah brought me some photographs of Jack!' She passed them over to me and I looked through them slowly. They captured the image of a young boy with the same oval face and pale blue eyes as his sister; the first four were of him at various stages of his life covering several years and the last two showed him now at almost eleven years old, one in his school photograph and another in cricket whites, holding a bat. The resemblance was striking and Lindy's smile mirrored Jack's in the photographs; there was no doubt that they were brother and sister.

'These are lovely, Jack's very like you, Lindy.'

'Do you think so? His face has changed since I last saw him but then he was little more than a baby with chubby cheeks. It'll take me a while to think of him like this but I knew it was him the minute I saw them. Sarah brought them as soon as they arrived at her office; she's been very kind and is helping me so much. She always seems so positive and thinks that I can move on with my life and make something of myself even though I've been in here. Sarah has more confidence in me than I have in myself!'

'Which is probably exactly what you need. You've got such a lot to offer, Lindy, and if you can put this time behind you and try to make something of your life, Sarah's just the right sort of person to help.'

'She's already found somewhere for me to live. The halfway house she's told me about sounds okay, I'll be happy with a little room of my own to keep clean and I'd like to learn how to cook. I don't share Sarah's confidence about getting a job though, Redwood might come back to haunt me when I'm applying for them, but I'll keep on trying until something comes up.'

'Good for you, you've certainly got the right attitude and there are employers out there who are sympathetic to people in your situation. You're only in here for stealing food to live on; someone will understand that, I'm sure.' I then went on to suggest that our meetings should be less frequent, perhaps every ten days or so, and I explained my reasons for this which Lindy seemed to understand.

'I'm going to find it hard to say goodbye to you, Maggie. Between you and Sarah you've made such a big difference in my life, it's been almost like having a family and I'm so grateful for everything you've done.' There were tears in Lindy's eyes and I had to swallow hard too. I would miss her but she needed to get out into the world, put the past behind her and build a new life. It would be wonderful to see her making friends and to eventually find love and a family of her own. Sarah would keep me updated on her progress for a little while at least, and I'd already decided that until she was released, I would ring her for a few minutes in between visits, just to keep in touch.

Norman Longstaff was next on my list that day and as I drove back to the surgery I wondered how his new job was going, hoping that he hadn't already fallen out with his employers. As expected he was sitting in the waiting room as I made my way to my office to grab a coffee; his appointment time was still forty-five minutes away but after hurriedly drinking the coffee I called him in early, as he was the only client that afternoon and afterwards I would be free to go home.

'How's the job going, Norman?' I bravely asked this to open our session.

'It's ace, Maggie! I've learned almost everything about the running of the shop and I think they're pleased with me.'

'Would you like to tell me exactly what you've been doing?' I ventured.

'Well, they put me in the stockroom for the first few days. It was my job to open the new bags of donations and sort them out. I put clothes in one pile, shoes and handbags in another, ornaments and china went into the staff room to be washed and books have to be taken downstairs and put tidily on the bookshelves. I needed to reorganise the bookshelves though, someone had put them on all wrong and I had to take them all off and put them back in order of colour.'

My heart sank when he said that. I had visions of books neatly in alphabetical order being moved by Norman into blocks of colour. I hoped the manager was an understanding man.

'I did ask if I could reorganise the clothes into colours as well but the manager said I was to leave them as they were. I did what you said though, Maggie, and waited until I'd been there for a full morning before asking but he still said no.'

'Perhaps they need to get to know you over a few weeks, Norman, maybe a few hours isn't long enough. Do you enjoy the work?'

'Oh yes, it's great and the manager said that next time the window display is due to be changed I can choose what to put in it. He said a colour theme would be good for the window so I've been making notes on what to do. Would you like to see them?'

'Yes please, Norman. A colour theme for a window display sounds a really good idea, I'm sure you'll do a good job.'

Norman took out a notebook, not his usual one, but he explained that a new job warranted a new notebook, to which I of course agreed. His tiny handwriting was punctuated by diagrams of the window and what he intended putting in it. It was obviously a summer theme which was to be red and yellow.

'It will be like a holiday theme with red and yellow summer clothes and yellow sand on the floor, like the seaside. I need some red and yellow hats, do you have any, Maggie?'

'Sorry, no, I'm not really a hat person.'

'That's okay but I'll let you know if there's anything else I need. So, what do you think?'

'I think it's a great idea, Norman, you've obviously put some thought into what you want to do and it looks good. Perhaps though if you asked your manager for his ideas and thoughts he might not feel left out, do you think?'

'Good idea, Maggie. I know it will be my display but people can be funny if they feel left out, I'll make a note to do that.' And he did, in the back of the new notebook went a little reminder to consult his manager. I smiled as Norman moved on to describe some of the others who worked in the charity shop, giving them a score out of ten for how efficient they were. Pretty soon Norman would be running that shop or perhaps even a chain of them! It did seem that the manger was an understanding man and for Norman's sake I was grateful. The new job had given him a purpose which in turn would stabilize his emotions, and as long as he managed to remain in work he would be happy. It was when Norman was idle that his problems were manifested; too much time to think upset him and sent him off on tangents which were not always healthy. There was the time when he tried to interfere in an argument in the town centre and the police were eventually called to what had been a simple disagreement between a young couple. Norman's ideas of right and wrong have no in-between areas and when he came across someone talking rather sharply as in this particular case, he felt compelled to interfere and show the young man where he was going wrong. Occasionally we've used role play as a tool to help him decide when it is right to interfere and when it isn't, and to educate him in how to express his feelings in a situation with which he is unhappy. Norman finds it difficult to accept that someone may not hold the same views as he does, especially as he is in no doubt that he is right. I'd like to think that our meetings help him to function in the wider world and over the time I have known Norman there has certainly been an improvement in his interactions with others. It's hard for him to live in a world which to him makes little sense and engage with people who are not always as honest and open as he is. This often makes me wonder who it is with the problem, and if the world would be a better place with a few more Normans in it.

Chapter 34

Alan was in work before eight o'clock the next morning, followed shortly by Della then Colin and Tony.

'Is he in?' Colin asked, nodding towards the door.

'I expect so, I was just going up to see. Moral support?' Alan looked hopefully at Colin.

'Of course, I've been looking forward to this.'

'You must be mad!' Alan said as they headed for the inspector's office. Alan was half joking; he got on well with the DI and was given plenty of autonomy in most cases, with the only proviso that the DI be kept up to date. He knocked on the door and the loud 'come in' confirmed that the DI had probably been in longer than they had.

'Good morning, Alan, Colin. Is this the update I've been expecting?'

'It is, sir, things have been moving quickly these last couple of days and we're expecting Mrs Jacobs and her solicitor to be here for interview at nine o'clock.' As they had arranged, Colin began to tell the inspector about the call from Pamela Clark and their subsequent visit. He gave the facts then added his opinion, which was the same as Alan's, that Pamela Clark was most likely telling the truth. Alan then went on to outline the visit from Liz Stewart and the questions it raised about Carol's father's death.

'And I suppose you've checked the details of that incident? Was it ever recorded as a suspicious death?'

'No, sir. The paperwork is good and everything was done according to the book but this one lie changes everything. If Carol had been truthful or if her sister had contradicted her version of events the case might have been looked at differently. However, due diligence was taken and with the information they had to go on the right decision was made. But now the 'accident' is looking a little more suspicious. Carol Jacobs was alone in the house with her father and he ended up dead at the bottom of the stairs eight years ago and now she was alone in the house with her husband and he ended up dead too. Of course it could be coincidence but with Pamela's take on the Jacobses' marriage and with Liz owning up to keeping her sister's lie, both deaths could be looked at in a different light.'

The inspector sighed.

'We've already had the trial by media and the general opinion is that Carol is the victim here. What do you think, Alan?'

'At first I thought so too. She had the bruises and even burn marks to prove the violence and she was pretty convincing. I began to change my mind when things didn't go as she expected and we looked a bit closer. I know I keep on about the breakages but she said several times that her husband had thrown them the night before but forensics only found Carol's fingerprints. When I persisted with this I could sense the anger beneath the poor little wife act, and then last night when I brought up her father's death she conveniently broke down and we had to stop the interview. She's had all night to think up an answer to that one and I'm rather looking forward to hearing what she's come up with. And as for Pamela Clark, I totally believe her. She has nothing to gain and seems to be the only one whom William Jacobs confided in.'

'What about you, Colin, do you agree with Alan?'

'Yes, sir, I do.'

'We'll need some pretty convincing evidence to alter public opinion and quite honestly, Alan, I don't think this is enough. It's circumstantial at best or even hearsay, you'll have to bring me more than this.'

'I could put a bit of pressure on this morning, see what happens?'

The DI nodded slowly. 'A confession would be good... for both deaths, but I don't think that's realistic.'

'No, sir, I don't think it is.'

'Well, see how it goes and let me know when you've finished. If you're looking to change the charge to murder we need a rock solid case, good luck.'

Alan and Colin left the DI's office and headed back to the incident room where Della was already making some notes for the coming interview. Alan peered over the DC's shoulder.

'Hopefully you're making my job easier, Della?' he said.

'Just trying to prepare, after last night I really don't know what to expect this morning.'

'We need to dig a bit more into the death of Carol's father. If you'd like to begin the interview with some soft questions, I'll take over to introduce Frank Stewart's death.' Alan told her how he wanted to play it.

'Ooh, good cop, bad cop!' Della laughed.

'When do you get the time to watch so much television, Della?'

Spot on nine am the phone rang to say that Carol Jacobs and her solicitor had arrived and were waiting in the interview room. Della and Alan exchanged a few more words before heading off to meet their suspect.

'Good morning.' Della smiled as she switched the tape on and identified the four people present.

'Are you feeling any better, Mrs Jacobs?' she asked with concern.

'A little, I suppose.' Carol looked as if she had slept badly with dark circles beneath her eyes. Her hair was a mess and she wore no make-up, not even the pale pink lip gloss she usually favoured.

'I could get you some coffee if you'd like?' Della was all concern.

'No thanks, I'd rather get this over with.'

Mr Albright interrupted here.

'Again I'd like to state for the record that my client is here voluntarily and throughout this investigation has always been willing to help. I would also respectfully request that all questions should relate only to the incident regarding the death of William Jacobs. Any questions which are not pertinent to the charge you have made against my client will not be answered, unless that is you have evidence to charge her with anything else.'

'Thank you, Mr Albright, we appreciate your concern for your client and will try to keep this interview short.' Della flashed the solicitor a wide smile.

'Carol,' she began, 'Have you had any thoughts overnight which could explain the anomaly of the smashed glass and crockery having only your fingerprints on the fragments we tested?'

'Yes. The events are still rather hazy but my prints would be on almost everything in the kitchen as I was the one who did all the cooking and cleaning, Bill never helped in the kitchen.' Carol was obviously pleased with this explanation.

'Thank you. That would explain your fingerprints but not the lack of your husband's if he was the one who had thrown them.' Della maintained eye contact with Carol, who simply shrugged as if that subject was closed.

'Could you try to think now about the morning your husband died. You said he was coming at you and was going to hurt you. How did you know he was going to hurt you?'

'The night before he'd raped me! Of course I thought he was going to hurt me again, Bill was out of control, he was throwing things and shouting at me!' Carol raised her voice and spoke quickly.

'I'm sorry, did you say he was throwing things? I thought he'd thrown the crockery the night before, can you explain that to me?'

'He'd thrown most of it the night before but he was still violent the next morning and began to do it again.'

'So as well as the glass and crockery thrown the night before he began to throw some more the next morning, is that what you're telling me now?'

'Yes.'

'So your husband threw several breakable items the day before his death and also on the following morning and we couldn't find a single print of his on any of the fragments we recovered?'

Mr Albright interrupted at this point.

'Haven't we gone over all this about fragments and fingerprints before? Do you have nothing new to put to my client?'

'Yes actually, we do.' Alan took over the questioning. 'Were you on the birth control pill during your marriage?'

'What the hell has that to do with anything?' Carol raged.

'Detective, this is totally inappropriate and my client does not have to answer that. Now unless this is relevant I suggest we move on to more pertinent questions!' Mr Albright had risen out of his chair with indignation.

'It is relevant, Mr Albright,' Alan said curtly then turned to Carol. 'A witness has told us that your husband wanted a family and that you led him to believe that was your wish too. It was devastating to him when he found out you were on the pill and you argued about it.'

'I wasn't ready for a family and Bill understood that. Whoever told you this nonsense is wrong, how would someone else know what went on in our marriage?'

'Because your husband confided in this witness, but we'll move on, shall we? Isn't it also true that it was you who physically abused your husband, not the other way round as you would have us believe?'

'Not unless you count fighting him off while he raped me as abuse!' Carol's face was growing red but Alan continued.

'Why did you lie to the police about your movements on the morning your father, Frank Stewart, died?'

Before Alan had time to interpret the raw anger that flashed across her face, Carol was on her feet, reaching over the table to dig her nails into Alan's face. He pulled back before she could get a good hold on him and she screamed as if she'd been the recipient of this painful act. Della was on her feet and around to the other side of the table within a second, wrapping her arms around Carol's body, pinning her flailing arms to her sides. Alan steadied himself after nearly falling off the chair, while Mr Albright scooted to the far corner of the room, afraid that he too might come under attack. While Della held on to a struggling Carol, Alan pressed the panic button and within a minute a couple of uniformed officers were inside the room, relieving Della of her charge. Carol refused to calm down, her screams could be heard all over the police station, and she was taken away by the two officers to a room where she would be left to compose herself.

Della turned her attention to Alan, looking at his face where the scratches had broken the skin in two places, one frighteningly near his left eye. Other colleagues had arrived to see what the fuss was all about and Della asked for a first aid kit which was with them in under a minute. She used some sterile gauze to clean the wounds and gave him a wad to dab on his face until the bleeding stopped. As officers left to go back to their desks Alan turned to a very white-looking Mr Albright, who still stood in the corner where he had taken refuge.

'Perhaps you need to talk to your client about what is and isn't acceptable behaviour during interviews,' he said flatly.

'Well I had warned you to stick to the case in point... it was you who asked about her father! The solicitor was defensive about his client and his own position. Della interrupted the two.

'Shall I ask the ME to come and have a look at Carol and you too, sir?'

'I'll be fine but yes, I'd like him to see Mrs Jacobs.' Della left the room.

'Well, I think continuing this interview will have to wait for another day, Mr Albright, but as we have received new information, reliable information that Carol lied to the police about her movements on the day of her father's death, I should warn you that I am going to pursue this line of inquiry. Feel free to wait and see your client after the ME has been or leave if you like but please excuse me.' Alan made his way to the bathroom where he looked at the damage Carol Jacobs had inflicted. The soft flesh beneath his eye was beginning to bruise but the bleeding had stopped. The other place where the skin had been broken was on his cheek where a scab was already forming. He looked at his reflection and wondered what on earth Sue would say about it. This was one of those things she would fuss over; ever since he'd been shot a few years ago she worried about his work, even though he told her constantly that injuries to police officers were very rare. Still this didn't rank with a bullet in his shoulder so hopefully Sue would see the funny side... if there was one.

Returning to the incident room, he motioned Della to go with him to see the DI. She was concerned for him but Alan's feelings were by then turning into embarrassment and he shrugged her sympathy off but of course the DI noticed the fresh wounds.

'What the hell happened to you?' were his first words. 'I know you said you'd put pressure on her but I didn't expect this.'

'It's fine, sir, Mrs Jacobs got a little angry and lashed out, but Della did a good job of restraining her then uniforms took her away to calm down and the ME's on his way.'

'Was it worth it, Alan?'

'Unfortunately not. Della opened the interview nicely but my first question about her father's death completely flipped her and she lashed out. I think any further questions are out for today at least but I'll wait until later when we see how she is and ring her solicitor to rearrange.'

'Well keep me informed and you'd better stay in the office for the rest of today, we can't have you being seen by the public like that.' The DI dismissed them without ceremony and Della insisted that she took Alan to the cafeteria for coffee and something sweet. Five minutes later, tucking into a Danish pastry, Alan said, 'Don't let my wife know I've been eating this, pastry's off limits in the Hurst household!'

'It's purely medicinal, sugar for shock, you know that, Alan.'

'Yup! And I feel better already.'

The news from the ME was not good. He had only been able to calm Carol down with the help of medication and was recommending a full psychiatric evaluation. With the patient's consent he admitted her to a residential psychiatric unit near York and it looked as if she would be unable to answer any more questions for some considerable time. Alan's team were frustrated; the case was gathering momentum and the end was in sight but with the question now raised over Frank Stewart's death it had become something other than straightforward. The DI agreed to look again at the supposed 'accidental' death in the light of Liz Stewart's information and the team would be tasked with this as well as anything else they could find out about William Jacobs' death.

By mid-afternoon when they knew the score, Alan told his team to go home and relax. They had worked hard over the last few days and a little rest and recuperation was in order. Taking his own advice and leaving early, Alan wondered what Sue would have to say about his now swollen and bruised eye.

Chapter 35
Maggie

It was the May Day bank holiday weekend and Peter, Mum and I headed for our cottage in Scotland with Jasper and Tara. With such a full car I was glad it wasn't too far to travel, and despite bank holiday traffic we arrived just over a couple of hours of leaving home. Pulling up into the driveway was a bittersweet experience for me and I knew it would be even more so for Mum as the happy memories the cottage evoked once again reminded her of the loss of Dad. Had he lived they would have been celebrating their golden wedding anniversary in the summer but it wasn't to be and Mum was too practical a person to allow herself more than a few moments of reflection. The first job was to turn the heating up; it had been left on low during the winter so didn't take long before we felt the heat coming through. For the first weekend of May it was still cold and we had driven through a few flurries of snow on the way here. As Peter and I unpacked the car, Mum busied herself in the kitchen, happy to be back in what had been her favourite room in the bungalow. Of course it was all new to Jasper and he bounded about, almost tripping us up with his excitement while Tara displayed her usual laid-back approach to life and found the chair nearest to a radiator to curl up on. Unsurprisingly, Mum had batch baked in anticipation of our long weekend away and had even brought a casserole ready to heat up for our first meal. The evening passed pleasantly as we enjoyed the good food and relaxed around the open fire, Mum half asleep and

Peter and I both engrossed in our respective reading material. It wasn't always easy to relax from the pressures of work and often took a few days to really wind down, so the advantage of our very own weekend cottage gave us the familiarity which helped us to do so almost as soon as we walked through the door. As Mum declared herself ready for an early night, Peter and I wrapped up in heavy coats, as it was always so much colder here than at home, to take Jasper for his evening walk.

Our little dog was so excited at having new territory to explore, and strained at the leash to sniff as broad a circle as he could. Night time had almost taken over the landscape but there was still enough light to guide us along the narrow paths. We came to a standstill to watch the sun setting, a brilliant display of orange-red sky slowly giving way to the darkness of night.

'I do so love it here.' I sighed.

'Me too, I loved it when you first brought me to meet your parents, which just happened to be when I first knew how much I loved you too.' Peter bent to kiss me. 'We're so blessed to have all this. Not just the cottage but each other, Helen, Jasper and Tara, our family!'

'And there's Jane and Rachel with their tribes!' I pictured all the people in our lives who meant so much to us; Peter was right, we were truly blessed.

The next day brought sunshine and the threat of showers so we planned to go to the shopping outlet near Gretna and treat ourselves to lunch out. As Jasper was still unused to being left alone for too long we took him with us; Peter would find somewhere he could take him in and have a coffee while Mum and I mooched around the shops. Afterwards we left Jasper in the car and went into a cosy pub for lunch. It was heaven not being tied to time, and I consciously disciplined myself not to think of my current clients who were nearly always on my mind. Peter found it easier to switch off than I did, because without the tools of his trade he could do nothing so was never worried about work. As we drove back to the cottage the rain had dispersed so Peter decided to do some gardening on our return. As ever I would watch him so that he didn't overdo things and perhaps dig over the borders while he mowed the grass. It wasn't a big garden and someone from the village managed it for us generally but it was pleasant to do a little ourselves and if I prepared the garden now, next time we came I could put in some bedding plants. The garden had been Dad's passion, which in itself gave us the incentive to keep it looking good.

We drove home on the Monday afternoon, refreshed from our weekend away. After dropping Mum at home and Jasper and Tara back at our bungalow, we went over to Sue and Alan's house to give them the cottage keys as they were going at the end of the week. Sue looked good, she seemed to be over the worst of her depression and once again resembled the friend I knew and loved. I was still taking Rose to school and would happily do so until Sue went back to work. As we chatted she told me that Laura, the practice manager, had been on the phone to ask if she would go back on a full time basis instead of the two days a week she had done since George was born.

'I don't think I'd manage full time,' Sue said. 'And the cost of a nursery place for George and James would mean I would be working for virtually nothing! Do you know it's now forty-five a day for George and it will be forty-eight pounds for James as he's younger? I'd look for a childminder but with not knowing them personally it's a bit of a risk. George really loves his days at nursery and he's come on so well there.'

'You've got a few weeks yet before you decide haven't you?' I asked.

'Yes but Laura needs to know as soon as possible. Oh, Maggie, can you smell that? I think my son needs changing!' She took James upstairs and I looked out of the window where Peter and Alan were playing football with Rose and George. I waved and when Alan saw that I was alone he came inside to give me a quick update on Carol Jacobs. What he told me sounded incredible but his eye still had the signs of a scratch and slight bruising.

'So what happens now?' I wondered out loud.

'She's staying in the psychiatric unit until they've completed evaluations. It could take a few weeks; they don't rush this kind of thing.'

'What's your thinking now, Alan?' I knew Alan wouldn't give me any details but I would appreciate knowing if I could expect another call from her, as we had parted without any arrangement to meet again.'

'We're looking at a different charge now to manslaughter.'

'No! Do you think she actually planned to kill her husband?' I couldn't believe what Alan was intimating. He looked at me and shrugged, I knew he couldn't tell me much more but it was so difficult to imagine that William Jacobs's death was anything other than self-defence on Carol's part.

'So do you doubt the abuse, because there were definitely signs on her body, those awful burns! Who hurt her if it wasn't her husband?'

'It wouldn't be the first time a woman's fabricated accusations of abuse but I can't really tell you any more except that I don't think you'll be hearing from her in the near future if at all. I'm not saying that she had a fully formed pre-meditated plan but the opportunity presented itself and Carol took it.'

I was speechless; it was difficult to take in. Had I been duped as part of a plan to attest to her being an abused wife?

Sue came back down the stairs with a sweeter-smelling baby who she passed to me.

'I'd better go and rescue Peter.' Alan grinned and went back to the garden.

'Were you two talking shop?' Sue asked.

'Yes but it seems that Alan's suspect will no longer be needing my services, things have moved on.'

'Well you probably know more about it than I do. All he told me was that the investigation, which has taken up so much of his time, is now on hold for psychiatric reports. He wasn't best pleased about it but I am! Apart from the scratches which he typically played down, he's gone back to working regular hours and even taken time off over the weekend to spend with us. Going to your cottage wouldn't have been an option if the investigation hadn't been interrupted so I'm pleased even if Alan isn't!' No wonder Sue looked so much better, she was back to the usual chirpy friend I'd missed.

'Have you come off the medication Tom prescribed for you?' I wanted to change the subject.

'I'm still taking one every other day. He told me to come off them slowly but I really have felt so much better, perhaps having Alan around more has something to do with it and I'm looking forward to getting away for a few days too.'

'Oh that reminds me, here are the keys.' I handed Sue the keyring. 'We've left the heating on low so it should be reasonably warm when you get there, just turn the thermostat up. There are a few bits to use up, some potatoes and carrots and feel free to use anything from the freezer.'

'You're an angel, thanks. I'm keeping Rose off school on Friday so we can go on Thursday night and we should be back the following Monday, or Tuesday, or never if we're having fun!' Sue laughed, something I hadn't seen enough of lately.

'I'm going to think about work while I'm away and decide what to do so that I can tell Laura when we get back. Perhaps we can compromise and I'll work three days. It's not that I don't want to be full time again, I love my job but it's the problem of childcare. What happens if one of them is ill? There's three times the chance of that happening now isn't there?' Sue laughed again.

'There's always Ruby!' I suggested.

'Oh yes, there's always Ruby!' Sue rolled her eyes. 'No, I have to admit she's been a great help. It's just her attitude, the 'I told you so' mentality, it drives me mad.'

Sue was back to her usual self and I was delighted. I rescued Peter from the garden to take him home before he exhausted himself and we headed off. It would be good to have Sue back at work, I'd missed her humour and our lunch time chats but I could see her problem with childcare arrangements. Hopefully something would crop up before her maternity leave finished.

Chapter 36
Maggie

My thoughts had often wandered to Lindy Baker since our last meeting, and as I drove again to Redwood I was unsure of what she would feel like doing. Understandably she found it painful to dwell on the past. Bad experiences had coloured her childhood but as we had only touched on them briefly I wondered if some more in-depth work would be appropriate. Thinking about the future was a subject also fraught with problems, as Lindy had no idea how having been in Redwood would taint her future life. Finding somewhere to live could prove difficult when her time at the halfway house came to an end; securing a job could also be a problem as many employers would be reluctant to take a risk on someone with a record. Knowing very little about how the future would pan out for this client, I had to admit that I cared, almost too much.

So what would today bring? I didn't want Lindy going out into the world with unresolved issues, so perhaps I would suggest looking at her past and exploring her feelings about some of those experiences we had touched on only briefly. Of course it was always up to the client to decide but I was aware that our times together were limited and I wanted her to be prepared for the next phase of her life. The most positive thing on the horizon of course was that Sarah Dent would be looking out for her and I had every confidence in Sarah.

The foyer seemed even larger than usual as I signed in before going to the room we always used; perhaps it was my uncertainty as I always wanted to do my very best for all clients but this one especially weighed heavily on my heart. I not only wanted to do my best, I needed to for her sake. She had somehow become special to me, whether it was that she had been let down so many times in the past, or simply that my maternal instincts were aroused, I don't know. If I'd been blessed with a daughter of my own she might have been about Lindy's age, but that was a ridiculous thought, I must be getting sentimental in my old age.

Lindy smiled as she entered the room, and it was obvious and gratifying that she looked forward to our sessions. When I asked how she was she admitted being a little sad as her friend Tracey had been released and left Redwood with her son. Knowing how much she cared for little Sam I could understand her feelings, but with pragmatism beyond her years she told me she would get over it and had been telling herself since they arrived that it was only a temporary friendship. I nodded and allowed a silence to settle upon us before I asked her what she would like to talk about.

'I don't honestly know, Maggie. I've felt a little down about Sam going but in a way he had become a substitute for Jack and although Jack is certainly not a baby anymore, I feel I've found him again and I now have hope that one day we'll be able to meet.'

Wow, I wondered, who was the therapist here, me or this young woman before me!

'What do you think we should discuss?' Lindy asked.

'Well you know it's for you to decide but I wondered about two things. Firstly the past; you've told me briefly about some of the foster homes you were in but we haven't got round to exploring your feelings about those experiences in any depth, how they made you feel and what if anything you learned from them.'

Lindy looked thoughtful so I continued.

'We could stay in the present and you could tell me how you're feeling day to day in Redwood, or we could discuss any plans or ambitions you might have for the future. Now that's really three topics, isn't it? The past, the present or the future but can I just say that if we look to the future much of it will be speculative. We can't predict what will happen although we can look at how you feel about moving on, so what do you think?'

'Both the past and the future seem a little scary but I think the past is the better option.'

I nodded and waited for her to continue.

'The foster homes I told you about weren't happy experiences for me and I've always thought it was best to try to forget them as there's nothing I can do about them. But then I began to think particularly about the last foster home I was in. That man got away with touching me and who knows what he's done to other children before me or even since? I've felt guilty that I didn't tell anyone about it, I just ran away and so he got away with it. Is it too late to tell the social services? I mean if that couple are still fostering children he could be doing all kinds of awful things to them and it was selfish of me to keep quiet just because it was the easiest thing to do.'

Even looking back to one of the worst episodes in her young life, Lindy's concern was for others. I could barely speak, there was a huge lump in my throat and I wanted to move over and hug this exceptional girl who deserved so much better from life than the horrors she'd endured. She continued.

'Is it too late, Maggie? I like Sarah and could tell her and I'm sure she would listen.'

I cleared my throat and blinked rapidly to compose myself.

'Yes, I'm sure Sarah would be the right person to tell and she would listen and take the appropriate action. It's a big step and you would be required to make a statement to the police, but they're very understanding in such cases and hopefully this man will be held to account for what he did.'

'What do you mean by 'held to account'?'

'Well at the very least he would be stopped from fostering any other children but if the police think they have enough information to charge him he'll go to court and be prosecuted and punished for what he did.'

Lindy nodded thoughtfully. Historic abuse is such a minefield to prove but I didn't want to go into details with her then. She seemed sure about this and I was happy to support her through the process, even if she had to become a private client when she left Redwood, pro bono of course. Sarah too would be a good support, believing in Lindy as I did; there was no guile in her whatsoever. I'd expected that if she began to look at her past she would discover hidden anger and bitterness, things which we could address with the use of 'chair work' where a chair, perhaps with a cushion on it, becomes the focus of anger and can be shouted at, pummelled or whatever else was necessary to get rid of the anger in a safe and controlled environment. I should have known better; in all the years I have been counselling there have never been two clients the same, but Lindy was in a different league altogether; even in recalling the abuse she suffered she was thinking of others and if she decided to take action it would be to protect them rather than out of any sense of revenge.

'Okay, I'll tell Sarah about it when she next comes. Will I have to go to court to give evidence?'

'You'll need to make a statement first to the police which would be videoed and if they still need you to go to court you could testify from behind a screen so you didn't have to see him, or even from another room through a video link. It would be a very brave thing to do and certainly not easy but there will be people there to support you through the whole process. You don't have to decide right now, talk to Sarah first and then take some time to think it over. It won't be an easy thing to do.'

'I know but he really should be stopped. It was cowardly of me simply to run away but I didn't think anyone would believe me if I spoke up. His wife certainly didn't want to listen and even blamed me. I'll think about it and let you know next time, shall I?'

'That's fine. Would you like me to talk to Sarah first or at least ask her to come as soon as she can?'

'No, I'll wait; it will give me time to think things through.'

Our time was at an end. I resisted the urge to hug Lindy before I left but when I got to my car I sat with my head on the steering wheel and sobbed for several minutes. When I eventually stopped to pull myself together, I realised what a profound effect this girl was having on me. Without being in the least aware of it she was intelligent, caring and compassionate with so much to offer. It would be criminal if she didn't get the chance to enjoy a normal life after all she had been through. Once again I could almost hear Joyce Patterson's voice telling me to keep my distance and remain professional. As to what would happen to Lindy in the future, I simply didn't know.

Chapter 37

The frustrations of the William Jacobs investigation being put on ice were offset for Alan by the opportunity of spending more time with Sue and the children. A long weekend at Maggie's cottage in Scotland was just the tonic they needed, and the weather proved kind to them enabling them to get outside in the fresh air where Rosie and George could run off some of their energy. Sue was almost back to her old self, which was such a relief, and their few days away did them all good. The investigation, however, was never far from the detective's mind. What more the police could do was now limited by the uncertainty of Carol Jacobs's mental health, but there were one or two things he wanted to look into and be certain about before he let the case rest. One of those niggling little things on Alan's mind was that he hadn't pushed Liz Stewart enough when she came to see him at the station. He'd been excited by her revelations and the possibility that Carol had been complicit in her father's death, which put an entirely different slant on the death of her husband. Surely the odds were slim against Carol being the only other person in a house on two separate occasions when someone died. Perhaps he hadn't asked Liz everything he should have and it was only afterwards that he felt he needed to further explore the relationship between Carol and her father. What was it that Maggie had said; something about transference of feelings? Did Carol hate her father so much that it had been transferred to her husband? It wasn't that simple, he knew, and he didn't understand the psychology behind it but he felt that the two deaths were linked, and perhaps Liz knew more than she had told them; after all it had taken her some considerable time to admit to covering for her sister, what more could she be keeping quiet about?

On the first morning back at work after his much-needed rest days, Alan decided to pay another visit to Liz Stewart. Colin Brownlow was on a late shift so he asked Tony Russell to accompany him; another opinion of Liz wouldn't hurt. Tony had chiefly been responsible for co-ordinating the investigation from the incident room, liaising with forensics and keeping the paperwork up to date. It was a glorious morning, much more like May should be after a cold wet start, and Tony appreciated getting out of the office.

'Is there anything in particular you think this girl can tell us?' he asked Alan.

'Yes, but I don't know what it is yet. She's been reluctant to talk from the beginning but I think she's troubled about what her sister might or might not have done recently and in the past.'

The betting shop was busier than it had been on Alan's previous visit, and it took Liz a while to spot them waiting for their opportunity to talk to her.

'I'm taking my break now, Simon,' she told a colleague when she did see the officers, and came out from behind the screen to meet them.

'Is there anywhere more private we can talk?' There were too many distractions in the shop.

'Come through the back.' Liz led the way through the door marked 'Staff Only'. 'No one's supposed to come in here except staff but I suppose with you being police we can trust you.' If it hadn't been for her deadpan expression Alan would have thought she was making a joke.

'What's happening to Carol now?' she asked. Alan noted that again she had enquired after her sister's welfare, he doubted whether Carol would have done the same had the roles been reversed.

'She's being treated at a psychiatric facility, undergoing tests, that sort of thing,' he replied, deliberately keeping things vague. Liz nodded then asked if it was because she'd told them about Carol's lie.

'When we asked her about it she didn't take it well.' Alan involuntarily touched the soft skin beneath his eye, remembering her clawing at his face, even though it had healed now. 'That's why she's being assessed and why we haven't got much further with the investigation.'

'So why are you here?' Liz was straight to the point.

'After you came to the police station and told us about the circumstances of your father's death we did a little digging. If you or Carol had told us the truth the death might have been looked at differently, as suspicious perhaps. What I'd really like to know is why you think your sister might have been involved, and what you think happened when Carol went back to the house that morning?'

Liz was chewing her bottom lip, avoiding eye contact and obviously deliberating on what to say.

'You were very young at the time, Liz, and have had plenty of time to think about what happened. Was there something which might have made Carol want to kill your father?' Referring to killing made Liz look up, surprised.

'They always argued but I never thought she'd actually pushed him down the stairs, I'd wondered why she lied to the police but you never think such a thing could actually happen, do you?'

'But you do now?' Alan asked.

'Well... with what happened to Bill and everything, it did make me wonder.' She was still playing for time, unsure whether to tell them anymore.

'So, you now believe she could have been involved in your father's death? What makes you think that, Liz?'

'I think Carol might have been pregnant and if she was and Dad somehow found out he would have thrashed her good and hard.'

'You only think she was pregnant?' Tony asked.

'Yes, when we were in town together, the weekend before Dad died, we went into a chemist's and Carol bought a pregnancy testing kit. I asked if she was pregnant and she called me stupid and asked why I thought she was buying it. I would imagine she used it but as she never spoke about it again I've always assumed it must have been negative.'

'Presumably she had a boyfriend if she thought she might be pregnant, do you know who that was?' Tony was fishing but for what, he didn't quite know.

'There was no one steady. Carol thought the boys at school were immature and although she hung around with them sometimes I don't think she had a particular boyfriend.'

'Did it surprise you that she'd obviously had a sexual relationship?' Alan asked.

'No not really, Carol would tease the boys. Although she never seemed to like anyone in particular she took a strange delight in egging them on.' From the way Liz spoke, it seemed that she didn't approve of her sister's actions.

'Did your mother know anything about this pregnancy scare?'

'I don't think so or we'd have never heard the last of it and it's not something I ever mentioned to Carol since.'

Alan sighed; they had yet another snippet of information but nothing solid. 'Can you tell me again, Liz, exactly what happened on the day your father died?'

'Well, Mum always left first for work, about eight o'clock and Liz and I left about thirty or forty minutes later. We generally walked to school together and when we left that morning Dad was in the bathroom. When we'd got almost halfway, Carol said she'd forgotten her homework and it needed to be handed in that day so she ran back home while I walked slowly on and she eventually caught up with me. It was when we got home after school that we found Dad at the bottom of the stairs. It was obvious he was dead so Carol phoned the police and the ambulance.'

'Just back up a little here, Liz. When Carol caught up with you on the way to school, did she seem upset or anxious about anything?'

'She was out of breath, but I presumed that was just from running.'

'And did she say anything about your father, seeing him, having a row with him perhaps?'

'No, nothing that I can remember.'

'And when you found his body, did she seem surprised at all?'

'Well yes, it was a shock for both of us. I remember crying and wanting to get out of the house, I'd never seen a dead body before. Carol pulled herself together quicker than me and made the telephone call.'

Alan thanked Liz and they left the shop.

'That was hard work,' Tony said, 'She almost drip-feeds you the information.'

'Yes, she's not very forthcoming but I think she's genuine.'

'So do you fancy Carol for the death of her father then?' Tony's eyes were wide.

'I do, it wouldn't have taken long to push him down the stairs, perhaps the opportunity presented itself and she took it. What if...' Alan paused, 'Fred Stewart, who we know was in the bathroom at the time the girls left the house, found the pregnancy testing kit and when Carol turned up, confronted her. An argument at the top of the stairs perhaps and a quick shove from Carol and he was out of her life for good.'

'It could be, it wouldn't have taken long to push him down the stairs and there was no love lost between father and daughter from what we know of the family dynamics.' Tony thought the hypothesis could fit.

'What I'd really like to know is who the father was,' Alan said.

'I don't suppose it matters really, it seems she wasn't pregnant after all.'

'But for a girl who didn't go for boys her own age, the pregnancy doesn't quite add up. I think I'd like to call in at the school again to have a little word with the games teacher.'

Simon Robbins's heart sank when the school secretary entered the gym to tell him the police wanted to talk to him. He dismissed his class five minutes early and then went anxiously to the office. The two detectives were talking to the headmaster, who narrowed his eyes when Simon came into view.

'Is there anywhere more private where we could talk to Mr Robbins?' Alan asked and the headmaster motioned to the room at the end of the corridor with *Staff Room* written on the door. The three entered in silence and took seats in the comfortable armchairs. This was obviously a much used room; a coffee machine in one corner was surrounded by a mish-mash of mugs which looked as if they needed washing, and a central coffee table was covered in dog-eared professional magazines. Robbins looked scared and Alan wondered if he knew why they were there.

'Sorry to bother you again, Mr Robbins, but this investigation keeps turning up almost as many questions as it does answers.'

'I don't think I can help you with anything, I've told you everything I remember about the Stewart girls and their family, which I know isn't much but it was a long time ago.'

'Yes, I know you have but something else has come up which you might be able to help us with. Apparently Carol Jacobs, or Stewart as you know her, was pregnant in her last year here.'

Mr Robbins's face paled and if he hadn't been seated Alan felt he might have collapsed. He recovered himself enough to sound indignant.

'I hope you're not suggesting that it was me who got her into that... err, predicament.'

'Well I have to ask. By all accounts she didn't have much time for the boys at school with her and there is that argument you had with her which was reported to us. Did you have a sexual relationship with Carol Stewart?'

'No, no way!' The teacher looked as if he might burst into tears. 'Look, she was a flirt and seemed to have a bit of a crush on me. There was one time, a silly incident which I knew was wrong and it never happened again... I kissed her. That was all it was, I swear, and I knew it was wrong as soon as I'd done it but she was flirting, teasing me and I was young and inexperienced. I suppose I was flattered but it never went any further than that one kiss, honestly!'

Alan was inclined to believe him; he felt sorry for the man but still needed to be convinced.

'So you at no time had sexual intercourse with Carol Stewart?'

'No, honestly, I would never do that.'

'But you did kiss her?'

'Yes, it was a one off, if anything I avoided her after that. Please believe me, I'm telling you the truth!' Simon was almost grovelling.

'Are you married, Mr Robbins?' Tony asked. Simon groaned.

'Yes, I'm married but I wasn't then. Please tell me you're not going to tell my wife about this, or the headmaster?'

'Well that depends on whether we think you're being truthful now, you certainly didn't tell us everything before, you led us to believe you hardly remembered the Stewart family.'

'I know and I'm sorry, truly sorry. I was young and inexperienced; you don't know how many times I've thought about that moment of madness, to my shame. I've never done anything like it again but if you tell Mr Wilson that will be the end of my career and probably my marriage. That's why I didn't tell you before, I've got so much to lose and it was a one-off stupid mistake.'

'So that argument you had with Carol, do you remember that now?' Tony asked. Robbins hung his head.

'Yes I do. Carol came to me and asked for money, she said she'd tell the headmaster that I'd tried to molest her if I didn't give her a hundred pounds.'

'And did you give her it?'

'Stupidly, I did, but I made it clear that it was all she'd get from me, I wasn't going to be blackmailed. Afterwards I realised that she could do it again if she wanted to but it was shortly after that her father died and Carol hardly came into school afterwards except to sit her exams. I was so relieved, but since you started this investigation it's all come back to me. One thing I'd like you to know is that when that incident happened Carol was already sixteen, it wasn't as if she was a minor.'

'And would that have made a difference?' Alan asked.

'I'd like to think so but I suppose none of us know what we would do in any given situation. I was stupid but I've learned my lesson.' A knock on the door interrupted them and Mr Wilson put his head into the doorway,

'Are you finished yet, we'll need this room shortly.' His frown spoke of his annoyance, which Alan thought was probably because he hadn't been invited to sit in on the interview.

'I think we're about through here, thank you.' Then addressing Simon Robbins he said, 'Thank you for your help, Mr Robbins, I appreciate your honesty.' Alan and Tony left, anticipating Robbins's discomfiture at explaining the reason for their visit to his boss.

'I'm inclined to believe him, are you?' Tony spoke first.

'Yes, I think it was as he said, he was young and inexperienced and probably lucky she didn't keep on blackmailing him. Our Mrs Jacobs is turning out to be anything but a poor abused wife.'

Chapter 38

Colin Brownlow began his career in the police force in York as a young, enthusiastic PC. He had met Jen, his wife, when he was the first officer on the scene of a robbery at a jeweller's shop where she was the manager. The robbery had been overnight but the shock to Jen was considerable when she arrived the following morning. Colin went over and above the call of duty when he called in at the shop almost daily afterwards, not with any news but to see if she had recovered. The attraction was mutual and eventually Jen agreed to go out with him, an action she told friends was to stop him calling at the shop and embarrassing her. The romance blossomed and they were married a year later and moved into a little flat which was convenient for both their places of work. It was a rented flat and they both worked hard saving to buy somewhere of their own but York, a beautiful city to work in, was expensive as far as property prices were concerned. Colin sat his detective's exams and when he passed learned of a vacancy for a DS in Fenbridge, a pretty market town not too far from York where the property prices were much more reasonable. The couple moved from their beloved city which held such precious memories to settle in Fenbridge but returned regularly to visit friends and family. On one such visit Colin and Jen had arranged to meet old friends in the 'The Viking' a public house not far from the city centre. Initially it seemed to be a dark, dismal place but as the name suggests was decorated heavily on the Viking theme. As with many buildings in the city, it was full of atmosphere with low beams and doorways through which most average height male customers had to duck. The smell was predominantly of beer but a tempting aroma from the kitchen encouraged Colin and his friends to order steak pie and chips for four. Like all pubs the smoking ban had improved the inside; no longer did the clientele have to suffer the fug of tobacco smoke. Whilst at the bar making the order, Colin turned as he heard his name spoken in a local accent. The owner of the gravelly voice was a small man, known as Jockey, who had been an informant for him in his uniformed days. No one actually knew if Jockey was a reference to the man's former profession or his diminutive height.

'Never expected to see you here, guv, thought you'd moved on,' the little man said.

'The old place still draws me, Jockey, how're you doing?'

'Not so bad guv, not so bad. You still in the force then?' he asked, making Colin smile, it sounded like a line from *Star Wars*.

'I am yes, a detective now though, over in Fenbridge.'

'Ah, not such a criminal hotspot then. Although I've been reading about your recent murder over there, or at least I think it's a murder.'

'What case would that be then?' Colin didn't want to give much away but was always interested in what Jockey had to say, as he had proved a most reliable source of information in the past. The little man chuckled.

'That poor little wife who stabbed her rich husband,' he replied.

'Yes, I know the case.'

'She was in here a few weeks ago, tried to hire a shooter but must have decided to do it herself after all.'

Colin was suddenly alert, wanting to know everything the man could tell him.

'How would you know that, Jockey?' he asked.

'She came to me, didn't she?' There was a sense of pride in his voice. 'Someone told her that I knew everyone in York and could help her out, but I told her this wasn't the 'Wild West'. I don't get involved in anything to do with guns, you know that, guv, don't you?'

'I do that, Jockey, you've never been a violent man.' It all sounded a little farfetched but Colin wanted to probe him some more.

'And could you help her out?'

'Nah, I'm semi-retired now, aren't I? I told her to go to the 'Pig and Whistle', this here's a more respectable hostelry.'

'And how do you know it was the woman in Fenbridge?'

'Recognised the picture in the papers afterwards, didn't I? Pretty little one she was, but maybe not so pretty on the inside. Mind you, she did tell me how he beat her up; bastard probably deserved all he got. You on the case then or what?'

'I know of it, yes. So when was this, Jockey?' Colin wasn't sure if the man was telling the truth or just making it up to pass the time of day.

'About a couple of weeks before she did him in, I reckon.' He stroked his chin thoughtfully.

'And is this true, or are you just having me on?'

'Honest, guv, it's true as the day is long, she sat in that very corner over there and told me this sob story about her husband.'

'Did you believe her, Jockey?'

'Not at first, I thought she was making up a tale but then she showed me the cigarette burns on her arms. What kind of a man does that to a woman, I ask yer!'

Colin was astounded; they had never made the information about Carol Jacobs's injuries public, and as far as he was aware it had never been leaked to any of the newspapers either. He slapped Jockey on the shoulder.

'Jockey, my old mate, how would you like a little trip over to Fenbridge to see my DS?'

'Would this trip be covered by expenses?' the little man asked.

'Of course! Be here on Monday morning at ten and we'll send a chauffeur for you, then it'll be an hour or two talking to my boss before lunch and a return trip on me.'

Jockey smiled and nodded; he knew there'd be a little extra for a few pints, Mr. Brownlow had always seen him right in the past.

Colin couldn't wait to tell Alan what he'd just learned. Excusing himself to Jen and their friends, he went outside to make a phone call. It was Saturday but he knew Alan would want to be disturbed with this new development so he rang him on his mobile.

'Alan, you're never going to believe what I've just heard!' Colin told him in detail about Jockey's story ending with the prize nugget, the burn marks on Carol's arm.

'Is this chap reliable, will he still be around on Monday?' he asked.

'If there's a pint or two in it for him he'll be around and I know where his usual haunts are.'

Alan was excited about the news but uneasy that this informer might disappear.

'Colin, I know it's your weekend off and you're out with your wife but could you possibly bring this man in now? I don't want to risk losing him, anything might happen before Monday. If it helps I'll meet you halfway and take him from there and you can be back with your friends in an hour or so.' Alan would also have to explain himself to Sue but this was the lead they'd been waiting for, they couldn't risk leaving it until Monday. Colin agreed, with only the slightest regret at the homemade steak pie he was looking forward to, and they decided on a rendezvous at about halfway between York and Fenbridge. Jen was so enjoying being with their friends again that she hardly raised an eyebrow when he broke the news that something had come up at work. She was learning that being married to a detective meant that regular hours were out of the window, not like when he was in uniform and she knew his timetable down to the letter. Jockey was surprised when Colin suggested they left now but agreeable after he had been promised lunch and a few more pints afterwards. They left the pub and set off to meet Alan, who was going to arrange for a video statement to be taken back at the station, and would call Tony Russell in to ride shotgun. If they were having their Saturdays interrupted, the whole team might as well be there.

After explaining to Sue that this was a major breakthrough, Alan set off to pick up Tony then meet with Colin and their witness as planned. Sue was gracious about it, as they'd managed to spend some quality family time together recently and she could sense his excitement at this development. Della was working that Saturday and was already in the station and able to set up for the video statement. This new development had lifted all their spirits and given a new enthusiasm for the case which until then appeared to be going nowhere. As she prepared the room it was with a new energy, an emotion the other team members shared. Hopefully Carol Jacobs would now be unable to claim self-defence for the death of her husband and the manslaughter charge could be changed to one of murder.

Chapter 39

Sarah Dent managed to squeeze in another visit to Redwood before she and her husband were off to sunnier climes for their two-week holiday abroad. Lindy was easy to visit, presenting no major problems and having used her time at Redwood wisely. The tutors were delighted with her progress and predicted good grades in the forthcoming exams. It was as if the girl was on a mission to catch up on the education she had missed and although the subjects available to study at Redwood were limited, she was studying with a passion and determination as if her life depended on it. In her bag Sarah had another envelope with two more photographs of Jack which she knew would bring excitement and joy to Lindy. They met as usual in the visitor's café, and Sarah bought them both a cup of tea before sitting opposite Lindy and handing over the photographs which elicited a huge, infectious smile. After discussing Jack's eyes, the colour of his hair and any other shared features Sarah asked about the forthcoming exams.

'I'm a little nervous; such a lot depends on the results. I'm already at a disadvantage being in here so I'm hoping that good grades will in some way make up for it.' Sarah understood what the girl was saying but refrained from telling her that she had other attributes which could make up for this blot on the copy book; it wouldn't do to make Lindy think too highly of herself, humility was part of her charm.

'Your release will be shortly after the exams, do you want me to reserve a room in the hostel I was telling you about?' Sarah had researched the limited options available and after talking them through with the girl they had decided on the hostel where she would have a room to herself and a shared bathroom and kitchen with five other girls. The best thing as far as Sarah was concerned was that the hostel was supervised twenty-four hours a day. Lindy had proved to be resourceful in the past but she wanted her to have someone to turn to who would be on site if needed. If the accommodation was settled and Lindy had a postal address she could claim benefits and use her time constructively to look for a job.

'Yes, the hostel seems the best option and I'm sure it'll be better than many places I've lived, including bus shelters!' Again, she had no expectations therefore would not be disappointed when confronted with the reality of the very basic, sparsely furnished hostel. Sarah, like Maggie, had been horrified at Lindy's aspirations to re-offend in order to get sent back to Redwood, and both women were relieved that she had moved past that stage and was hoping to find a job and become a valued member of society.

Sarah had some experience of career guidance and used this to find out what the girl would be suited to regarding employment.

'Well, while here I've spent most of my time between reading in the library and helping Tracey look after baby Sam. I've done some sessions in life skills working in the kitchen which I quite enjoyed but I'm not sure I'd like to do that as a job.' She looked thoughtful.

'Catering is an area in which there are always jobs so let's not rule that out entirely. Working in libraries would probably suit you well but as some libraries are under threat of closure due to budget cuts I think any vacancies will be like gold dust. Maybe you could think of training in childcare, an NVQ perhaps?'

'I had thought of that but don't you have to be police checked for anything to do with children?'

'Yes you do but I think they'd only be looking for offences relating to children. Your time in here is for shoplifting and you were a minor so you might still be acceptable. I'll look into that one, Lindy, and let you know next time I see you.'

Before Sarah left she told Lindy that she would be away for a couple of weeks and would see her on returning to work. On the way home she thought it would be as well to ring Maggie to let her know that she wouldn't be visiting Redwood for a while.

'Hi, Maggie, it's Sarah Dent, how are you?'

'I'm fine thanks, Sarah, and you?'

'I will be in a couple of days, Phil and I are off to the Seychelles for a couple of weeks.'

'Wonderful, you lucky thing!'

'That's what I wanted to tell you really, I've seen Lindy today but obviously won't be going for a while. I didn't know if you'd want to bear that in mind when you're visiting her.'

'She's in my diary for next week anyway but I'll make a point of ringing her, she'll be sitting the exams by the time you get home, won't she?'

'Yes, we spoke about her future today. I'll be booking a room in a halfway house for her for when she gets out. It's nothing salubrious but she pointed out herself that she's lived in worse places.'

'What's her train of thought now?' Maggie asked.

'Working in a library would be her dream but as many are closing down I can't see that as a viable career. I suggested she look for training in childcare; she loves children and she'd be ideally suited to caring for them but she'll have to make a good impression to get on a course, and disclosing where she's lived for the last few months might go against her but she'll have to be honest.' There were a few moments of silence and Sarah thought Maggie had been cut off.

'Sorry, Sarah, you've just given me an idea, one that's been staring me in the face! I'll have to go, I need to speak to Lindy but I'll tell you all about it when you come back if it works out that is, so have a great time, bye!' Maggie left Sarah completely baffled but couldn't tell her of the plan which was forming in her mind until she'd looked into the possibilities herself.

'Hi, Lindy, it's Maggie,' she said as if the girl had endless telephone calls. 'I've been thinking about what you'll be doing when you leave Redwood and I need to ask your permission again to talk to someone about you.'

'This sounds very mysterious, why would you want to tell someone about me?' Lindy was puzzled.

'Because it's just possible they might have a job which would suit you very well. It would be as a nanny for three children, would you be interested in that kind of job?'

'Oh, Maggie, it would be a dream come true, tell me about the children, how old are they?'

'I don't want to get your hopes up and you know it won't be easy and even though I can speak for you they might not want to consider you.'

'Because I'm in here.' Lindy sounded dejected.'

'It's always going to be the case but we would need to be completely honest with this family and that's why I'm talking to you first.'

'I know you're on my side and I trust you, Maggie, so tell them whatever you feel they should know. One thing you can say is that I would be honoured to look after their children and I will work as hard as possible to make them happy, children have a right to be happy.'

Chapter 40
Maggie

Lindy's parting words really touched me. Here was a girl who had been neglected, abandoned by her own mother, let down by a supposedly caring society and left in the care of people who took advantage of her vulnerability, yet she had stated with candour that children had a right to be happy! How did she know this? Had she been reading books on psychology and child development? I knew she hadn't but Lindy has extraordinary empathy with children and I get that, I really do.

When I trained in therapeutic counselling we had many lively discussions in our group as to why people are what they are. Freud, together with many of his peers and successors, takes it all back to childhood, which makes sense to a degree. But it's not only our childhood experiences which determine which of us will be well-adjusted adults, there's more to it than that. Neither is it due to our genes that we become the people we are. If a child is abused and neglected in childhood one school of thought is that he or she will grow up to be an abuser and neglect his own children. I cannot go along with that and neither can many clients I have worked with over the years, who have overcome abuse and neglect yet grown into the most caring individuals and parents it's been my privilege to know. I remember a lady called Janet who had suffered sexual abuse in childhood and remained silent about it until she was fifty years old, when she suffered an emotional breakdown and finally disclosed the pain of her past. Janet had raised two wonderful, well-adjusted children and had been an exemplary mother. The only trait lingering from her own personal hell was that she had been an overprotective mother, which was due to a very real fear that her children might be molested in the same way. This woman would have been horrified to hear theories that abused children grow up to become abusers themselves. Of course it does sometimes happen but there are also many men and women who have experienced happy, loving childhoods yet for some reason turn into adults who abuse others. There are no hard and fast rules to this. One of my fellow students had a theory that an abused child would draw from their experience and either grow up to become like their abuser or swing completely the opposite way to be determinedly not at all like their abuser.

But all this is me on my little hobby horse again, so why was I revisiting all this confusing psychology? Because I wanted to persuade Sue and Alan to take on Lindy as a nanny to their precious children. It would give Sue the opportunity to work as many days as she liked and I was convinced that Lindy would do everything in her power to give their children the happy childhood they deserved. I was hoping that having spoken to her she wasn't dreaming too much about new possibilities. I'd tried to make light of the idea but she was bound to be thinking about it.

So, at seven pm I rang Sue to ask if I could go over to see both her and Alan, knowing that by the time I arrived the children would be in bed, which would give me the opportunity to present my improbable suggestion to their parents. I left home telling Peter where I was going but not what it was all about; if all went well I would explain later.

'This all sounds rather mysterious,' Sue chuckled as she answered the door. 'It's not like you to be so secretive, Maggie!' Again I tried to make light of my visit, but the idea had taken root in my own mind and I kept thinking of the wonderful happy ending this could bring for Lindy and how it could solve Sue and Alan's childcare issues too. But where to start was slightly problematic. I'd rehearsed various opening lines during the drive over but none seemed appropriate and when I was actually sitting with them in their lounge with both of them waiting for me to talk, the best I could do was to come straight out with it.

'I have a client, a seventeen-year-old girl who is quite incredible considering the tough breaks she's been handed in life. Lindy is instantly likeable and has an interest in children, something which she would like to develop into a career. It struck me that possibly she could help you with your childcare issues and maybe become a nanny for you?' I looked hopefully at my two dearest friends knowing this had come out of nowhere and was something they would need to think about. There was also much more they should know about Lindy but hey, one step at a time. I looked at them both for a reaction.

'This is a surprise, Maggie. We've never thought about getting a nanny but it might be something to consider.' Sue spoke first. 'Alan's occasionally expressed a wish for a Swedish au pair but only in fun I hope! What do you think, Alan, is it something we could consider?'

'Why not? It would probably be cheaper than nursery places for George and James and they'd be cared for here in their own home, I'm certainly happy to explore the idea.'

'I know you can't tell us why you're seeing this girl but what can you tell us? Is she local, does she live in Fenbridge?' Sue had asked the inevitable question and there was nothing to do but come clean.

'No, at the moment she's in Redwood, but will be out soon.'

Alan's eyes widened at the mention of Redwood and Sue looked from him to me before asking,

'Am I missing something here? What is Redwood?' she asked.

'It's a young offenders' institution on the York road.' His expression was unreadable but Sue was instantly horrified.

'You're not seriously suggesting that we put our children in the hands of a criminal, Maggie, are you?' Sue rarely raised her voice at me but she was on the edge of being angry now and who could blame her? I knew how this must look to them.

'I am suggesting that, but do you think I'd be doing so if I thought Lindy was unsuitable? Will you let me tell you more about her before you decide?'

'It won't make any difference, Maggie, it's a risk I'm not prepared to take!'

'Let's hear her out, Sue.' Alan placed his hand on his wife's arm to calm the anger rising in her. 'I know Redwood and I also know that some youngsters end up there more from circumstances than anything they've done. Can you tell us why she's there?'

'Yes, I've got Lindy's permission to tell you anything you want to know. She was caught shoplifting and received a six months sentence, as much because she had no permanent address than because the crime warranted the punishment. She was taken into care as a six-year-old, along with her brother Jack who was just a baby. He was adopted fairly soon afterwards whilst she began a round of being shunted off to a series of unsatisfactory foster homes where she never felt loved or wanted. Her biggest regret was that she lost touch with her brother; Lindy had been his main care-giver as their mother was an alcoholic. It was Lindy who'd asked for help when Jack was critically ill and she couldn't rouse her mother from a drunken stupor. Baby Jack was rushed to hospital and if she hadn't taken action he would probably have died. The social services took her to a place where she was initially bullied before being sent to the first of a series of foster homes. In the fifth one the 'father' began to sexually abuse her, which led to her running away and living on the streets for a while and the shoplifting was the alternative to going hungry. When the police first found her, they returned her to social services with only a caution but Lindy feared another round of foster homes and ran away again. Another shoplifting charge resulted in her being sent to Redwood where she has been taking advantage of the teaching available and is about to sit her exams. During the time I've been seeing her I have become very fond of her, she's intelligent and very capable with a natural gift for getting along with children; she's been helping a young mother who was in Redwood with her baby son and by all accounts Lindy is gifted with children.

'Sadly she seems to have slipped through the net as far as social services are concerned and when I tried to speak to them on her behalf it turned out that her designated social worker had left the job and no one else had been appointed to take her place. That has since been rectified and I'm in touch with her new social worker, who has the same high opinion of Lindy as I do. I know this might seem like an insane idea but honestly, I wouldn't suggest it if I thought she wasn't a fit person to look after the children. I love them too, Sue, and some kind of arrangement could be mutually beneficial, if I didn't think that we wouldn't be here having this conversation.'

Sue was much calmer then and Alan backed me up when he said, 'I've known kids who've been in Redwood, often because of association with the wrong people and they haven't all been innately bad. They've just made stupid mistakes or been persuaded by others to do the wrong thing, and many of them regret it. It sounds as if Lindy is there because of circumstances which as a child she had no control over.'

I could have kissed Alan for those words and Sue was obviously thinking about them.

'During my first meeting with Lindy I asked if she had any hopes or aspirations for when she was released from Redwood and her answer was that she would do her best to get back there even if it meant shoplifting again because it was the best place she had ever lived. She appeared to have no hopes or expectations of a better life than being in Redwood.' Those words seemed to have an effect on Sue, whose expression was so much softer now.

'I'm sorry, Maggie,' she said, 'You must think me terribly bigoted, I spoke before I'd given you chance to explain. I'm not saying we'll do this but I think we'd like to look into the possibility.' She looked at Alan, who smiled and nodded his agreement.

'Will we be able to visit her in Redwood?' Sue asked.

'Yes, that can easily be arranged, the only visitors she does get are me and her social worker.'

'But that's awful. Did the girl's mother ever try to get her back?'

'No, Lindy never saw her again after the day she was taken into care. She was told that her mother had moved to another town and didn't want to see her and Jack again.'

'That's dreadful! No child should be let down like that!' Sue's concern was increasing. 'So where will she live when she gets out?'

'Sarah Dent, her social worker, has found her a place in a halfway house which is a hostel where she'll have her own bedroom but share the facilities with other girls.' Another look was exchanged between Sue and Alan, and if I read it correctly they were thinking about the attic room in their home, which was as yet untouched by them but which I had thought would make a super room for a nanny. Nothing was said on this subject and I decided to leave it at that and let them draw their own conclusions. I'd said enough to make them think and I was feeling positive about the way they had listened and been prepared to consider it. Assuring them that whatever their decision I was grateful to them for listening and considering what I'd said, then I left my friends to think about it and headed home to Peter.

It seemed appropriate to tell Peter why I had been to our friends so I basically shared the same information with him as I had with Sue and Alan without disclosing Lindy's name. Having done so, my husband would not feel excluded if the four of us were together and it would enable a discussion to take place to which he might even be able to contribute. I felt sure it would take several days for them to think about it and decide whether they wanted to meet Lindy and if they did I would gladly take them to a regular visiting time. Having not wanted Lindy to be too hopeful I now had to rein in my own feelings, finding myself dreaming and planning what might be in the not too distant future.

Chapter 41

Alan could hardly believe what Colin Brownlow had just told him. The good fortune of Colin being in the same pub as this Jockey fellow was incredible but the icing on the top was the information the man had given about the burns on Carol Jacobs's arms, burns which he now believed to be self-inflicted. Specific injuries had not been shared outside of the team and certainly not to the newspapers, which validated Jockey's claim that he did actually meet Carol when she tried to find someone to kill her husband. The wait to put this new information to their suspect was going to be frustrating; there was no information forthcoming from the medics as to when she would be fit to resume answering their growing list of questions. In the worst possible scenario Alan imagined an indefinite time period elapsing and the case lying dormant while Carol avoided two possible charges of murder, and the list of offences was growing with soliciting someone to commit a crime now being added.

When Alan and Tony met up with Colin, Alan thanked him for taking the time out of his rest days to bring Jockey in for questioning, saying he was blessed with an exceptional team who were both enthusiastic and dedicated to the job and he could not ask for more. The little man with the gravelly voice solemnly shook hands with Colin before getting into the back of Alan's car.

'We appreciate this, Jockey, it's a weekend and I know you'd probably rather be doing something else,' Tony said.

'It's no trouble and Mr Brownlow said you'd make it worth my while.'

'Oh did he, well I suppose we can have a whip round to buy you a couple of drinks but after we've asked our questions, mind, we can't have you worse for wear on our video, can we?' Alan wondered if the man was already inebriated but a few cups of the station's coffee should help with that.

'Mr. B didn't say I'd be starring in a movie.' He chuckled 'That's a first for me!' He then sat back and closed his eyes. Tony opened the window; an aroma of unwashed flesh was beginning to fill the car.

Della was ready and waiting for them and happily went to fetch coffee from the canteen before they began the interview. Jockey seemed to be an easy-going man although he professed a preference for beer rather than coffee which Alan said they could get after the interview. Della had a pack of six photographs, one of them Carol Jacobs and the others women of similar age and appearance to show Jockey for identification. After handing them to Alan and when the coffee was drunk Della left them to it and Tony switched on the video recorder. With the photographs spread before him Alan asked Jockey if he could identify the woman who had approached him in 'The Viking'. Without hesitation he pointed to Carol Jacobs's picture and said emphatically, 'That's the one.' Alan had to suppress the smile which was forming on his face as he asked if Jockey could tell them in his own words exactly what this woman had asked him.

'She'd asked at the bar for someone who was in the know in the underground world and the bar-man directed her to my little corner. Brought me a beer over she did, then asked where to find someone to do a job for her, and she didn't mean a plumber! Said that her husband was a cruel bastard and she was desperate to escape his beatings. Said that money wasn't a problem either and if someone was prepared to shoot him she would pay well. At first I thought the woman was having a laugh but then she went all doe-eyed on me and showed me those marks on her arms, cigarette burns they were, sure as eggs! I told her she'd got the wrong man; I won't have anything to do with that sort of stuff and I suggested she tried 'The Pig and Whistle', there's some shady characters hang out there... and then she left.'

'And can you remember when this was?' Tony asked.

'Like I told Mr. Brownlow, it was about a couple of weeks before I saw her picture in the papers and I said to myself, *blow me down if she hasn't gone and done it herself!*' Alan asked a few more questions but Jockey had provided them with a clear, if short, account of what had happened. After taking the man's full name, Jockey Burns, and an address in York where they could reach him, Tony took him out of the station to the nearest pub to purchase the promised beer and a pork pie. After Jockey had quickly downed a couple of pints, Tony's mobile rang. It was Della to tell him there was a car waiting with a couple of uniformed officers to take Jockey home.

'But I've only had a couple of pints!' Jockey complained, munching his way through the pie, so Tony took out his wallet and gave the little man two twenty-pound notes for his trouble.

'And you've had a good day out on such a lovely sunny day.' Tony steered him out of the pub and back to the police station. When the car set off Tony went inside to the incident room where Della and Alan were viewing the tape.

'At least he doesn't appear to be drunk, we should be thankful for that,' Della observed.

'Yes, he's a man of few words but they're certainly the right words for us. I find it incredible that Carol would even attempt to hire a hit man; this is Fenbridge, not the London backstreets,' Alan said.

'I suppose that's why she went to York, it's the nearest city but surely still too close to home and a huge risk to take,' Tony added.

'And it paid off but for us, not Carol, thanks to Jockey. He's quite a character. I only hope he comes over well in the witness stand if we ever get that far. Do you think we'll be able to see her again soon to question her about these new claims?' Della asked.

'It's entirely in the hands of the medics. We'll keep this information quiet for now, just the team and the DI of course to be in the know, and then when we get the okay to speak to her again we'll put it to her. Of course it could be some time before that happens but if she gets an inkling of this she'll probably take sanctuary in the psychiatric hospital indefinitely.' Alan honestly had no idea of what would happen with this case. He was, however, certain now that Carol Jacobs was not the victim she wanted them to believe she was and had planned to kill her husband at least two weeks before actually stabbing him. They were dealing with a cold, calculating woman and he sincerely hoped that justice would be done and she would get the punishment she deserved.

Alan left the station to return to Sue and the children. His wife looked at him studiously and asked,

'Why is it that going into work on a Saturday puts such a smile on your face?'

'What do you mean, it's coming back to you that makes me smile,' he lied. 'Believe me, Sue, this last couple of hours has been important to the case, in fact I'd go as far as to say that it's watertight now and it feels so good!'

Chapter 42
Maggie

Having given Sue and Alan a few days to think about my suggestion, and knowing that Lindy would be released in just a few weeks' time, I was a little anxious as it seemed sensible for my friends to meet her as soon as possible. I'd seen Sue only a couple of times since that evening when I called to pick Rose up from school. She was her usual self and neither of us seemed to want to open the dialogue about Lindy; me, because I didn't want them to think I was pushing them into a decision and Sue... well her reason could be anything, simply to make me squirm or just because she hadn't decided yet. On Saturday Sue rang me.

'Would you believe Alan's gone into work?' she opened the conversation.

'Well it must be important to leave you on a Saturday.'

'I'm hoping he'll be back soon, I wanted him to make a start on decorating the attic today.' A silence followed Sue's words. Was she trying to tell me something or just teasing in the way she often did? I didn't rise to the bait and waited for her to speak again.

'Aw, Maggie, don't you want to know why?'

'Of course I do but I'm trying to be patient.'

'Well, we've chatted about your suggestion, in fact we've hardly spoken about anything else since you came round and we've decided to meet Lindy. Not that I'm making any promises but we need to meet her before we can make a decision. Is there visiting at weekends?'

'Yes, and a couple of evenings, I think. Were you thinking about tomorrow because I'll be free to go with you then?'

'That would be great. How will you let her know?'

'I'll ring, they've got telephones in Redwood and I believe they even have the internet,' I teased.

'Funny. You know what I mean, Lindy will need to know we're coming, won't she?'

'Yes, I'll ring straight away and let you know the time later. Is Alan okay with this?'

'It's him who's pushing it. I have to confess to having more reservations than he does but he's persuaded me that we have to meet her before we can make any kind of decision.' Sue sighed.

'Yes, of course you do. I'll ring and find out visiting times then get straight back to you and thanks for this, Sue, I really appreciate it.'

'There's nothing to appreciate yet, we haven't made any decisions and I was only winding you up about the attic; we're certainly not at that stage yet.'

'And here I was getting all excited!' I was a little cross with her for that.

'Sorry, I couldn't resist, you're so gullible. But we are talking about it and when we've met Lindy we'll have more of an idea if we could go along with this.'

'Okay, you're forgiven. I'll ring you back shortly, bye.' I quickly told Peter the gist of my conversation with Sue then looked up the number for Redwood. Lindy was surprised to hear my voice, especially because it was Saturday but when I told her the reason why I was calling there was a silence at the other end of the line.

'Lindy, are you okay?' The silence worried me.

'Yes, Maggie, but I won't know what to say to them and what if they don't like me?'

'Just be yourself. They'll probably want to ask you a few things so simply answer as best as you can.'

'It feels like such an enormous thing, I'm more nervous now than I am about sitting my exams!'

'You'll be fine and I'll be there too. Sue and Alan are good friends of mine and they're very caring people. This visit is only to see if they think it's worth serious consideration, it doesn't mean they've reached a decision but they rightly feel they can't come to any decision until they've met you.'

'Yes, I understand that but I've already got a zillion butterflies in my tummy!'

I laughed; all she needed to do was to be herself. If my friends thought there was a chance that Lindy would be able to become their nanny there would have to be several more visits. It wasn't like an ordinary job interview which was over in one go. The fact that she was in Redwood put her at a disadvantage before they even met but I knew they would be fair. Alan in particular seemed to be sympathetic to the circumstances which led up to her being placed in Redwood and if Sue took to her Lindy would have a friend for life.

Visiting was from two pm, and ten minutes early the three of us entered Redwood, all with our own thoughts and feelings. Alan had insisted on driving; he always preferred to drive rather than be a passenger and I sat in the back seat wondering if this really was such a good idea. In the foyer we walked into a full blown row between a forty-something woman and a warder. The loud woman, who had managed to squeeze her rather large behind into tight leopard print leggings, was shouting about her rights as a mother. Her bare arms were covered in tattoos and her face dripped with piercings. We couldn't tell what the argument was about and I didn't particularly wish to know and signed us in as quickly as possible, then we went through the metal detector into a waiting area. Sue rolled her eyes at the commotion and I wondered what she was expecting of this visit. Resisting the urge to tell her that Lindy was nothing like this raucous woman, I thought it best to let her draw her own conclusions. Eventually we were herded into a room laid out with comfortable chairs in groups of twos and fours around low coffee tables with a self-service hatch at the side offering drinks and light snacks. We settled ourselves at a table in the far corner under the window with a view of the recreation area at the back of the facility. It was all new to me, having been used to the small impersonal room in which we usually met. The girls were brought in a few at a time, Lindy in the first group looking pale and nervous. Standing to greet her, I introduced her to my friends and she sat between Sue and me with her tiny hands clasped in her lap. Alan offered to go for coffee, and Lindy thanked him and managed a smile which transformed her face and gave me a degree of hope that this meeting would go well. It was awkward and I found myself holding my breath as if I was somehow on trial here, when it should have been me who facilitated the conversation to help Sue and Alan see Lindy at her best.

'Lindy's sitting her exams over the next couple of weeks.' I threw these words into the centre of our little group. 'How are you feeling about them?' This probably wasn't the best topic to start with but at least it gave her the opportunity to speak.

'I'm pretty much prepared and spend every spare minute revising but I don't know how I'll do, I've never sat an exam before.' Her voice was quiet, solemn.

'But the tutors are pleased with your progress, aren't they?'

'Oh yes, they're predicting high grades which will be great if they're right.' The silence crept in again, sitting on the coffee table like an unwelcome intruder. Surely

Sue must want to ask her something but she was holding back. Alan was the first one to break the ice.

'Maggie tells me you have a brother?' He smiled, prompting the same response from Lindy, as she was on her favourite topic now.

'Yes, he's called Jack and is nearly eleven now. I brought you some photos if you'd like to see them?'

'Yes please. He'll be in secondary school, is he?' Alan continued the conversation while Lindy fished in her pocket for the photographs.

'He'll be moving to secondary school in September. Here he is; of course I haven't seen him since we were very young but it's nice to have these pictures.'

'Where's he living?' This was Alan again, I wondered when Sue was going to take part in this conversation.

'He was adopted and lives in Leeds. From what my social worker's told me he's very happy there and doing well at school.' Alan passed the photos on to Sue, who studied them for a minute.

'And you were never adopted?' She finally spoke.

'No. I had a few different foster homes but generally people who want to adopt are looking for a baby.' She spoke without malice; it was a fact that was all. 'How old are your children?' Now this was Sue's territory!

'Rose is the eldest, she's five going on fifteen and is at school. George is two and goes to nursery a couple of days a week and James is just a couple of months old now. I've got a few pictures in my bag if you'd like to see?' Sue offered, and I could feel the thaw in her attitude.

'Yes please, I'd love to see them!' Lindy took the photos Sue offered and looked intently at them. 'Rose is very like you, isn't she?' Her comments made Sue smile. 'And George is just like his daddy! James looks as if he'll favour his daddy too.' She was genuine in her comments, nothing was put on for show and I hoped Sue and Alan could see this as I did.

'Lindy's been helping one of the other residents here with her baby son,' I offered.

'What, people have babies in here?' Sue was astonished.

'Yes, I was surprised at first but the facilities are really good. She had her own little bedsit with a bathroom and a microwave to prepare food. It was probably better than where she was living before she came here,' she answered.

'And what will happen to you when you get out of here?' Alan asked.

'Well I'm a little more confident now that I have a new social worker, which is thanks to Maggie, and she's reserved a place for me in a hostel until I can find somewhere better and she'll be helping me to look for a job. I'd love to work with children and train for qualifications to do so, but I'll take whatever comes along. Having been in Redwood won't make it easy to find something, but I've told Sarah that I'll happily do voluntary work to gain experience.'

Alan nodded thoughtfully and Sue again joined in.

'I know Maggie's told you that we might be interested in hiring a nanny. What would you be able to offer our children if we took you on?'

Lindy's face radiated with a smile,

'I love children and would do everything in my power to keep them safe and happy. I looked after my brother when we were very young and I know how important being loved is. Being with children makes me happy and would most certainly be my dream job. As for having been in here, I don't know exactly what Maggie's told you but the shoplifting was only to feed myself after I ran away and is not something I'm proud of, but I've learned my lesson and won't do anything so stupid again.'

The rest of the visit seemed to go reasonably well but as I hadn't known what to expect it was difficult to judge. Naturally I asked my friends' opinion as we travelled home and although Sue was rather guarded Alan seemed to have taken to Lindy.

'She's not what I expected,' Sue eventually said. 'At least there was no ring through the nose and a body covered with tattoos, not that I'm against them but some of the subjects, particularly skulls, I fail to understand. You told us that she was seventeen but quite honestly she could pass for fourteen or fifteen. It makes me wonder if she's responsible enough to care for the children.'

I understood where she was coming from but still wanted to defend my client.

'Looking so young will be an asset when she is older but her life experience has given her a certain wisdom and her love for children has been central to many of our conversations. She understands what it feels like to be neglected and unloved and therefore is determined that any child she comes across should never have to know that feeling. Lindy may look younger than her seventeen years but in wisdom and common sense she is much older. I don't want to push you into a decision and I know you must feel really comfortable about her ability to care for the children. Please just talk it through, visit again as much as you like, they have visiting on Tuesday and Thursday evenings as well as Saturday and Sunday. Thank you for going today and giving her a chance, I appreciate it and naturally whatever you decide I'll happily go along with.' Alan dropped me at home, declining to come in for coffee as Ruby needed to get off somewhere as soon as they got home. I decided not to bring the subject up again and leave it for them to do and I honestly didn't know what they were thinking. If I was so on edge about this I could only imagine how Lindy must be feeling.

Chapter 43

Monday morning brought good news to the team on the Carol Jacobs case. Apparently the woman had been discharged from the psychiatric unit and declared fit to answer questions. Wasting no time, Alan rang Carol at home and asked her to come to the station as soon as possible. After some prevarication on her part it was agreed that she would contact her solicitor and they would let Alan know the earliest time they could come. Ten minutes after that call Mr Albright was on the phone, laying down the conditions under which his client would answer questions. Alan kept his cool but in no way intended her or her solicitor to dictate the questioning in what was now a murder inquiry. He kept the news of Jockey's evidence to himself and would enjoy seeing the look on both their faces when that evidence was introduced.

By ten-thirty, the agreed time, Alan was getting antsy as they were nowhere to be seen. The whole team had been in since eight that morning and were eager to know the outcome of this interview. At ten forty-five the front desk officer rang through to say that they had arrived and he'd put them in interview room eight which was the coldest room in the station. Alan asked Della to sit in with him but they waited until eleven before making their way to the interview room where, as expected, Carol was agitated and her solicitor angry.

'We've been here for nearly twenty minutes!' Albright glared accusingly.

'Sorry about that, we were ready at ten-thirty but as you were late other things took priority,' Alan lied. It was perhaps a bit immature, a tit for tat situation but the detective wanted to stamp his authority on this interview and was determined to be in charge of the proceedings. Della switched on the tape recorder and reminded Carol of her rights then commenced the interview with an opening question enquiring about Carol's health. Before the woman had a chance to reply Mr Albright butted in,

'I would like to remind you that my client's mental health is still very fragile. She has suffered much with the death of her husband and the doctors are now looking at PTSD as a diagnosis.'

'Thank you, Mr Albright, but we would prefer it if your client could speak for herself.' Della smiled sweetly.

'I'm better than I was, thank you. The introduction of my father's death triggered painful memories and I'd like to apologise for my behaviour.' Carol was acting like the perfect interviewee.

'Apology accepted,' Alan said curtly, his eye twitching where she had clawed him.

'As you've mentioned your father, perhaps you could answer the question which we asked on that occasion; why did you lie to the police about your movements that day?' Della asked gently.

'It's a long time ago and I was very young. I don't remember deliberately lying to the police, I must have simply forgotten that I'd gone back to the house, it was a traumatic experience to find my father dead like that.' Tears glistened in Carol's eyes, and Alan drew in a deep breath; he was not in the mood for games.

'Let's try something not so long ago then, shall we? Why did you go to York a few weeks before your husband's death to try to hire someone to kill him?' The ensuing silence was palpable, and oh so satisfying to Alan and Della. Carol turned pale and stuttered, unable to find any words to speak while her solicitor too looked ashen with his mouth open in surprise. He recovered from the shock first and asked,

'DS Hurst, is this another one of your fishing expedition or do you have any solid evidence with which to charge my client?'

'We have a positive identification and a videotaped statement which puts Mrs Jacobs in York a few weeks before her husband's death, asking around the pubs for a hired killer. We would now like to change the charge of manslaughter to murder with a further charge of soliciting a third party to commit murder. Della, would you read Mrs Jacobs her rights please.' Alan could barely keep the satisfaction out of his voice as Della read Carol her rights and arrested her for murder. Carol's eyes met Alan's for the briefest of moments and in them he saw pure hatred. Not only was Carol Jacobs revealed for what she really was, but Mr Albright too had the wind taken out of his sails. It was a good feeling, his team could be proud of their hard work and a conviction looked to be in the bag. Alan left the room as two uniformed officers arrived to take Carol into custody and Mr Albright was running after them shouting instructions to her to say nothing unless he was present.

The interview had been short and very sweet, and when Alan and Della returned to the incident room there was coffee, real coffee, and donuts which they ate in celebration. The DI, whom Alan had briefed before the interview, was also there to congratulate them on the result.

'So what happens to the Jacobses' fortune now, then?' Colin asked.

'If she's convicted of murder it will go to the next of kin, his mother. I should think that in itself will be a punishment to Carol.' Alan smiled.

'I wonder how long she'd planned this. It's incredible that she would fake being an abused wife and set up her home to look as if he'd attacked her,' Della pondered. 'The poor sod, thinking he'd got himself a lovely young wife only to be murdered for his money, I can't understand how anyone could be so cold-blooded.'

Thinking of how Carol Jacobs had tried to fool them reminded Alan of Maggie, and he felt he should ring her to update her on these latest developments. He excused himself and left the room to make the call.

'Maggie? It's Alan, just thought you'd like to know that we've charged Carol Jacobs with murder. Obviously I can't go into details but we're pretty confident we've got a watertight case.'

'Murder, as in planned, pre-meditated murder?' Maggie was astounded.

'Yes, it was planned alright. The more we dug into the case the more I became convinced she had known what she was doing all along but over the weekend we got a lucky break, a witness to her intentions. I can't say much more than that but I thought you'd like to know. She certainly won't be coming back to you for counselling.'

'Can I tell Tom?' she asked.

'Yes of course but wait until it breaks in the press before you tell anyone else will you?'

'I will and thanks for letting me know.' Maggie hung up and Alan went back to enjoying the celebrations with his colleagues by having another donut.

Chapter 44
Maggie

It seems that I have been duped but it's not the first time in my career and surely won't be the last. With each new client my default position is one of belief, I listen and believe no matter how wild or fantastic their stories are. It would be impossible to support them if I didn't believe them, even though the law of averages dictates that a small percentage of clients will lie to me. But that's the point of counselling, the client needs me to be wholly on their side and sometimes they lie to ensure that, although they don't need to, I'd be right there with them whatever.

Carol felt the need to lie to me for purposes known only to her but the trouble with telling lies is that it becomes almost impossible to pick out the truth from the same source. It seemed that Carol had fabricated a web of lies to show that her husband was abusive. Now I was wondering if any part of her story was true. Was she ever abused? If not then she took drastic measures to convince me that her husband was violent. Did she inflict the injuries on herself? I could picture those six perfectly round blistered burns on her left arm, could she really have done that to herself? It's a chilling thought and as yet I don't know but Alan seems confident that she is a charlatan and hopefully the truth will eventually come out.

Admittedly this case is probably the strangest I've ever had. Generally if a client lies to me I won't challenge them as often those lies are designed to gain my support, which is what they most need at that point in time. Generally as the counselling relationship continues I am able to strip away the lies and probe the reasons why they felt it necessary to lie in the first instance. The untruthful client may be seeking sympathy but what I try to give is empathy, which is not the same. Sympathy is expressed by platitudes, even if they are well meaning and I don't do platitudes. When a client pours their heart out to me I listen but my role is not to say, 'how awful' or 'poor you'. Empathy takes a step closer to the root of a client's problems and is an attempt to get alongside them. My role is to listen and understand then to help the client explore their feelings, their relationships and their emotions, and empower them to make changes or not, it's entirely up to them. When I connect with a client and have true empathy with them I can walk in their shoes and see through their eyes and in doing so we travel the journey together and I can form a solid base for them to reach out to when things become overwhelming.

Carol Jacobs never wanted counselling in the true sense of the word. She was seeking someone to back up her lies and so now I understand why we didn't connect, why a relationship didn't evolve from the time we spent together. Carol had her own agenda and was using me, Tom Williams and even Alan and the police force to bear witness to an abusive husband... but it was all lies and now she will have to pay the price for her cold and calculated actions. And how do I feel at having been used in such a way? I have to say that I am saddened by all that has happened.

I was still calling for Rose each day to take her to school, and dreading the day when Sue felt able to do this again herself. On the Monday after our visit to Redwood nothing was said about Lindy or if she had discussed the matter at all with Alan. We concentrated on getting Rose ready, she always had so much to tell me that she forgot she was supposed to be getting her shoes on or brushing her teeth. It was the same on the Tuesday morning and I resigned myself to waiting until Sue was ready to talk to me but on Wednesday she took me by surprise.

'I went to visit Lindy last night.' My friend casually dropped this information into a conversation about peanut butter or cheese for sandwiches. I looked at her, amazed.

'You never said!' It sounded more accusing than I meant it to.

'You never asked!' A typical Sue response.

'So how did it go?'

'Very well actually, she sat the first of her exams that morning and felt it had gone well. We had an interesting conversation about books; Lindy seems to be reading anything she can get her hands on. I've said I'll take her some in next time I go but don't worry I'll not take the Jackie Collins ones.'

So, she was going again, I couldn't help smiling.

'Don't grin like that, Maggie, I haven't made my mind up yet.'

'I'm just glad you're giving it serious consideration, thank you for that, Sue.'

'Well I'm afraid it's going to take me a long time to decide, both Alan and I feel we need to know Lindy much better than a few visits to Redwood can give us, it's a big thing leaving our children with a stranger.' Sue was frowning.

'Oh, right... it is perhaps rushing it a bit but maybe you can visit regularly, she doesn't have anyone else who goes to see her.' I was disappointed; although I understood what Sue was saying I'd hoped for a quick decision, which was unrealistic of me I know.

'So I've asked her to come and live with us when she's released in three weeks.' Sue dropped this bombshell quite casually as if we were back to deciding on the peanut butter.

'You've what?' I almost shouted. Sue grinned at me, she could be so annoying at times.

'It's impossible to offer the girl a job looking after our brood unless we know her really well. Alan liked her and admittedly I did too but visiting in Redwood is hardly the right setting to really get to know her is it? Anyway, Alan was telling me about these halfway houses like the one where they're going to send her and it sounds awful. The poor girl needs a home and what better way to get to know her than by having her living with us? It means Alan will have to get his finger out and decorate the attic room but it's all arranged.'

'Well, what did Lindy say?'

'She said yes, of course! We had a woman to woman talk, there were too many of us there on Sunday, it must have been overwhelming for the poor girl, and she agreed to moving in with us without the commitment of a job offer from us, or that she'll stay from her, it'll be like we're all on trial. This really is the only way I can see it working; I'm not prepared to leave the children with someone I barely know.'

I flung my arms around Sue; she's a pain at times but I do love her and it's the perfect solution. I knew Lindy would be excited by this offer and only hoped it didn't put her off her exams. Three weeks wasn't long to wait and I was so much happier thinking of her living with Sue and Alan than in some kind of hostel. I'd ring Lindy later and I could hardly wait for Sarah Dent to get back from holiday, she'd be thrilled, I was sure.

Chapter 45
Carol

Fenbridge only has one council estate, a relatively small group of houses on the east side of town, conspicuous by their uncared-for appearance. The council in their wisdom designed these two- and three-bedroomed homes with a small forecourt at the front and a generous sized garden at the back, but the majority of the residents neither wanted nor maintained these gardens. They became dumping grounds for an assortment of unwanted items from fridges to furniture and it wasn't unusual to see abandoned cars in various states of disrepair. Local cats and dogs used the gardens as their toilet and vermin were simply a fact of life. There were few exceptions to this neglect and the house I had the misfortune to grow up in wasn't one of them.

My most abiding memory of my mother was of her sitting on the sofa watching television and eating crisps and chocolate washed down by a litre bottle of cola. Her idea of a family meal consisted of shop bought pies with tinned processed peas or if she had spare cash, chips from the fish shop with fried eggs. When my sister Liz and I reached our teens we were pretty much left to fend for ourselves at meal times, using whatever we could find in the kitchen to stave off hunger. I suppose there are many who've had worse breaks in life than this but I learned from an early age that the only person looking out for me was me.

My father was a monster, which is why when the opportunity presented itself I killed him. It wasn't planned although it was one of my fantasies to watch him die and I have never been plagued by remorse, the bastard deserved it. He was a drunk, a disgusting slob of a man who was too quick with his fists and would hit out at whoever was nearest to him. My sister and I learned to keep our distance so it was usually Mum who was in the line of fire and I like to think I did her a huge favour when I killed him. That morning is still crystal clear in my mind; Liz and I left for school as usual but I'd forgotten some homework which needed to be handed in so I ran back to the house while Liz walked slowly on. Dad was coming out of the bathroom as I reached the top of the stairs and when I saw what he was holding I knew I was in for a thrashing. He'd found the pregnancy testing kit I'd bought and was waving it at me in a furious rage, his eyes bulging and spittle on his chin. He shouted some choice names at me, 'slut' and 'whore' to name a couple and was launching himself at me in anger. All I did was to press myself into the corner of the landing, hard against the wall and when he got within touching distance I launched myself towards him using the wall for leverage and pushed him as hard as I could. Dad was at the top of the stairs with no place to go but down and I stood watching as he tumbled and landed in a heap at the bottom. My initial thought was, *I hope he's dead*, because if he wasn't and he recovered I would be in serious trouble. I experienced no feeling of remorse, no sadness or guilt, just a sense of pure relief that he was finally out of my life. As I went tentatively down the stairs, the open staring eyes confirmed that he was dead so I grabbed the pregnancy kit, stuffed it into my bag and ran out the door to catch my sister up. It had taken less than five minutes and if Liz noticed anything wrong with me she didn't say. The pregnancy kit had shown negative, it was a false alarm and suddenly my day was looking good.

When we arrived home from school I went through the motions of being shocked and upset. I dialled 999 and gave our address to the operator and the wheels were set in motion. A policewoman went to pick Mum up from work and we dutifully answered all their questions as Dad's body was taken away in a black car. I neglected to tell them that I had gone back to the house and if Liz thought about it she didn't say anything. Even Mum didn't appear to grieve; we were hardly a family in mourning and got through the next few days doing all that needed to be done. When the funeral was over and the police eventually left us alone, satisfied that it was a tragic accident, we readjusted our routine and continued living without Dad. From everyone's point of view it was an accident but from mine it was the most significant thing which had ever happened to me. I was empowered by it and knew that I had the ability to make anything happen, a realisation that would change my life, for the better of course.

I went back to school to sit my exams but I knew my future would be far away from the grime and despair of the council estate, yet to live the kind of life I wanted would take money. Mum rarely had any in her purse when I checked so I began to dream up other ways to make money. The boys at school were eager to give me a few pounds for favours exchanged but I got bored with them leering at me and wanting to touch what I only allowed them to see so I decided to try one of the teachers. Mr Robbins the PE teacher was the perfect target, fresh out of college and rather good-looking, he responded to my flirtations. It was no hardship to let him kiss me which was playing right into my hands. That kiss earned me a cool hundred pounds but I wasn't sure he'd part with any more than that. I hated those last months at school with the teachers putting pressure on us to do well in the exams, pretending they were concerned for our futures when they were actually thinking of their statistics. The day I left for good was one of the happiest in my life. Working in the local supermarket was a stopgap until I formulated my plan to reinvent my life, and the paltry wage was spent on new clothes and make-up which were the tools to make my dreams become a reality.

Bill Jacobs was a virgin when we met, which initially I thought was rather sweet and he told me that he wanted to wait until we were married to have sex. As for me, I'd have been happy to wait forever as Bill really didn't do it for me. He was old and losing his hair and more than a little overweight but he possessed the one thing I really wanted, money, which to me represented freedom. I'd dreamed of being rich for years and escaping the drudgery of poverty. Repeating the pattern of so many who lived on our estate, and turning into my parents, was most certainly not for me. I wanted so much more from life and felt that I deserved it too.

On our first date Bill offered to pick me up at home but I couldn't let him see the dump where I lived so we arranged to meet in the town centre. He turned up with an orchid in a box; I'd have preferred something with more intrinsic value, jewellery perhaps but it was evidence that he was trying to please which boded well for the future. From our exchange of emails I knew Bill owned his own company, something to do with computer software. I didn't fully understand all the ins and outs of his business but judging from the brand new, top of the range Audi he drove, it seemed to be paying well. His suit too was certainly more Saville Row than Man at C&A, which was the best any of the lads round our way wore. Bill was shy too and obviously unused to talking to girls. I was the one to make conversation but that seemed to be the way he liked it and as he asked to see me again I reckoned the night had been a success.

Back at home I Googled his company and learned that although a small firm it was certainly up and coming. The area he lived in was in the better part of town and when I looked at the street on Google earth I was amazed; compared to our house it was a palace and I knew then I'd met the right man for me. Our dates were to places I'd only ever dreamed of, fancy restaurants with white linen tablecloths and silver cutlery, the theatre in Manchester; this was the life I wanted and being nice to Bill was such a small price to pay. Choosing the ring seemed to give Bill as much pleasure as it did me. He took me to the Victoria Quarter in Leeds where I could choose anything I desired without checking the price, which in itself was quite a heady experience. I chose a three-diamond ring of round brilliant cut diamonds set in platinum and when Bill slipped it on my finger I silently vowed never to take it off, which was not for sentimental reasons.

Bill lived with his mother and inevitably he suggested that I should meet her, something I could hardly refuse. A formal invitation for Sunday lunch was conveyed through her son who picked me up, again from the town centre. I took a bunch of chrysanthemums for Mrs Jacobs, which she hardly looked at as she inspected me closely. From the look of disapproval on her face, I saw that I was not what she wanted for her only child and she was cool with me all through the meal, talking to Bill about people and subjects of which I knew nothing. When she did glance my way it was with undisguised suspicion in her cold, watery eyes as if she could see that I only wanted her son for his money, which was actually spot on and quite perceptive for such an old lady. Our mutual hatred of each other grew each time we met, which when I got my way wasn't very often. Bill confided that she threw a tantrum when he told her we were to be married, the knowledge of which brought me a perverse sense of satisfaction. Looking into the future it seemed that this old biddy was to be my nemesis and I could only hope she would not live to a ripe old age. At her insistence I was presented with a pre-nuptial agreement to sign, an unexpected obstacle to my plan but to refuse would have caused suspicion; after all as a newly engaged woman I should be planning to live with my husband forever. It was a hitch I would overcome at a later date and an indication of how stubborn the old lady was.

Her son, however, was like putty in my hands and our hasty wedding was an extravagant affair albeit with few in attendance. Reluctantly the guest list included my mother and sister and I was only glad that Dad was not alive to attend with them. Bill, of course, was not a bit like my father had been. Dad was a bully, for him women and children were put on the earth to serve him and to kick about when the mood took him. He spent most of his earnings on beer and cigarettes and we made do with the loose change at the end of the day. I was never going to live like that again and was prepared to do whatever it took to get what I wanted. The house we bought before our wedding was delightful and I loved it. In an exclusive avenue of individually designed homes with a drive leading to a double garage, it boasted four bedrooms and three bathrooms, a kitchen to die for and immaculately landscaped gardens. This was my dream home and with an unlimited budget to furnish it, I was in heaven. The power of money is totally and utterly seductive.

We honeymooned in Barbados before returning to settle into our new home. The intimacy of our marriage was a small price to pay in the long term but I quickly tired of Bill pawing me and wanting sex on a regular basis. He talked about children all the time too, joking about making babies being such fun. There was no way I wanted a baby and so I remained on the pill with my husband completely unaware that we would never have children. As time passed Bill thought we should seek medical help but I cajoled him into believing that we just needed time and I was still young enough to wait until it happened naturally.

It wasn't as easy as I'd assumed it would be to live with someone you didn't like, and the dislike soon turned to hatred. Looking back, I was frustrated and bored. I picked arguments with Bill and treated him shamefully in the hope that he would want a divorce but it wasn't going to happen. The terms of the pre-nuptial agreement stated that it was only if Bill initiated the divorce that I would be entitled to a share of his wealth, but he seemed determined to stay with me no matter how badly I treated him. It was in a mood of frustration and anger that I began to formulate a plan, a serious effort to permanently free myself of my husband; yes, to kill him. Extreme, I know, but I had done it before and knew I was strong enough to do it again. Firstly I needed to gather around me sympathetic allies who would vouch for me. I began hurting myself, targeting areas of my body I knew would bruise easily and then going to my GP to 'reluctantly' admit that my husband abused me. It was surprising how readily Dr Williams accepted my story and sympathised with me. He tried to persuade me to leave Bill but I played the frightened little wife who knew he would only come after me and make things even worse. After a few visits the doctor offered me counselling, a gift for my purposes of another witness to my domestic abuse. The counsellor too accepted everything I told her without question and like the doctor explained that there were options and I didn't need to stay in an abusive relationship. The plan was going well. It was painful to bang my head on open doors or hit my leg with a hammer but the injuries needed to look authentic and they did. As a final act to cement the sympathy and trust I decided to burn my arm with a cigarette. It took three stiff whiskeys before I plucked up the courage to do it and needless to say it was excruciatingly painful but the small circular burns were so effective. The counsellor, usually a straight-faced woman, winced when I showed them to her and she even had tears in her eyes as I told her how Bill had done it for no apparent reason.

The scene was set and it was time to act but my nerves were getting the better of me. I'd considered pushing him down the stairs but if the police put two and two together it might look suspicious, two deaths in the same manner. I thought about hiring someone to do it for me, as the world is full of people who'll do anything for money, so I decided to look into it. A trip to York proved fruitless. I'd hoped to find someone who would arrange some kind of 'accident' to befall my husband and I was prepared to pay well. Carefully phrased questions in some of the seedier pubs of York led me to a little weasel of a man called Jockey, whom I was told had his finger on the pulse of York's underground scene. Obviously I used a false name when approaching him and he readily let me buy him a few drinks, toying with me as I tried to find out the information I wanted. I even attempted to play on his sympathy, showing him the burn marks on my arm and telling him of the abuse my husband made me suffer but it was to no avail and I left without achieving my goal. So, it was down to me, I would have to kill Bill and make it appear to be self-defence. Of course it was his mother's fault, if only she hadn't suggested that pre-nuptial agreement, a divorce would have been much more civilised.

I steeled myself to act, my mind on the freedom and wealth the action would bring; I knew it would be unpleasant and messy but anything worth having is worth making an effort for. I got up earlier than usual and waited in the kitchen until I heard Bill coming down the stairs. To get his attention I dropped a tray full of glasses and shouted as if I was hurt, knowing he would come running into the kitchen. He barely had time to take in the scene before I plunged the knife into his chest. The look on his face was one of utter surprise and confusion. It was sickening, his blood felt warm on my hands as I watched him drop to the floor, reaching out to me for help. There was no need to stab him again, I must have wounded him fatally with the one action and as the blood pooled on the Italian tiled kitchen floor I knew he would not survive. To set the scene even more I threw items of crockery around the kitchen to give the impression of a huge row and then dialled 999.

The plan had seemed so simple; everyone has sympathy for an abused wife and most people would agree that the husband deserved all he got, but things didn't work out as planned. I'm assuming that my sister was the one who told the police about my lie on the day Dad died; she was the only one who knew. Then the stupid sergeant became fixated with the broken glass and crockery, bringing it up time and time again until I hardly remembered what I'd told them about it. But the final blow was struck by that awful little man in York. Who would have thought he'd connect the dots when he happened upon my picture in the paper, a photo which Bill's mother had given to the press?

My solicitor tells me that a self-defence plea is no longer feasible and has suggested I plead guilty with diminished responsibility. So now it all hinges on whether a jury believes that I was a victim of abuse and didn't comprehend the consequences of my actions or if they believe the story of my seeking a hired assassin. Either way I lose. It will be prison or a psychiatric facility and Bill's mother will get everything that I worked so hard to obtain...

Chapter 46
Maggie

It was a blisteringly hot Saturday afternoon at the end of August, and James Hurst was nearly six months old. Peter and I were at Sue and Alan's enjoying a barbeque in their large garden and as I looked around at the small gathering it struck me how much had transpired in the last four months. Rose and George were bouncing on the trampoline, their latest obsession which they used whenever they could. Lindy was close by, watching to see they remained safe and laughing as if in competition with Rose. I caught Sue's eye and she smiled at me, that knowing smile which told me all was well in her world. Lindy had been living with them for nearly three months now and the arrangement was going well. The decision to keep her on had been made, which as Sue was starting work in a week was perfect. She and Alan were delighted with Lindy who appeared to know exactly the right balance to make her presence in their home comfortable. She loved her large attic bedroom which now incorporated an en suite with a shower for her sole use, and Alan had bought her a television for evenings when she wanted to be alone. Her love of reading meant that she happily spent time in her room reading too, which gave Sue and Alan the privacy they needed. But it was obvious that she fitted perfectly into the family and as something more than a live-in nanny. She had found a home filled with the kind of love she had only ever dreamed of, the children adored her as she did them and it was the ideal arrangement. I must admit to feeling a little smug that it had been my idea, but then

Sue had made the whole thing do-able by giving Lindy a home first before considering the job. Looking at it now with hindsight it would have been too big a risk for them to take on a girl straight from a remand centre and leave their three precious children in her care. Sue's plan B was so much better and gave them all the time and opportunity to bond over a longer period of time without the pressure of my plan A, although I hated to admit it!

Alan dropped into the seat next to mine.

'Penny for them?' he smiled.

'I was just thinking how things have worked out so well, it's really generous of you and Sue to take Lindy into your family as you have.'

'I think we're getting as much out of it as she is. It's a relief to know the children will be so happy; she's like a big sister to them already. We've you to thank for that, Maggie.'

'Any news on Carol Jacobs?' I changed the subject while I had Alan to myself.

'She'll be up in court towards the end of September and will remain on remand until then. The CPS are confident of a conviction and hopefully she'll go down for a long time. She must be one of the most heartless women I've ever come across.'

I resisted the temptation to defend her to some extent. I know what she did was evil and inexcusable but her early years had shaped her into what she became and I think her mind was sick. It was to be hoped that prison would change her and she would begin to feel remorse for all she had done. If I voiced any of that to Alan I know he would have shaken his head and tutted at me. He was fond of telling me that I'm too soft with people but I prefer to look for the good in everyone rather than the bad. Lindy ran over to join us.

'Has he told you, Maggie?'

'Told me what?' I asked.

'Oh, that, it's nothing special is it?' Alan teased and she pulled a face at him.

'I've been accepted at college to do a B-Tec in nursery nursing from September!' Her face showed pure delight.

'That's brilliant, Lindy, well done.'

'And Sue's only going to work four days so I can have the time off to go to college on Fridays.'

Sue's voice interrupted as she asked Alan to answer the door and as he stood to go, Lindy sat down beside me.

'This is really all thanks to you, Maggie, I can't possibly say how grateful I am.'

'Your smile says it all for you; I'm so pleased things are working out so well,' I answered then turned towards the sound of Alan coming back into the garden with a group of people following on. Squinting against the sun, I was surprised to make out Sarah Dent and immediately wondered what on earth she was doing here. Lindy too had turned to look and a cry came out of her mouth as she recognised her brother, Jack, and flew at him almost knocking him over. I assumed the couple with him were his adoptive parents, which Sarah confirmed with introductions. Sue and Alan must have known they were coming but had obviously kept it to themselves and I thought Lindy was going to burst she was so full of happiness! Jack was smiling shyly but seemed pleased to have found his sister and I would find out more from Sarah later, I'd grill her for every detail! Presumably the fact that Lindy had a permanent home and a job with a policeman and his wife was much more acceptable to Mr and Mrs Simpson than a girl in Redwood or a halfway house.

Peter came and stood beside me, slipping his arm around my shoulder.

'Are you crying?' He grinned at me.

'No... I think I've got some sun cream in my eye,' I lied.

The End

Other books by Gillian Jackson

'Abduction'

At what point do you abandon hope? An idyllic summer's day, a children's birthday party and a simple, innocent game of Hide and Seek.

What should be the happiest of occasions for the Bryson family turns into their worst nightmare as three-year-old Grace disappears from their own garden, devastating the family and changing their lives forever. But fourteen years later when her sister Elise sees a young woman in a department store she becomes convinced that it is Grace. How can Elise, heavily pregnant with her first child, convince her family and the police that she is not mistaken? Could Grace still be alive and if so, where has she been since disappearing, and what really happened on that summer afternoon fourteen years ago?

'The Counsellor'

The unexpected death of Maggie Sayer's husband shatters her perfect world. Struggling to make sense of the overwhelming grief, a complete change and a positive focus seems to be the only thing which will enable Maggie to carry on with life. Training as a therapeutic counsellor provides this focus, bringing her into contact with people who desperately need help.

Julie is living in fear of an abusive husband, Janet is crumbling under the weight of a secret she has kept for over forty years and Karen has never recovered from her mother's violent death.

Maggie is drawn into each client's problems as she seeks to empower them to move on with their lives. And then she is faced with an ethical dilemma when she meets Peter...

Sensitively written, poignant and compelling, 'The Counsellor' is the first book in the 'Maggie Sayer Series' by British author Gillian Jackson.

'Maggie's World'

Ellie Graham wakes from a coma to a strangely different world than the one she remembers. Sarah is a newlywed whose fairy-tale romance and marriage is turning into a nightmare, causing her to doubt her sanity. Ruth, desperately longing for a child of her own, is inking beneath the weight of a long kept ssecret.

Therapeutic counsellor Maggie Sayer is no stranger to grief herself and uses her skills to help these three young women. But Maggie's own life has its complications too. Her new husband is suffering from a degenerative illness and a past client returns to her door with problems she is unable to solve. Maggie uses every possible approach to give the very best to her clients but not every story can have a happy ending.

'Pretence'

For Rae Chapman the months before her wedding should be the happiest time of her life, but the same troubling nightmare that disturbed her sleep in childhood has returned once more. Could something from the past be trying to resurface? Are they only dreams, or long-lost memories? Rae begins a journey to find out more about her past and discovers a family secret which throws her world into turmoil.

Lydia appears to have led a life of ease and privilege but now has a decision to make, one she has put off for nearly forty years and one which will shock her family and friends. As time is running out she turns to Maggie Sayer for help but is it already too late?

Linda thought she had escaped an oppressed life when her husband left, but has she simply exchanged one difficult situation for another and how can she support and protect her only child but still do the right thing?

As always, therapeutic counsellor Maggie Sayer seeks to give her best to these clients but is shocked by an unexpected turn of events in her friend's life and finds that her support is needed much closer to home.

'The First Stone'

Would winning over eight million pounds on the Lottery be your dream come true? It is for Jenny and Malcolm Grainger, but their delight quickly turns into a nightmare when secrets from the past resurface, resurrecting painful memories and provoking conflicting emotions within their family. Jenny struggles to accept what her husband has been hiding for over thirty years and with counsellor Maggie Sayer's help begins to look at the issues from a different perspective.

For as long as she can remember, Alice has been intent on remaining single, a decision based on an unhappy childhood. There is, however, a vital piece of information not in her possession which may make her think again. How can she persuade her mother to reveal the truth and what will be the effect on Alice of learning this shocking secret? Alice embarks on a journey of healing and accepting the past in order to move confidently into the future.

Maggie's involvement with these clients comes at a time when her own family need her more than ever as they are confronted with an insidious, heart-breaking illness.

'A Measure of Time'

What would your 'bucket list' be if you knew when you were going to die? When Helen Reid is diagnosed with terminal cancer, time suddenly became a precious commodity, a gift not to be wasted. Attempting to make the most of her few remaining months, Helen plans to travel to Canada and enjoy time with family and friends. But the past is drawing her back to the very worst period in her life, to an incident which even now, years later, brings shame and regret. Is it possible to make restitution for that awful event which has haunted her over the years? Revisiting her home town brings Helen into contact with people she would rather not meet again but determination spurs her on to do what should have been done forty years ago, something which will hopefully bring the peace Helen so desperately needs.

The First Snow of Winter   A romantic novella.

Victoria Patterson is in love with Josh Harper and daring to hope that she has at last found her soul mate. With the perfect job as a nurse on the ICU unit in a Manchester hospital, her future looks rosy, but is Josh really the man for her?

Sarah Jamieson is a midwife in Edinburgh and happily married with two beautiful children. Her participation in the making of a television documentary about maternity care in Edinburgh, resurrects painful memories of one of the worst times in her life.

One cold autumn evening, an extraordinary event stuns Victoria and changes the course of her life completely, eventually bringing the two women together and fulfilling the dreams of them both.

'Moving On From Victim to Survivor'

Non Fiction

If you, or someone you know, has been subjected to sexual abuse in childhood then this book is for you. It has an easy-to-read format and is presented in a simple way, cutting through jargon to offer down to earth help and support.

Moving On From Victim to Survivor is born out of the author's personal experiences. It offers positive help and practical ideas for dealing with the trauma brought about by an abusive childhood. The text is purposely short with chapters which can, if desired, be dipped into rather than read from cover to cover. It is a guide to the journey of regaining your self-respect and love of life, in order to live your life as a whole person and finally shake off the shadows of the past.

See more of Gillian's work @

www.gillianjackson.co.uk

Twitter;   @GillianJackson7

https://www.facebook.com/gillianjacksonauthor/

Lightning Source UK Ltd.
Milton Keynes UK
UKOW02f0053210916

283443UK00002B/7/P